AUTHOR	CLASS
MYERS, A.	F

TITLE	Murder makes an entree 05254803

MURDER MAKES AN ENTRÉE

MURDER MAKES AN ENTRÉE

Amy Myers

HEADLINE

First published in 1992
by HEADLINE BOOK PUBLISHING PLC

10 9 8 7 6 5 4 3 2 1

British Library Cataloguing in Publication Data

Myers, Amy
Murder makes an entree.
I. Title
823.914 [F]

ISBN 0–7472–0477–2

Typeset by Medcalf Type Ltd, Bicester, Oxon

Printed and bound in Great Britain by
Richard Clay Ltd, Bungay, Suffolk

HEADLINE BOOK PUBLISHING PLC
Headline House
79 Great Titchfield Street
London W1P 7FN

For my mother
and in memory of my father
upon whose shelves
I first met Mr Dickens.

The Imperial Hotel Broadstairs Kent

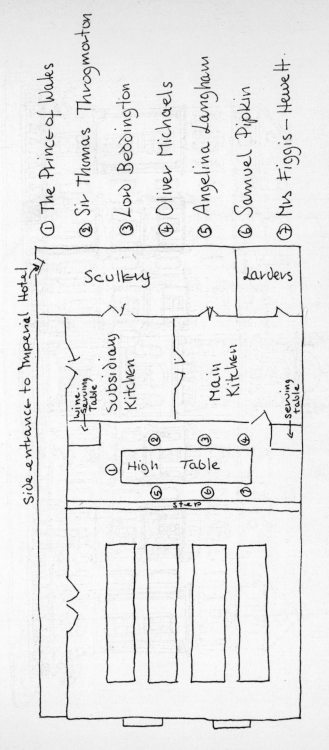

Side entrance to Imperial Hotel

Sculkery

Larders

Wine serving table

Subsidiary Kitchen

Main Kitchen

serving table

① High Table

② ③ ④

⑤ ⑥ ⑦

step

① The Prince of Wales

② Sir Thomas Throgmorton

③ Lord Beddington

④ Oliver Michaels

⑤ Angelina Langham

⑥ Samuel Pipkin

⑦ Mrs Figgis – Hewett

Plan of Dining area and Kitchens of the Imperial Hotel with Inspector Egbert Rose's table plan

Author's Note

Broadstairs today is very much the same delightful place as when Auguste Didier visited it, and the Royal Albion Hotel with its Dickensian history flourishes in Albion Street. The latter's inhabitants in this novel, however, are fictitious, as is the Imperial Hotel.

My gratitude for their help is due to Mr Peter Roger (Royal Albion Hotel), Mr Alan Robinson, and the staffs of Lenham, Broadstairs and Margate Public Libraries; among written sources to Cedric Dickens's delightful *Dining with Dickens* (Elvendon Press, 1984); to Natalie Greenwood who so expertly sketched the Imperial Hotel for Inspector Rose; to my mother for her help on Victorian dress; and to my agent Dot Lumley and editor Jane Morpeth for their constant enthusiasm and support.

Chapter One

'Who,' screamed Auguste Didier in anguish, 'is responsible for *this*?' His six apprentice pupils cowered, as he regarded in despair the ornate silver platter and the creation it bore.

'In five minutes, *mes amis*,' he continued grimly, as the culprit showed no signs of admitting his or her guilt, perhaps because none of the six could see anything amiss, 'the Prince of Wales will be dining on this – this – abomination.' He pointed a finger of scorn at the chicken stuffed with foie gras and truffles from Perigord. 'Le Maître Escoffier created *Poularde Derby* as a tribute to His Royal Highness, and you choose to make a mockery of his dish. That pupils of the Auguste Didier School of Cuisine could descend to such abomination!'

'What's wrong with it, Mr Didier?' asked James Pegg stolidly; he was braver than the rest, a slow-thinking Englishman of thirty who saw no harm in calling a *Poularde Derby* a Chicken with Liver.

Auguste glared at them. 'The jelly,' he said shortly, amazed that it was not immediately obvious.

'Oh, that was me, Mr Didier,' said Alice Fenwick gaily.

'You, Mademoiselle Fenwick?' Auguste was bereft of adequate words. Of all of them, he looked to Alice for attention to detail. She had a gift of competence rivalled by few, perhaps instilled into her by her upbringing as an army officer's daughter, Auguste had decided. But then even Homer nods and even he, Auguste Didier, had occasionally

1

been guilty of even quite major sins, such as insufficient attention to the importance of the pudding in English cooking. 'This horror is from your hand? I do not call it an aspic. It bears no resemblance to one.' He regarded the bonny-faced Alice sternly. Surely she must be aware of the enormity of her error? True, her heart was unhappy. His attitude softened in fellow feeling.

'It's only a garnish, Maître,' announced Algernon Peckham superciliously.

'Only' was not a word to use to maître chefs, particularly not to Auguste Didier. 'Only a garnish,' he repeated through gritted teeth. 'Only the most important part of the dish, only the garland to proclaim the arrival of the boar's head, only the candles that heralded a feast by Monsieur de La Reynière himself, only the chief advertisement of delights to come. By its garnish shall ye know the dish,' he thundered. 'Meat jelly, Mademoiselle Fenwick, should merely coat the back of the spoon in consistency. The end result should not bounce as does Monsieur Pegg's *blanc-manger*; it should be as tender and yielding as a woman's arms,' he proclaimed, carefully and speedily removing the offending blobs of jelly and replacing them with more croutons bearing slices of foie gras. 'Never forget that, *mes amis*.' He added a last Madeira-soaked truffle. '*Voilà*. Let it depart. Maître Escoffier shall have no reason to be ashamed of his creation.' Auguste gave the signal to the two footmen clad in the bright blue livery of Gwynne's Hotel. Nothing subdued for Emma Pryde, its flamboyant owner.

Dear Emma. He had been unable to disregard her plea to take over her kitchens for the evening in order to cook this very special dinner given for the Prince of Wales, for she herself had been laid low by the unbecoming illness of chickenpox.

Gwynne's Hotel in Jermyn Street alternated between a raffish reputation and one of sobriety with a hint of daring.

2

The attendance of the Prince of Wales was a boost to the latter, especially as on this occasion His Royal Highness would be dining, not discreetly in a very private room with a lady of his choice as in days of old, but making a more public entrance with the ultra-respectable members of the Society of Literary Lionisers. Only a dinner of first-class excellence could tempt the Prince of Wales to endure this ordeal for all he was the Society's president for this year of 1899, and this Emma, at the request (and generous payment) of the Lionisers, had guaranteed. Unfortunately not even Emma could ignore her spots to superintend the kitchens with her usual authoritarian rule and so Auguste had agreed to come to her aid on one condition. He could not work with unknown staff; he would bring in the six pupils from his cooking school. In his innocence, he now thought grimly, he had assumed this would be both a credit to him and good experience for them.

Now he despaired. Had he done right? For the Society of Literary Lionisers, he was not concerned. For the Prince of Wales he was. His spirits rose slightly as he cast his eyes over the empty dishes coming back from the preceding course, the soup, the *sole à la Batelière*, the grouse pudding remove, the other entrées. Perhaps there was hope yet. With the pragmatism of the true artiste, Auguste promptly dismissed the departed chicken from his mind, and turned his attention to the now urgent approval of *entremets*, both sweet and savoury.

But his heart was not fully in it. It seemed to him that his life must surely be a failure. Yesterday, 24 July 1899, had been his fortieth birthday, and how had he spent it? Alone and a failure. True, he had kept his slim figure; true, his dark eyes could be used to great effect as when they cast their spell over the kitchens of Stockbery Towers, and true, his career was considered by many outstanding. Yet now he must face the fact that in six months he, the master chef,

3

could not teach pupils how to make a correct clear aspic. And for it to be Alice at fault, of all people! Commercial gelatine. Never would he have believed her capable of it. It must be his fault. Yet how could a heart that was sad produce the heights of a chef's art? Tatiana — no, he would not think of his black-haired dark-eyed Russian princess, so nearly for one tantalising moment within his grasp, only to flutter beyond it for ever. Even Natalia — he winced. No, he must devote himself to his art, alone. Never again should woman darken his heart — or commercial gelatine his store cupboard.

His thunderous face alarmed his pupils.

'Everything is correct, *ja*?' enquired Heinrich Freimüller anxiously. The oldest of the class, in his early fifties, he often protectively appointed himself sheepdog to his five colleagues.

Auguste cast his eye over the *entremets*: a small crayfish salad, a *timbale de macaroni à la Mazarin* — and what difficulties *that* had caused. In vain he had argued with Emma that His Royal Highness disliked such starch-filled foods. Emma had merely smiled in her maddening way and pointed out that she was an expert in what the Prince of Wales liked in *everything*. To which he had no reply.

There was a Charlotte Romanov — no mere Charlotte Russe for tonight but his own receipt (with vodka) in honour of his patron the Grand Duke Igor of Russia, who had made it possible for Auguste to leave his employment at Plum's Club for Gentlemen, albeit with much regret, and to launch the Auguste Didier School of Cuisine in a house in Curzon Street. It had been a rare fit of generosity initiated, had Auguste but known it, not by Igor himself in gratitude for Auguste's help in the unfortunate happenings that had dogged the Grand Duke's last season in Cannes, but prompted by Natalia Kallinkova who had danced her way out of Auguste's life with some guilt.

And, lastly, there was a *pièce montée* of the royal coat of arms in meringue and spun sugar, a triumph of the confectioner's art.

'Thank you, Miss Dawson,' Auguste commented appreciatively. How strange that such exotic delights should prove to be the skill of Miss Emily Dawson, a former governess in her late twenties. Where in her previous dismal existence looking after the children of others could she have acquired the art of creating such exotic desserts? Not in nursery fare that was for sure. True, the wistfulness in her eye suggested dreams far beyond a governess's role, and perhaps for this reason she had joined the school.

'Monsieur Soyer was of the opinion,' observed Algernon Peckham, 'that one should never attempt to astonish guests with any extensive wonders of nature or art in the matter of eatables.'

Auguste flashed him a look of pure dislike. 'Thank you, Monsieur Peckham,' he snapped. 'Monsieur Soyer however was not called upon to entertain the Prince of Wales, who was, fortunately for him, still in the nursery then.'

Peckham's addiction to the sayings of Alexis Soyer was a perpetual thorn in Auguste's side, even more annoying than his conspiratorial attitude with Auguste when discussing the cuisine of France, to which he considered a two-week visit made shortly before the commencement of the course entitled him. How, Auguste often reflected, could he have had the misfortune to alight on a disciple of Alexis Soyer for his class: nay, not only a disciple but a fanatical devotee, against whose dicta, though he had been dead over forty years, all Auguste's pronouncements had to be measured. Alexis Soyer, master chef to the Reform Club, feeder of the poor, inventor of soup kitchens for the famine-stricken Irish, caterer to rich and poor alike, saviour of the Crimea, inventor of the Magic Stove, creator of the splendours of the Gastronomic Symposium of All Nations at Gore House,

5

had dogged Auguste's footsteps. With his own maître to whom he had been apprenticed in Cannes, Auguste Escoffier, he enjoyed a happy friendship, but Soyer, taking advantage of the fact that he was dead and thereby immortalised, meanly still sneaked up on him to cloud his days. To see him reincarnated in a jaunty, pretentious young man such as Algernon Peckham was the last straw. He tried hard to be charitable, to tell himself that Peckham was only twenty-three, but charity came hard when an aspiring Soyer silently criticised his every dish.

The school had been operating for six months now, and he counted himself fortunate in his first six pupils. All of a high standard, and a mixture from all walks of life, all co-operating together dedicated to the high calling of food. Four men, Heinrich Freimüller, from the German embassy, James Pegg, the tall and burly son of a veterinary surgeon, the pretentious Algernon Peckham, so anxious to conceal the fact he was a butcher's son, a fact made obvious from the first time he cut a joint of meat, and Lord Alfred Wittisham, Emma Pryde's amiable and somewhat vacuous protégé, who had come to Auguste at her urging. He announced disarmingly that as there seemed nothing else he could do, Emma thought he might be good at cooking. To his own surprise as well as everyone else's, he turned out to be extremely good at it.

Two women, Alice Fenwick (who had resolved to become a new Emma Pryde and Lady Wittisham into the bargain) and Emily Dawson, completed the group. The latter two were much of an age, but to the onlooker this was not apparent. Twenty-nine year old Alice, bright-eyed, pretty and good-humoured, made a strange contrast to the quiet Emily whose only relapses into animation tended to be sparked off by references to her grandmother's vast repertoire of home remedies.

An odd mixture and, he was bound to admit, an

6

unexciting one. But then so seemed many recipes at first, Auguste thought. It took the art of a master chef to create an exciting unity out of uninteresting ingredients. Yet here he had not achieved it. He sighed. Yes, he needed a holiday, lest here too he saw only failure.

'*Nein*,' roared Heinrich Freimüller. 'What are you doing, Fraülein?' His usual joviality deserted him as he turned to see Emily Dawson in the act of applying a tacky mess of cream to his dessert. 'My Nesselrode pudding do not need cream!' he shouted.

'There's nothing like a nice bit of Chantilly,' said Emily unusually firmly. 'And I'm responsible for garnishing the desserts. I *know* about desserts.'

'This is not garnish. This is desecration. It is ruined. Carême did not demand cream in his receipt, nor Francatelli, nor even your Miss Acton. No, only Miss Emily Dawson demands cream.' His voice rose in a wail of frustration, as he pounded the table in anger.

Emily burst into tears and dropped her cream bag on top of the *Canapés de Prince de Galles*, where it spat out globules of cream on top of the anchovies and gherkins.

'My canapés,' screamed Algernon Peckham, clutching his head. 'This is what happens when you let governesses into the kitchen,' he stormed at Emily.

'You can't talk to a lady like that,' said Lord Wittisham, shocked, offering an impeccable handkerchief to Emily.

Alice Fenwick glared.

'Only a butcher's son could say such a thing,' sobbed Emily, goaded out of her usual timidity.

Algernon turned red at this double attack on his pedigree, and opened his mouth to retaliate, but was frustrated by Auguste's frenzied: '*Les anges*,' called forth not in supplication for external and higher assistance, but from the smell of burning. Alfred Wittisham promptly detached himself from Emily and rushed for the stove, colliding with his two admirers, Alice Fenwick and James Pegg. The latter acted as a sort of bulldog protector to his lordship, who had won his devotion quite accidentally by inviting him to dine at Plum's under the impression that Clubland was James Pegg's usual evening haunt. At the moment James's chief object was to protect his lordship from the attentions of Alice Fenwick, whether through jealousy at his own rejected suit at the hands of Alice, or an altruistic desire to preserve his lordship from matrimony was not clear. In any case, it was immaterial, since his lordship, oblivious to these efforts on his behalf, had matrimonial plans of his own, unknown to any of his fellow pupils.

In silence the six apprentices of the Auguste Didier School of Cuisine regarded the three ruined *entremets*, while their maître stood by unable to speak through shame. But, rising to emergency, Auguste dexterously dressed the Nesselrode with *marrons glacés* to hide the white smears of removed cream, arranged the cream on the canapés to resemble a recent brainwave on the part of a master cook and despatched a fresh set of angels on horseback to the frying pans.

'A chef,' he told his pupils severely, 'must be at all times prepared for disaster.'

The immediate damage was repaired, but Auguste's worries were not so quickly dispelled. For six months they had worked together in apparent amicability, and now suddenly it seemed to be breaking down. Perhaps they *all* needed a holiday. And thank goodness they were just about to have one.

It had been an inspiration on his part to go away with his class on a Fish Fortnight. It was July, and so they would combine the pleasures of work with those of a holiday. They would go where all the English went in the summer: to the seaside. What fun it would be. He had never been to The Seaside in the sense in which the English used it, and he was

8

eager to try its delights. To the French, it was a strange idea to wear odd clothes, to watch marionettes when this could be done equally well in the Tuileries *jardins*, even odder to climb into clumsy damp bathing machines, where one changed into unbecoming, vulgar garments, and was pulled by a large horse into the water. Why not take the waters in more elegance at an inland watering place, argued the French, where respectable food might be obtained and enjoyed with the comforting thought that any unhealthy humours resulting from it might be disposed of the following day at the spa?

Nevertheless, Auguste Didier was willing to try all experiences, and he wished to see what this Seaside was like. Moreover the Bank Holiday Monday would occur while they were there. He had passed many bank holidays in his years in England, but these, he had been told by dear Egbert, were a mere nothing compared with one spent at The Seaside. Very well, he would go. And moreover they would have the advantage of being able to cook with fish freshly caught from the sea, bought from the local fisherman or from local markets. What pleasures were in store there. No tired, flabby, dull-eyed offerings, as so often found in London. No more smoked fish, so prevalent in the cities. But *fresh* John Dory, fresh crabs—

'Mr Auguste,' a voice broke in on his musings, 'what's the Prince of Wales like when you meet him?'

'A flounder,' replied Auguste dreamily.

The sight of Alice's surprised face brought him back to reality. Auguste blushed. He had been guilty of absent-mindedness in the kitchen. How often had he reproved his pupils for this heinous crime. He brought his full attention back to the important matter in hand: food. Broadstairs must wait.

Interesting touch, this cream. Several floors above them the

Prince of Wales was giving due attention to the canapés named after him. He did not appear to be doing so, for he had long cultivated the art of apparent courteous attention to his companions, while musing to himself on far more enjoyable subjects. For once, however, he did allow his thoughts momentarily to be deflected to the matter on hand. Why on earth had he allowed himself to be elected honorary president for the year? Literary Lionisers indeed. It didn't seem too much of a chore when you dictated a letter about how pleased you'd be, and so on, but just see where it could end up. It wasn't all *Poularde Derby*. Far from it. What it meant in the end was that you couldn't arrive at Goodwood in decent time for the start tomorrow, and then you had to be dragged away hard on the heels of Cowes, deprived of celebrations at the Royal Yacht Club for what must undoubtedly be a victorious week for *Britannia*. All to go to some bally literary dinner. Dickens indeed. And at Broadstairs of all places, which he always associated with Mama, since she was always going on about what fun it had been in her youth. Fun! Not a good game of baccarat anywhere. Thank heavens, he'd be leaving for Marienbad shortly. Mind you, they didn't have angels on horseback at Marienbad. Not like these anyway. He concentrated on food again. That Poularde Derby took him right back to his own younger days and Monte Carlo. He sighed. He was getting on he supposed. Nearly sixty. His Monte Carlo days were over. Thank heavens Poularde Derbys went on for ever. My word, but this chef was good.

He shuddered at what Broadstairs might produce. Glancing round the table at the six committee members of the Literary Lionisers, he had little faith in their ability to ensure a tolerable Brown Windsor, let alone a Poularde Derby; it must have been Emma behind tonight's fare. A good chap she'd hired. What a group these were. The young woman had possibilities perhaps, and that young fellow, for all he had the cheek to wear a short dinner jacket. Where the devil did he think he was? America? In all these societies it was the old 'uns ruled the roost, though. Right and proper too, except when it came to matters affecting Albert Edward's stomach.

'You will truly enjoy the evening, Your Royal Highness,' trilled one frightful-looking woman. He'd a notion he'd met her husband once, poor devil. Something in the city. 'Especially the readings after the banquet. Such a pity you cannot arrive for the afternoon walk around Broadstairs. Where *he* trod and laid his head, you know.' She lowered her voice in appreciation of this year's hero. 'Our English Watering Place, he called it. Oh, *how* he loved it. As you would too, sir. Would indeed you could attend for the whole week?' Her voice rose in enthusiasm, while the Prince of Wales hastily made a note to make sure that Mama invited him to lunch at Osborne on Sunday and that his yacht *Osborne* (tactfully allotted the same name) arrived well after the appointed time for the afternoon torture.

'Indeed a pity, madam,' he sighed. 'A most worthy writer, Mr Dickens.'

'My own tastes are for Thackeray,' put in a rounded gentleman who, for all his preferences, resembled Mr Pickwick in girth.

For once Albert Edward, his mind still running on the glories of the food of Auguste Didier, picked up the wrong word, and was about to enquire whose chef Mr Thackeray might be, but was saved from this unfortunate gaffe by the intervention of the Society's chairman, Sir Thomas Throgmorton.

'I myself,' said Sir Thomas pompously, 'consider Mr Dickens a giant who stands alone. Imagine a series of readings from Thackeray.' The Prince of Wales could not. 'Compare this to the gamut of Mr Dickens from the immortal Pickwick to the majesty of *Bleak House*. From the humour of Scrooge to the savage glories of *Oliver Twist*. I myself,' he coughed deprecatingly, 'shall be reading from this dramatic work after the banquet.' A repressed snort from 'Mr Pickwick', as the Prince had mentally named Thackeray's advocate.

'You are always so brave,' said That Woman in hushed tones, though with a slight note of sarcasm, so it seemed to the Prince. He brightened up. A little bit of discord in the hen coop sometimes cheered these events up. 'It was,' she informed the Prince sweetly, 'the reading from *Oliver Twist* that is supposed to have led to *his* death.'

'Whose death?' asked the Prince bewildered.

'The Great Man's,' explained That Woman. 'His doctors advised him that the strain of these readings was too much for him, but he persisted. His public came first.' She wiped a tear from her eye with a lace handkerchief. A hurmph of a snore greeted her remark. The Prince of Wales turned a frosty eye on the offender, as he awoke from his peaceful refuge. Albert Edward took a dim view of social lapses in his presence, even from elderly gentlemen.

'I myself,' intoned That Woman remorselessly, 'in the character of Agnes Wickfield, shall be reading from *David Copperfield.*'

The Prince of Wales in a rare fit of flight of fancy thought the literary lady from *The Pickwick Papers* might suit her better, but his air of polite approval did not betray this for one second.

'And you, madam?' He bent his eye with relief on the decent-looking female, who answered complacently:

'I shall take The Death of Little Nell, sir.'

'The harrowing scene from *The Old Curiosity Shop*. You will recall, sire, the American public crowded at the quayside as the ship arrived from England with the latest instalment demanding to know whether this brave child still lived,' added the young man.

Albert Edward looked at him sharply. Did he detect a note of parody in his voice? Perhaps so, for there was a distinct edge to Sir Thomas's voice, as he quickly replied: 'A natural death, of course. Unlike my death of Nancy at the ruthless hands of Bill Sikes.'

This literary conversation was getting too much. A spark of annoyance crossed the Prince of Wales' face, just as Sir Thomas added: 'At Broadstairs, sir, you will hear of murder. A most foul and harrowing murder.'

Auguste sank back in relief. It was over. He and his pupils sat down around Gwynne's largest kitchen table to partake of their own supper before vacating the premises to allow Emma's staff to embark on the somewhat less rewarding task of washing up. Normally Auguste would insist on this being done by his pupils, even himself, but this evening was different. They were guest artistes. Each of his pupils was now engaged on silent appraisal of how successful the others' dishes had been. An ill-assorted group they might be, Auguste thought, but, he put it to himself in all modesty, they were at one in appreciation of the standard of cuisine which only Auguste Didier could impart to them. Cooking had made strange kitchen-fellows, however. Who would have thought that that somewhat vacuous but patrician Lord Wittisham would befriend the stolid and definitely non-patrician James Pegg? Although the slowness of Pegg's movements concealed the intelligence of his brain, Auguste suspected. His thoughts were speedily removed from such considerations as the door opened with a crash, and seven pairs of startled eyes turned to the newcomer.

'Ah, it is only Monsieur Sid,' said Auguste resignedly.

'Sorry, Mr Didier.' Sid, or Mr Sidney Hands, to give him his full name, dressed for the evening in the livery of

Gwynne's Hotel, was Auguste's general factotum at Curzon Street, a nineteen-year-old from Stepney. Normally a lively eel, under everyone's feet and in everyone's way, this evening he had been detailed ostensibly to remain on duty at the doors of the suite, but in fact to report on the company's reactions to the delights before them.

'One of 'em said I was like Sam Waller, Mr Didier,' Sid offered cheerfully. 'Who's 'e? I've 'eard of Lewis Waller.'

'Weller, Sid, not Waller. And Mr Sam Weller is not related to the eminent and popular actor. He is a character from Dickens.'

'Dickens.' Sid was struck by a happy thought. 'That wuz 'oo they was talking about up there. Some banquet they're going to have. 'E's a writer, ain't 'e? Saw one of 'is plays at the penny gaff once. The *True Story of Oliver Twist*. It wasn't 'arf long – took twenty minutes. There wuz only me left in the place at the end and I wuz only there, 'cos I was with—'

'Enough of your romantic revelations, Sid,' said Auguste sternly, well aware of the reason for the popularity of penny gaffs. 'Kindly tell us what comments you heard about the food.'

But Sid was not to be deflected now. 'They said there was to be a murder, Mr Didier.'

Murder! Auguste was oblivious to the gasps from his pupils as they interrogated Sid. The word murder made him recoil. All too often murder had appeared in his life. At Stockbery Towers, at the Galaxy Theatre, at Plum's Club for Gentlemen; it had even followed him to his native town of Cannes. And see how it had ended there! He firmly dispelled the spark of misery at the thought of Tatiana, lost to him for ever. It was true that in exchange murder had brought him the warm friendship with Inspector Egbert Rose of Scotland Yard, and his wife, dear Edith, but at what price.

14

'I wonder what it's like to murder someone?' Algernon was murmuring as he elegantly sipped soup.

'I shall have great pleasure in finding out, Mr Peckham,' said Auguste exasperatedly, 'if you retain that disparaging expression whilst partaking of my *Consommé à la Prince de Galles*.'

'You've investigated quite a lot of murders haven't you, Mr Didier?' Alice regarded him admiringly. 'I read about you in the *Harmsworth Magazine*. The new Auguste Dupin, they call you.'

'Yes,' said Auguste shortly. Not the great cook, no, just a penny-halfpenny detective. Not even one in his own right, but merely 'a new Dupin'. For this he was to be renowned. At times it gave him great pleasure, for it was indeed true that his powers of detection were extraordinary, but this was not one of those times.

'You must be very clever,' said Emily timidly.

'*Non*,' said Auguste, pleased. 'Ah, perhaps just a little, for it is like cooking, you understand. You have the ingredients, the evidence. You put them together, you stir them, you have the solution – *voilà* the dish is ready. It is a matter of logical deduction, plus a little bit of the extra genius of the detective, or the cook. I am a maître chef of detection,' he ended grandly.

'Yer a marvel, Mr Didier,' commented Sid cheerily. 'His Nibs up there liked that chicken thing you sent up,' he added, recalling at last his duty for the evening. 'I expect that's what he wants to tell yer.'

'When?' asked Auguste bewildered.

'Now, I s'pose. 'E asked to see yer. 'Course,' he flung after Auguste's retreating figure, rushing wildly out of the door, hurling imprecations behind him that did not betoken well for Sid on his return, 'it might be because 'e thought it was orf.'

The Prince of Wales, already hatted, cloaked and

15

walking-sticked, was leaving. He had reached Gwynne's foyer when Auguste's figure hurled itself to stand to attention by the door.

'So you're the cook?' Albert Edward paused. Pity his punctuality wasn't as good as his cooking. Nevertheless: 'Fine supper, fine supper. That Poularde—' The Prince of Wales paused. His brows knitted. 'Haven't I seen you somewhere before?'

'In Cannes, Your Royal Highness. The – er – cricket pavilion,' Auguste murmured apologetically.

The royal eyebrows shot up. Albert Edward had no wish to be reminded of that most unfortunate episode.

Their eyes met in unspoken agreement to drop the subject.

'You run a cooking school, so Mrs Pryde tells me.'

'Yes, sir.'

'No French holidays this year, eh?'

'No, sir. We are about to leave for a Fish Fortnight Holiday of Instruction. At Broadstairs.'

Royalty regarded Auguste Didier thoughtfully. 'Broadstairs, eh?'

Inspector Egbert Rose of Scotland Yard turned over a pile of files in his small office in Scotland Yard overlooking the Embankment. He was pleasantly happy. July was no month to be working in the Factory; July was a time to be out enjoying those blue skies. And in three days he would be. Meanwhile he had the enjoyable task of handing all these old chestnuts over to Twitch, or Sergeant Albert Stitch, to give him his correct title. Let him earn his eagerly desired promotion if he could with this lot. Rose chuckled evilly to himself.

He was looking forward to his two weeks' holidays in Ramsgate though, and was even more pleased now he knew Auguste would be in next-door Broadstairs. Edith had wanted to take rooms, even do her own cooking, but at that

16

Rose had rebelled. He didn't want any landlady cooking dinner for him, and he certainly didn't want Edith cooking herself. That was part of what a holiday meant, to get away from Edith's cooking. Moreover he looked forward to partaking of some of Auguste's cooking – thank goodness holidays, for Auguste, did not involve abstinence from the kitchen range.

Twitch strutted in, rather like something out of a Gilbert and Sullivan chorus, Rose decided, eyeing his subordinate amusedly. Pity that he was invaluable in some ways, otherwise he'd have him out of his department quicker than a three-card trickster off the steps of the Athenaeum.

'Are you ready to hand over the files, sir?' Eagerness barely concealed, twitching at the nose.

Rose glanced down at the gems Twitch was so eager to take under his control: report from Special Branch on the supposed setting up of a German naval spy ring, latest juicy wanted criminals list for the Paris Sûreté. He had no great faith in Inspector Chesnais' not having confused victim and suspect. Nothing much new here anyway. It was notable that the theft of a necklace formerly belonging to Madame de Pompadour from the château of the Comte de la Ferté (thief thought to be English) took precedence over the recent mysterious death of William Hugget, circus performer (thought to be murdered by one of his colleagues, all British). It certainly took precedence over the death of a thirty-year-old groom, Joseph Smith, in Bordeaux, believed to be a murder by the wife (both thought to be English), the quite definite murder of three young ladies for gain of person and possession by an unknown hand (thought to be English) in Brittany, and the murder of a chef in Grenoble by one of his apprentices (two of whom were English); these last three cases had by now accumulated as much metaphorical, if not literal, dust over them as his own 'dead crimes' files. Theft of Madame Pompadour's necklace indeed. No more

17

burglaries for him. The last one led him to Cannes, and a whole heap of problems. A nice spy or murder and you had something to go on.

'Here you are, Stitch — and welcome to 'em. When I get back,' Rose added straightfaced, 'I expect to see progress.' Progress? He hadn't made any himself for months on those files, and Stitch knew it.

His face glowed with enthusiasm. 'You will, sir,' he said smugly. 'You will.' Modesty was not his strong point.

Rose left the Factory a happy man, a man about to be set free from investigation and care, a man shortly to leave for Ramsgate.

The house in Curzon Street retained its elegant appearance outside, but inside the whole of the basement and ground floor had been converted to kitchens. The ground floor formed Auguste's teaching area, the basement was for the pupils' own experiments. The first floor housed a library, and here Auguste lectured his pupils on the theory of cookery. The rest of the house was his own domain, a far cry from his former lodgings in King Street. From time to time one or other of the pupils remained overnight, even Alice on occasion, though she had remained disappointingly aloof. It had not been a tribute to his charms.

On this Wednesday morning, the so-called Isle of Thanet, in particular its seaside resorts, was as much in the air in Curzon Street as at Scotland Yard. Messrs Carter Patterson would shortly be calling for the advance luggage. The card had been placed in the window in ample time, the first visible statement that the holiday season was here. Most of the pupils' luggage and Auguste's was in the hall, ready to go. Even Sid's modest baggage managed to appear in time. Essential kitchen equipment had also been lovingly packed under Auguste's anxious supervision. Much would be provided in the house he had rented in Broadstairs, but he could not expect a rented house to possess sufficient refrigerators, bains-marie, salamanders and salad basket. Ah, but this all took so much organisation, and his pupils thought his fees were expensive! They were cheap. Besides, you could put no price on art.

'Where is the boning knife?' he cried.

'Don't worry, Mr Didier, I've got it,' came Alice's reassuring voice.

'Mademoiselle Fenwick, happy the man who marries you,' said Auguste fervently.

He saw Alice blush slightly, as she glanced at Alfred Wittisham. He wished her luck, but privately doubted Alfred had even noticed. Besides, had he not seen his lordship dining at the Savoy with a young lady recently? A somewhat large young lady, in personality as well as size, beside whom Alice in her subdued grey poplinette working dress would stand little chance. He had been visiting Maître Escoffier, and Alfred and his companion had seemed deep in conversation – if ever Alfred could be said to be deep in anything.

The sound of the door knocker boomed through the house. 'There is the excellent Mr Carter Patterson,' exclaimed Auguste thankfully, tired of clambering over boxes and baggage.

But it wasn't Carter Patterson that greeted Sid. Outside was a carriage, not over-ornate but one unmistakably marked with the arms of the Prince of Wales.

On the step a soberly clad gentleman in black tail-coat and dark grey trousers was handing a missive to Sid, which was speedily removed by Auguste, who had come quickly up behind him.

'I am to wait,' announced the visitor, stepping inside, and averting his gaze from the luggage that took up nine-tenths of the space.

'You are not Carter Patterson?' enquired Auguste unnecessarily.

19

Eyebrows were raised. 'No, I don't believe I am. I am—'

But there was no need for Auguste to listen, for he had seen, with a strange, sinking feeling, the royal coat of arms on the seal of the letter. He ripped it open with scant respect for the thick cream paper hand-made in the Maidstone mills.

Seven pairs of eyes fixed on him interestedly, crowding him in the narrow hallway. Word had gone round about the carriage.

'It seems,' announced Auguste slowly, looking up at his pupils at last, 'that—'

'Your reply, Mr Didier,' interrupted the courier courteously but firmly. 'I take it I may tell His Royal Highness you accept?'

Auguste bowed his head in acquiescence, and the door closed behind the envoy.

'It seems,' Auguste said in a voice heavy with foreboding, 'that our Fish Fortnight holiday is to be interrupted. His Royal Highness has com— requested that we should cook the banquet for the Society of Literary Lionisers on Saturday week. Apparently, Sid, the event to which you heard them refer is to take place at Broadstairs.'

'Murder, Mr Didier?' asked Sid eagerly.

'No,' said Auguste hastily. 'The Grand Dickens evening. I am to see the chairman Sir Thomas Throgmorton to discuss the menu.' He managed a wan smile. This was not going to be the carefree seaside holiday he had imagined. 'Very well,' he continued melodramatically, 'but I shall tell this Sir Thomas that if I, Auguste Didier, sacrifice part of my holiday to this banquet of which I am in charge, then I am to be in complete control. We, *mes amis*, shall do *everything*. We shall shop, we shall prepare, we shall wait, we shall clear, at least on the Prince of Wales's table. This way and this way alone we are assured there will be no disasters at Broadstairs, unless,' he added grimly, 'you forget yourselves as happened yesterday evening.'

20

For all his brave words, however, Auguste remained sunk in gloom, even after Carter Patterson had called to alleviate his mind of one problem. What unfortunate luck that this wretched banquet should occur at Broadstairs of all places! Normally the words 'wretched banquet' would never emerge in juxtaposition from Auguste's lips, but just now holiday had an even more attractive sound than banquet. Last time he attempted to take a holiday it had ended in disaster. True, this time, for all Sid's prognostications − goodness knows what he thought he'd heard − murder could surely not again take the stage, but all the same, cooking for, he gathered, sixty people, was not the best of all possible ways of spending a holiday weekend.

For the Prince of Wales, he would do it. He would achieve miracles no matter what the fare. He felt no enthusiasm for Mr Dickens himself. He had read with some difficulty several of his novels in his youth, since his English mother was a champion of his works. Reading of the rookeries of London, however, amid the green fields of Provence redolent with the perfumes of Grasse, the words made little impression on him save that they were too long and, for someone struggling with the English language, distinctly tedious. The great Mr Dickens had taken a tumble in Auguste's estimation, and it was years before he read another, inveigled into doing so by a stage performance of *Nicholas Nickleby*. Now he enjoyed the novels. Even so, he did not understand this English habit of making clubs for everything. A society just to appreciate literature? Would respectable Parisians form a society to appreciate Flaubert and travel to *eat* in a town he liked? Why not eat in Paris?

No matter. This was an English form of enjoyment. Like the seaside. The dinner would be but a brief interlude, one dinner to be cooked and then the rest of the holiday to enjoy, with the smell of the fresh fish early in the morning. He smelled again the fish markets of Paris and of the fishermen of Cannes. The smell of the sea. His spirits began to rise. He looked at the boater and blazer lying on his bed, ready to be packed in his hand case. He tossed the boater in the air, caught it, and executed a little dance with it. Away from cares and dull everyday grind. He was going to The Seaside.

Chapter Two

The noble Society of Literary Lionisers had come into being almost twenty-five years previously, founded by a group of gentlemen who, indignant at being unable to gain admittance to the Literary Club, convinced themselves that the proud traditions of Dr Johnson's Club were being eroded. The Society set itself the modest ambition of instilling in the masses, or such masses as could afford their membership fee, a greater appreciation of the works of the literary giants of Great Britain, with a passing acknowledgement to the achievements of less favoured nations. Alas for good intentions: the Lionisers found their ideals somewhat more difficult to sustain than they had supposed and, moreover, since lovers of literature are not necessarily noted for their organisational abilities, the committee in particular suffered from squabbling and undercurrents no less vicious for their being somewhat concealed than they had been in former times when David Garrick was so brutally blackballed from Johnson's Club.

Only the presence of the Prince of Wales had prevented the passions of the present committee from overspilling into open warfare during their dinner at Gwynne's. The committee numbered six, an awkward number for efficient functioning, but the founders of the Society had blithely assumed that between men of culture no quarrel could possibly arise that could not receive amicable resolution.

Although the monthly meetings held at St George's Hall

or the Savoy Hotel fulfilled the original aims of the Society, the committee meetings held in a private suite in nearby Gwynne's Hotel most definitely did not. Occasionally, especially since the appointment of Mrs Langham and Mr Michaels, accord was achieved without verbal bloodshed. However, the meeting to which the six members were now making their way was, they all knew, not going to be one of those occasions.

Each year a literary figure was chosen (by the committee) as the Lion of the Year. For twelve months the members would study the works of the great man (or, occasionally, woman), listen to learned authorities discussing his work and to actors declaiming it, and endeavour to instill in various dignitaries the overwhelming case for statues, monographs, busts and commemorative china, and, most importantly, the need for preservation of buildings and places known to and described by the current Lion.

The highlight of the Society's year was the Week of the Lion. En masse, the Society would descend on his 'Lair', the haunts where the Lion had roamed in fact or in his imagination on his pages, in order more fully to appreciate his every word, and to ensure that his homestead and/or other locations described by him were being maintained in the proper respectful spirit.

At first the choice of the Lion of the Year had been sacrosanct; now, regrettably, impure considerations were creeping in to his selection. Before he received the accolade of the Society, it was necessary that thought should be given as to whether he had been sensible enough to reside in or describe in his works a suitable venue for the Week of the Lion. A particularly zealous committee had one year lit upon Daniel Defoe as a subject, thereby consigning the Society to a choice of a week's holiday in Stoke Newington, an unknown desert island, or a Tour through the Whole Island of Great Britain. The following year, Lord Byron, with his more enticing prospect of foreign travel, was hastily selected by a more practically minded committee.

Obligingly, Mr Charles Dickens presented no such problem. After some anxious debate as to whether the location for the Week of the Lion should not more suitably be Rochester, it was unanimously decided that Broadstairs, with a day visit to Rochester, would be blessed with the Society's presence. This discreet resort, presenting none of the disadvantages of crowded Ramsgate or merry Margate, was a highly suitable venue and Mr Dickens was silently congratulated by the committee for his convenient choice of watering place. True, he had ceased to visit it long before his demise, having complained it was spoiled by increasing numbers of visitors and, even worse, the noise made under his windows by itinerant musicians in the streets, but forty years on people were more accustomed to such annoyances.

The overriding concern of the committee this evening, however, which threatened to tear the Society apart and indeed bring about its entire disbandment, if certain threats were carried out, could not be laid at the door of Mr Dickens. It was next year's Lion who was to blame: Mr William Shakespeare. He had been selected as the obvious choice of Lion for the prestigious year of 1900, the first year of the new century (despite vigorous argument on this point in the columns of the press). The Society's year conveniently began on Shakespeare's birthday, 23rd April, St George's Day, and the chairman's four-year reign being at an end, Sir Thomas Throgmorton would have stepped down and a new chairman preside over the day's festivities.

Or would he?

'To Gwynne's, Hobbs.'

Sir Thomas Throgmorton had gazed, displeased, at the usual dusty roadway exacerbated by the hot dry weather and summoned his carriage. It might only be ten minutes' walk

25

from his Mayfair home to the hotel, but for this all-important meeting, he needed to present himself impeccable in both appearance and argument. He had half the committee on his side (counting himself). He frowned. Perhaps he had made a mistake in alienating Gwendolen? Surely she would not waver in his support, however? How could he have foretold what illusions the foolish woman was harbouring? He had had no choice but to act as he did. Beddington would be sure to support him. After all, Throgmorton told himself, he had right on his side. His years as a manager of an international bank had taught him the value of that. True, there was a small flaw in his argument, but with luck no one would see it. People would overlook anything, however obvious, if you were confident enough of your case – or appeared so. He'd learned that in banking too. Perhaps even Angelina would see the justice of his case, if he put it to her once more. He had found her dissension quite inexplicable. When they were married, he would gently and firmly make this plain to her.

Angelina Langham had no intention of changing her views. Accompanied by fellow committee member, Oliver Michaels, the young playwright with whom she had just shared a most enjoyable dinner at the Savoy, she too was thinking about the Lionisers. As a newcomer to the committee, and moreover one championed by Sir Thomas himself, and as a 'young' woman – she was twenty-eight – she was aware that she was expected to know her place. As was Oliver Michaels, elected to represent Youthful Attainment (at thirty he was already a successful playwright). For her part, she had no intention of remaining in her place. That was not what had made her seek Sir Thomas's acquaintance after the death of her husband nearly three years ago. A middle-aged and mild-natured poet of some distinction, he and not Alfred Austin would undoubtedly have been next Poet Laureate, had not circumstances decreed otherwise. His distinction, although he was deceased, vicariously entitled her to sit on the committee, where she was naturally not expected to play an active role.

Oliver Michaels handed Angelina down from his pride and joy, his recently acquired Peugeot, and approved once more her slight, golden-haired figure with its air of Madonna-like calm hidden at present behind a rather ugly motoring veil. He held on to her hand, remarking as he glanced at Gwynne's portals:

'Oh Sairey, Sairey, little do we know wot lays afore us.'

'You, Oliver,' replied his madonna sweetly, throwing back the veil, 'to quote from the same immortal work, "will make a lovely corpse" if you compare me to Mrs Gamp.'

Oliver laughed. 'Very well. Shall I compare thee to a summer's day, instead, dear Angelina?'

She shuddered. 'This evening, Oliver,' she remarked firmly, 'I fear Mr Shakespeare is *not* a welcome thought.'

'Very well, let us beard the Lions in their den, and meet our end with dignity.' Offering her his arm, he escorted her into the foyer of Gwynne's Hotel.

'The female of the species,' Gwendolen Figgis-Hewett muttered to herself in the hansom cab.

She had no escort. Even when Mr Figgis-Hewett was alive, she had frequently had no escort, for his interests outside making money were not hers. Drinking and gambling were no occupations for a lady of literary talent. Her poem had been accepted by the *Ladies' Companion*. True, they had not published it, but acceptance was the important thing. Mr Figgis-Hewett had been dead five years now, and his widow was tired of being alone, however pleasant it was to be so wealthy. Since Sir Thomas was a widower of about the same duration, she had seen no reason why they should not pool their common grief. Even now she could not quite believe what had happened on that dreadful evening after the Prince of Wales's dinner.

Mr Rudyard Kipling never wrote a truer word. Now she felt much deadlier than the male.

'We're here, sir.' The disembodied voice of the cab driver boomed through Lord Beddington's dreams, as he reclined dozily on his way to Gwynne's. The Garrick dinner had been pleasantly relaxing and only with difficulty did he recall that he was bound for Gwynne's and not the Reform this evening. He was not quite sure what all the fuss was about, but he had no doubt Sir Thomas was right. Anyway it was more sensible to vote for him, for matters were more quickly concluded that way. It was probably only that fellow Pipkin making a mountain out of a molehill. Sitting on committees was rather like the Lords or the magistrate's bench; you could think your own thoughts, and just wake up for the vote.

'Oh me, oh my. Your time is nigh,' said Samuel Pipkin triumphantly to himself, his mind full of Thomas Throgmorton.

The secretary of the committee of the Society of Literary Lionisers almost bounced down in glee from his cab outside Gwynne's Hotel. The time of reckoning had come. With the enthusiasm of a Pickwick in pursuit of a Jingle, he launched his corpulent frame through the doors of the hotel, eager for combat. Like Angelina, however, he would not have welcomed the Dickensian comparison, for Samuel Pipkin was not a Dickens man. Far from it. He was through and through dedicated to the works and memory of William Makepeace Thackeray. He disliked Dickens and everything to do with him, and in particular his own undeniable resemblance to Mr Pickwick. This was merely physical, however, for it is by no means an infallible rule that all fat

28

men must be benevolent and Samuel was seldom benevolent. Resemblance to cartoons of Thackeray he deemed an honour, references to Pickwick an insult.

Since the choice of Charles Dickens in preference to his own idol, Mr Thackeray, as this year's Lion, relations between himself and Sir Thomas had reached a low only equalled by those that existed for many years between their respective heroes. Sir Thomas was of course a Dickens man, deliberately cultivating the grave aspect of the author presented in his later portraits and ignoring all evidence of the younger, sprightly, exuberant writer. The thought of what Sir Thomas was now proposing was beyond endurance for Samuel Pipkin. Outrageous! Greater even than the affront to the immortal Mr Thackeray by that common upstart Dickens. 'Tis strange what a man may do, and a woman yet think him an angel,' he mused. How truly Mr Thackeray spoke when he wrote that. He might have had Sir Thomas in mind. Throgmorton must be exposed, and this evening was the time or his name was not Pipkin.

Sir Thomas looked round at his five colleagues, whom he had carefully positioned to separate the opposition. True, this involved his directly facing the obnoxious Pipkin, but no matter. Angelina was by his side, conveniently placed for him to exert his full charm upon her.

He beamed at the committee, exulting in the almost palpable tension. Ah, the power of being able to mould people to his way of thinking. The thought of those who had sworn vengeance on him over the years gave him particular pleasure, for he knew they would never succeed. Conversely, few ever got the better of him, and he never forgot the rare occasion they did, just as he never forgot a face. Sooner or later they would pay − and especially one. He'd been made a fool of, and it would never happen again. Particularly not tonight, much as Pipkin was eager to try.

29

Already, his chest puffed out in happy anticipation of Sir Thomas's downfall, Samuel Pipkin was reading the minutes of the meeting that had heralded the crisis. 'Although the Society's year runs from 23rd April to the following 22nd April, and the chairman holds his position for four years, Sir Thomas Throgmorton moved that his chairmanship should end on 23rd April 1900, and not 22nd April, relying on Rule four bee bracket small roman three unbracket of the Society's constitution. It was agreed after discussion that further consideration be given to the matter and that it be resolved at our next meeting in order to allow plenty of time for suitable plans to be made for the Event.'

Sir Thomas glanced confidently round the table. 'And has anyone had further thoughts on the subject before we vote?' he asked off-handedly, as though expecting silence. But it was patently clear from the voices that immediately broke out that anyone had, if not everyone. (Beddington was asleep.) The indignant bellow of Pipkin, however, carried the day.

'I still maintain your suggestion is preposterous, sir, preposterous. The rule makes it clear that the chairman shall hold the post for four Society years. Your chairmanship, sir, was inaugurated on 23rd April 1896 and you, sir, therefore desist from being chairman on 22nd April 1900.'

'I disagree, as you know, Mr Pick – er Pipkin.' (He did it on purpose, seethed Samuel.) 'The rule also clearly states that the chairman shall hold the position for three years of three hundred and sixty-five days and one leap year. The year of 1900 is not a leap year. My case is, therefore, that, my fourth year being one day short, I remain chairman until and including 23rd April 1900. The chairman elect, yourself, sir, will take over the position on the 24th. This is the law.'

'Then, sir,' sneered Pipkin, 'in the words of your Mr Dickens, the law is an ass.'

30

'You are the ass, sir,' said Sir Thomas calmly, 'if you cannot understand plain English.'

'I think, Sir Thomas,' Oliver put in, doing his best to keep a strictly serious face, 'that your point overlooks rule four bee bracket small roman two unbracket, which states that the Society's year shall run from 23rd April in each year until the 22nd the following year; it makes no allowances for variations in the calendar; this must surely take precedence over rule four bee bracket small roman three unbracket.'

Sir Thomas fixed an unsmiling eye on Oliver. Young figureheads on committees were meant to be seen and not heard, particularly since it had not escaped his notice that Oliver had arrived with Angelina. He was a playwright; he should leave legal matters to his peers. Sir Thomas turned his best Dickensian frown on the young man. 'They are two separate rules, Mr Michaels. I see no reference' – ostentatiously he studied the parchment sheets before him – 'to any link between the two rules. Common sense decrees that rule four bee bracket small roman three unbracket is spelled out so precisely for good reason. Do you not agree, Lord Beddington?' Sir Thomas raised his voice, and with a harumph of a start Lord Beddington was restored to consciousness.

'Quite,' he grunted, and collapsed back into semi-oblivion.

'Mrs Langham?' Sir Thomas turned graciously to his neighbour. 'Do you have a comment?'

'Oh,' replied Angelina, fluttering her eyelashes and looking modestly down. 'I'm only a woman, of course, but it does seem to me, Sir Thomas,' bestowing a bright ingenuous smile on her chairman, 'that it might be rather difficult for the Society to do full justice to the memory of Mr Dickens on the birthday of Mr William Shakespeare in a centenary year to be devoted to the Bard of Avon.'

31

'It is my intention,' explained Sir Thomas loftily, then paused. Dear Angelina could not possibly have seen where this was leading her, but it would be unwise for him to provoke further outbursts of hysterical jealousy by divulging that he had no intention of celebrating Mr Dickens on 23rd April 1900, but of leading the Bard's important birthday celebrations himself in such a dramatic year. That would come later. 'I have my plans. No need to worry your pretty head about that,' he said graciously, patting her hand in avuncular fashion.

Dear Angelina tried to restrain herself from pulling her hand away, and smiled understandingly. Her plans, after all, needed longer to mature. She could not bring herself to vote with him, but she would not alienate him − not yet. Her chance would come at Broadstairs.

'And Mrs Figgis-Hewett.' Sir Thomas bestowed another gracious smile, this time of forgiveness, on Gwendolen. But Gwendolen had no intention of being forgiven. There had been no question mark in his voice, she noted. Very well. Thomas should suffer. She was going to show him that she had a mind of her own.

'I haven't really decided,' she cried shrilly, and a ripple of surprise ran round the table. 'There is a great deal to be said for both sides, it seems to me.' What it was, she didn't know, but Sir Thomas was seriously alarmed. No trace showed in his voice, however.

'Very well,' he announced smoothly, 'we will reflect further whilst we are at Broadstairs and—'

'No,' interrupted Samuel triumphantly, victory in his grasp, so he mistakenly thought. Mathematics was not his strong point. 'We vote now, as already decided. All those in favour of Sir Thomas's argument that his office as chairman expires on 23rd April 1900 kindly make your views known.'

With years of practice at waking up at the psychological

32

moment, Lord Beddington jerked into consciousness. 'Aye,' he said in a pleased voice. Gwendolen sat in a miasma of conflicting emotions.

'Mrs Figgis-Hewett.' The full force of Sir Thomas's personality was brought to bear on her. It was too much for a mere female. She shivered. If she disagreed, he would never speak to her again, never hold her arm as they walked the lanes of England in search of past literary glories, never clasp her hand as at that particularly exciting reading of Wordsworth's *Prelude*, never again stride the moors as Heathcliff and Catherine Earnshaw, never — ah her heart quickened — never again a swift brushing of her lips as in the dark of a Mediterranean evening they trod in the steps of Shelley. No, *she* would remain true, even if he had proved a rotten apple. But somewhere, some time he would pay. At Broadstairs.

'Aye!' she yelled out suddenly, making everyone jump.

Sir Thomas relaxed, forgetting to flash her a smile of gratitude, something he never failed to do in banking diplomacy. 'And I myself make three in favour. Any abstentions?' There was none. 'Very well.' Sir Thomas paused impressively. 'So that is three in favour, three against. I therefore propose the only alternative allowed for in the rules. We must put the matter to His Royal Highness the Prince of Wales in Broadstairs. As president for the year he has the casting vote.'

Samuel was stricken, victory snatched from him. Having heard a little of the interesting scene between Gwendolen and Sir Thomas after the Prince of Wales's banquet, he naturally assumed her allegiance to him would be broken. Now, he was aghast. The Prince would be sure to support Throgmorton; he had the right background — well, half right. He was a banker and an important influence in Europe. What had he, Samuel Pipkin, inheritor of a fortune

33

made in corsetry, to set against this? True, there was his own invention of the Pipkin's Patent Health Corset, but they never awarded honours for that sort of thing. If they had a woman as prime minister now . . . Never, never should Thomas Throgmorton usurp his place as chairman on 23rd April 1900. Over his dead body.

Whose, he did not stop to think. But at Broadstairs, Throgmorton should not escape him.

Now that the matter was as good as settled, Sir Thomas relaxed. The Prince of Wales would be sure to support him, with Beddington on his side. Her Majesty was well known to be partial to Beddington's company, incredible as it seemed. He had paid court to her in his young days. Hard to imagine that Beddington ever had any younger days, looking at his peacefully slumbering, reddened face, bearing traces of years of good and ill. Sir Thomas complacently considered his own middle-aged locks, plentifully adorned with Macassar oil. He was only fifty-three after all, and a catch as far as Angelina was concerned. He was looking forward increasingly to Broadstairs.

Auguste Didier fidgeted impatiently in the anteroom adjoining the private room, awaiting his summons. When he had arrived, he had already had a few doubts about the wisdom of this enterprise. Now, thanks to Emma Pryde, he had grave misgivings. Lacking the strict upbringing of Auguste's Provençal father, Emma had no compunction about listening to the conversations of others – particularly when they might affect herself. In this case, she was fond enough of Auguste still to take at times an almost maternal interest in his affairs, particularly his romantic ones, which irritated him greatly.

'It's only another of these daft societies,' she had explained to Auguste. 'They meet here once a month just to have a good old shout at each other. Old Boney sounds

34

better on his night off than that lot yelling at each other I can tell you.' Old Boney was her pet parrot.

'But if His Royal Highness the Prince of Wales is president, Emma,' Auguste had said, shocked, 'surely it must be a highly honourable society.'

'Old Albert Edward,' remarked Emma, with scant respect for her next sovereign, perhaps born of past intimacy, 'is a good sort. He agrees to these things, then he regrets them once they're done and he has to get off his bum and do something. Generous, is Bertie,' she said absently, perhaps remembering past favours. 'If you want to hear what this lot's like, you come and listen to this.' She had taken him from her private dining room into the anteroom. Putting her fingers to her lips, she drew him over to a small serving hatch. ' 'Ere.'

At first scandalised, then intrigued, Auguste found it impossible to resist the lure of the cut and thrust of battle from within. Thus, by the time his summons came, he was considerably more gloomy about interrupting his precious Fish Fortnight holiday than he had been earlier, even for His Royal Highness. He tried to encourage himself by thinking of the delightful fish menu he had selected, calculated to please everybody, and began to look forward to its getting the accolade it deserved.

'Ah, Mr Didier.' Sir Thomas rose, greeting him expansively, almost shaking hands with him before he realised that, chef to the Prince of Wales or not, Didier was merely a cook, and hurriedly directed him to a chair discreetly repositioned well to the side of the table, where he could not contaminate the committee. Angelina politely turned her chair to face him, earning Thomas's displeasure. Lord Beddington dozed on.

'And how is Norfolk?' enquired Sir Thomas blandly.

This nonplussed Auguste, who had no idea that he had been appointed in his absence chef to His Royal Highness.

35

Fortunately he was saved from rendering the Prince of Wales's tactful gesture to the Society void by Sir Thomas adding: 'Or are you part of the Marlborough House set?' laughing at his little joke. Servants did not have sets.

Auguste opened his mouth, reflected and acquiesced. It could do him no harm to accept this undeserved royal patronage. One for Emma! He murmured something deferentially indistinct, which seemed to satisfy Sir Thomas, and moved on to safe ground: food and his menu.

'*Voilà!*' With a flourish he handed the results of his day's labours to Sir Thomas, who stared at it blankly.

'What is this?' he enquired politely.

Auguste was taken aback. Fancy anyone not knowing what a *mousse de homard* was. 'It is a delicate warm mousse of lobster, monsieur, followed by turbot with quenelles of crawfish—'

'No, no, no, my man. Why are you handing me a menu?' Sir Thomas interrupted impatiently. 'You are here to receive a menu, not give me one. You are here to get your instructions.'

Auguste gazed at him, heart sinking. There had been some mistake. To get instructions? Was this what Auguste Didier had descended to? Was it for this that Auguste Didier was proposing to forgo a precious portion of his holiday? He would leave immediately. Then he reflected. How could he give offence to the Prince of Wales? He was, after all, half English. His English half might be committing treason by so doing. He gulped. He must try what reason could achieve.

He would point out that he was on a fish-cooking-instruction holiday – no, he could not do that now that he had been classified as chef to His Royal Highness. Subtlety was called for.

'Only the very best of fare must be provided for such an important banquet, monsieur, and in Broadstairs only fish surely may be considered.'

36

'But unfortunately Mr Dickens rarely mentions fish, Mr Didier,' said Angelina, smiling, 'save in the plainest of references.'

'No, no, no,' interposed Sir Thomas as though this was entirely Auguste's fault. 'I'm afraid you don't understand at all, my man. It is not *us* who choose the menu, it is not *you*. It is Mr Dickens.'

'*Pardon, monsieur?*' Auguste was completely lost now. Surely this gentleman must know Mr Dickens died some time ago?

'This is the Society of Literary Lionisers and it is the custom that the Grand Banquet should include only food approved and mentioned by the subject of the year. This year our Lion is Mr Charles Dickens. The choice of food is selected from his writings and our knowledge of his likes and dislikes.'

'It hasn't been easy, Mr Didier,' said Angelina cheerfully, with a sidelong glance at Oliver. 'Mr Dickens's characters seem to have had very plain tastes in food.'

'Nonsense, my dear Angelina,' said Sir Thomas, for once irritated by her. 'One has only to read the novels with care to see what appreciation lies behind every mention of food. And consider the fact that Mrs Dickens herself penned a cookery book, that she and Mr Dickens were visitors at Gore House—'

Auguste stiffened. 'At Gore House?'

'Mr Alexis Soyer's Gastronomic Symposium of all Nations eating house. If you, Mr Didier, cannot find the recipes for anything on our menu, you should refer to the cookery books of Alexis Soyer which were approved by Dickens himself.'

'Steak *à la Soyer* is included in *What Shall we Have for Dinner?* by Lady Clutterbuck, Mrs Dickens's *nom de plume*. So, Mr Didier, you need have no *fear* at using this recipe,' trilled Gwendolen.

Auguste had received a double blow. Not only had the dreaded name of Soyer been uttered, but Dickens had chosen the menu. Yet to the best of his recollection, he could remember no succulent descriptions of food in the novels, no overpowering sense of its central place in the affairs of men. An appreciation of food yes, but of cuisine? No.

Now his worst suspicions were confirmed. This Dickens was an admirer of Soyer and his cooking, and he, Auguste Didier, was commanded by his future sovereign to cook a Dickensian banquet *à la Soyer*. He could not endure the humiliation. Some escape must be found.

As if understanding his thoughts, the lady referred to as Angelina was looking at him with compassion. 'I'm sure, Mr Didier, you will succeed very well. You have not earned your reputation for nothing. My friend Lady Jane Marshall was mentioning your name to me the other day,' she emphasised innocently.

He almost smiled; the young Lady Jane from Stockbery Towers, now married to Walter Marshall and the mother of three budding politicians aged six, three and one.

'I am most grateful, madame,' he replied genuinely. Had she not spoken, he might have committed *une bétise*.

'Soup,' declared Sir Thomas, anxious to get on with the matter of the moment. 'Mutton broth or Scotch broth. Understand, Didier?'

'But it is July,' expostulated Auguste, all his good intentions of calm deserting him.

'I know that,' said Sir Thomas testily, angry that his idol had not produced lighter alternatives. 'Any suggestions from your readings of Dickens?' he asked sarcastically.

'Fish soup,' intervened Samuel Pipkin brightly. 'A sort of soup, or broth, or brew,' he quoted dreamily from the Great Master, in his case Thackeray. 'The Ballad of Bouillabaisse,' he added for those not fortunate enough to be so well acquainted with the immortal works as he was himself. Auguste's interest quickened. This Thackeray sounded a more sensible writer than he had thought him.

'Pah, Thackeray,' snorted Sir Thomas. 'A mere plagiarist.'

Samuel leapt to his feet, spluttering with rage. 'You will retract that, sir. You will apologise.'

'My dear fellow,' Sir Thomas smiled condescendingly, 'you must agree that many of his scenes and characters are based on Mr Dickens's—'

'You lie.'

'Mr Pipkin,' said Angelina softly. 'This is not the place.'

Samuel glanced at Auguste, and subsided into his chair. But the look he turned on Sir Thomas was inimical. Another unforgivable sin had been added to the catalogue of his crimes.

'Any other suggestions?' enquired Sir Thomas complacently.

There was none.

Auguste racked his brains wildly, but they failed to produce any suitable Dickensian memories. He sighed. 'Soup,' he wrote down. 'Mutton broth.'

'Dimpled over with fat,' added Oliver Michaels, 'to make it a true Dickensian dish.'

Sir Thomas looked up. 'I feel we can dispense with the fat dimpling, Mr Michaels.'

Here Auguste was in horrified accord.

'A barrel of oysters,' Lord Beddington woke up suddenly. 'Read that somewhere in old Dickens. Sensible fellow. Don't do things by halves, eh?'

'And oysters,' amended Sir Thomas, aware of the need to placate his one stable supporter.

'They are out of season, sir,' murmured Auguste weakly. 'But I will try.'

'Kippered salmon,' suggested Samuel sulkily, thus revealing a knowledge of Dickens that he would never otherwise confess to – save in an attempt to out-Dickens Sir Thomas.

'No!' thundered, Sir Thomas. 'Lobster salad to follow. As in *The Pickwick Papers*.'

Auguste relaxed. Here, at least, was something one could present to the palate of the Prince of Wales. But would lobsters be obtainable by then? He would ensure they were. He would talk to the fishermen.

'Now. The entrée. I think we're all agreed?' Sir Thomas looked triumphantly round the table before announcing their verdict: 'Mrs Crupp's dish of kidneys.'

Howls of laughter followed from all save Samuel. Auguste looked blank.

'Mr Didier,' explained Oliver, 'the joke is that David Copperfield's housekeeper sent for all her dishes from the pastrycook, so you—'

'*Non*,' stated Auguste simply. Here Horatio must stand firm to guard his bridge. 'Everything for the Prince of Wales is cooked by *me* – not by a Broadstairs shopkeeper.'

Perhaps it was something in his eye which told them their joke had fallen flat, but no more was said on the question of Mrs Crupp's dish of kidneys, it being tacitly agreed that the dishes of kidneys would be *à la Didier*.

'Now, the goose,' said Sir Thomas casually.

'This too is a joke,' said Auguste confidently.

'No, my dear fellow,' he retorted testily. '*A Christmas Carol*. Either goose with sage and onion stuffing and onion sauce, or turkey.'

'Oh, Sir Thomas, do you think you ought?' enquired Gwendolen anxiously. 'With your delicate stomach—'

Sir Thomas glared. 'I am not prepared, Mrs Figgis-Hewett, to abrogate my duty to Mr Dickens. It is to be goose, madam, goose.'

Auguste gazed at him, wondering whether he were mad.

'But this is a Christmas dish,' Auguste said at last. 'Not

a dish for August Bank Holiday Saturday.' His voice was almost calm.

'Quails,' suggested Pipkin. 'Dolby tells us Dickens ate them in America.'

'Veal cutlet and taters,' said Angelina with relish.

'Lovely, lovely beefsteak pudding made with flour and eggs,' put in Gwendolen, who had never made one, and rarely eaten one.

'Simoon of roast,' said Oliver. *Master Humphrey's Clock.*'

'*Mais—*' Auguste tried, but broke off to gather his strength for the plan he had in mind. 'May I suggest your goose if you wish, sir, but for those for whom this is just a little heavy, His Royal Highness for instance, how about raised pies? I am sure' – clutching wildly at his recollections of Dickens – 'he mentions pies.'

'Indeed. Jolly meat pies. Pickwick,' said Sir Thomas lugubriously. 'But does His Royal Highness—'

'Pies and pickles are beloved by His Royal Highness,' said Auguste, without proof but certain he was correct in assuming His Royal Highness would find them preferable to goose on an August night. Already his fertile mind, having got the measure of the monstrous problem confronting him, was rearranging the menu so that it might not disgrace the Prince or himself, and yet *appear* to conform with Mr Dickens's predilections.

'Mr Dickens does not seem to have had a sweet tooth, unfortunately,' Sir Thomas droned on. 'Charlotte Russe – Lady Clutterbuck has a recipe. I think that would be allowable in default of anything better.'

'Raspberry jam tarts are mentioned in *Martin Chuzzlewit*,' offered Oliver, earning a glare from Sir Thomas for his erudition.

'And we can drink ginger beer,' shrieked Gwendolen. 'What fun it will be.'

41

Fun was not the word that Auguste could associate with the Prince of Wales's discovering that he was expected to drink ginger beer with his dinner. Fortunately, Sir Thomas here intervened with Auguste's full approval. 'The rules of the Society,' he pointed out, 'do not specify that the drink has to be as noted in the works by the Lion. We will of course have porter and stout available for those who wish it, perhaps even mint julep and hot elder wine, but for the banquet itself,' just as Auguste's alarm was once again rising, 'I feel we may safely partake of French wine. Do you not agree, Mr Didier?'

Mr Didier did.

'Then we need not detain you, Mr Didier. We leave you to your plans. I recommend you to Mr Soyer's recipes. You won't go far wrong there.'

Auguste left the room, trembling with emotion, with Sid's words coming back to him. Now he had a shrewd suspicion how and why murder would be committed at Broadstairs. By him. Or perhaps, unless this menu were radically adapted, by the Prince of Wales with himself the victim.

Chapter Three

Auguste opened one eye, and closed it again as the full force
of his dilemma returned to him. True, it was the first day
of the Fish Fortnight. He firmly refused to consider it a
holiday, with such an inauspicious start, firstly as he had
no strong faith in the English seaside as a suitable venue
for such an event, and secondly, because the last time he
had set off for a holiday, murder had awaited him. Not that
he could seriously envisage that happening in this case, but
nevertheless the word holiday was rapidly regaining its
unpleasant ring. Moreover, there was the matter of the
Dickens banquet. Visions of roast goose floated before his
eyes, and he groaned. Then his natural optimism reasserted
itself as the sun shone invitingly through the window. Who,
after all, would wish to remain in London in such tropical
temperatures? The seaside might prove quite acceptable,
even if it did bring with it such major disadvantages as a
Soyer banquet to cook.

He sprang out of bed with sudden resolution, prepared
to greet Saturday, 29 July 1899. But the dilemma still
remained: should he don suitable travelling clothes for
departing from Victoria railway station, considering the
inevitable coating of smuts from the engine smoke that these
would acquire, thus arriving at his destination looking as
out of place as a bouillabaisse in a Smithfield eating house,
or should he brave the worst and don his new holiday
apparel. He eyed the boater wistfully, but replaced it in its

hatbox. However tempting, he could not depart from Curzon Street adorned in a brightly striped blazer and sporting a boater. This afternoon, he vowed, they would make a proud appearance, however. Perhaps even his new blue bathing costume would join them.

'Kipper an' corfee, Mr Didier,' came Sid's cheerful shout from below.

'*Je vous remercie*, Sid,' Auguste called, and in due course duly descended to face Sid's usual offering of kipper (ritually rejected by Auguste and eaten with relish by Sid) and muffins. At first Sid had tried hard to entice Auguste into the delights of kidneys and kedgeree for breakfast, but had been forced to admit failure. Strong coffee and a brioche had been Auguste's simple demand, reduced to a compromise of muffins after prolonged negotiation. In the days of William of Normandy, the Conqueror as he was known here, Auguste reflected, 9 a.m. was the hour of dinner not breakfast. He shuddered, glad that he lived under the rule of the good Queen Victoria.

'My granny allus said, "Wittles inside, walk with pride. Without no peck, watch your step",' contributed Sid.

Auguste's opinion of Sid's granny was not enhanced by this tribute to her poetic powers, but in the interests of Anglo-French co-operation he submitted as usual to the muffins.

'Tomorrow, Sid,' he pontificated, adding a dollop of quince preserve, 'we will rise early and greet the fishermen as they return with their catch. We will purchase your beloved kippers as herrings.' Sid greeted the prospect without joy.

Later in the day, Auguste planned happily, he would perhaps go to see dear Egbert and Edith at Ramsgate. A brisk walk over the sands . . . His spirits rose again, and most of his former forebodings about Broadstairs fled with the speed of Sid's granny's immortal dicta.

44

Victoria railway station bustled with an excitement only rivalled at Christmastime. Those who could afford hotels, lodgings or boarding houses by the seaside mingled with mere day excursionists in a mass departure in search of less polluted air, a need heightened this year by the exceptionally hot weather. Frustrated husbands, unable to leave their offices for two weeks, or wishing to appear as if this were the case, waved their families off. Buckets and wooden spades were clutched by tiny hands as symbols of veteran travel, sailor suits were sported by every male under twelve, and ladies of high fashion bound for the respectable haunts of Broadstairs or the Cliftonville Hotel at Margate pursued their porters bound for first-class carriages. Their less affluent sisters swarmed cheerfully towards second- and third-class carriages, clutching ancient grips and eyeing their battered trunks possessively, while the excursionists scurried for their own cheap fast train.

Auguste and Sid followed their porter to their reserved first-class carriage. The Auguste Didier School of Cuisine did not do matters by halves. Like in a recipe in which ingredients suddenly assume a different identity when mixed together according to instructions, he was interested to see what would happen when this odd mixture of pupils was together for a whole fortnight. Holidays were strange occasions. Those you thought you knew well turned out sometimes to be quite unlike that at all. Others you had previously set little store by could turn out to be shining jewels of companions. And what, after all, did he really *know* about these six people?

As Auguste climbed up into the teak carriage, he tripped over Sid's feet, his spirits tumbling with him as he saw his six pupils squeezed together in the one carriage. Alas, who could believe these six geese might in a few hours' time become happy swans? No one could have guessed this quiet group was bound for the seaside. True, Broadstairs was apparently decorous, even dull by Ramsgate and Margate standards, yet surely not this sombre.

Auguste seated himself next to Alice Fenwick, who was sandwiching Alfred Wittisham between herself and James Pegg. Alfred was sporting his Old Etonian waistcoat, but beyond that showed no signs of holiday festiveness. James, too, with brown boots and heavy suit, was subdued. By the corridor window Auguste was opposite Emily Dawson, clad in an unbecoming dark brown cotton dress, unrelieved by touches of colour. What would she wear at the seaside? he wondered. Black bombazine? Algernon Peckham sat next to her ostentatiously reading Carlyle. Various other levels of reading matter adorned the other laps, including, he noted, the inevitable *Harmsworth* in Alice's lap. Auguste's spirits fell further. Despite a lack of excitement, there was a definite tension. But why? He told himself that he was imagining things, but the impression would not go away.

'My book says,' remarked Emily brightly, 'that there was a murderer from Ramsgate thirty years ago, killed five people. Ramsgate's near Broadstairs, isn't it?'

'Quite near,' replied Auguste repressively. He had no wish to encourage talk of murder.

'Is that vy ve go there?' rumbled Heinrich Freimüller with interest.

'*Non*,' said Auguste. 'Certainly not.'

'It said in one of my *Harmsworth Magazines*,' announced Alice, 'that if you walk along the Strand from Charing Cross to Temple Bar and back any day at any busy hour, you'll pass a man who has either done a murder or who will do a murder before he dies. It says that somehow you will sense it. Is that true, Mr Didier?' She found it necessary to clutch Alfred's arm for protection against such horrors.

'This I do not know, Miss Fenwick,' answered Auguste

grimly. 'I work during the busy hours. I do not have time to wander along the Strand gazing at my fellow man when I have to teach pupils as difficult as yourselves.'

'We're not as bad as that, are we?' drawled Algernon. 'I thought my veal curry rather excellent yesterday.' Too late he realised he had betrayed an interest in meat cookery.

'You used curry paste,' Alice retorted disapprovingly. 'You can't make a real curry like that. You have to use the proper spices — red pepper and cardamoms, and garam—'

'Nor,' said Auguste breaking in, 'do you use a *Soyer* recipe for curry. Miss Fenwick is correct, Mr Peckham. For curry you use perhaps Colonel Kenney-Herbert's *Culinary Jottings for Madras*—'

'My grandmama had a cholera recipe that used cardamoms,' volunteered Emily.

'I did not know your family came from India, Fraülein Dawson,' said Heinrich. These were about the first words he had addressed directly to her since the unfortunate affair of the Nesselrode pudding, at which she had taken great offence.

'No, she lived in Dover. They had a cholera outbreak near there.'

'That is near vere ve are going?' enquired Heinrich anxiously.

'*Non,*' said Auguste resignedly. 'Not vere ve are going.' Really, for a so-called holiday, there was a remarkable harping on illness and death in the conversation.

'Nasty thing cholera. I was in the army you know, over there,' announced Alfred.

'In Dover?' asked James with interest, earning himself a rare black look from his hero.

'No. India. The Guards. Only for a year or two. Had to resign for ill health.'

'Were you wounded?' breathed Alice tremulously.

47

'No,' said Alfred cheerfully. 'Caught chickenpox from the Colonel's youngest. They thought it was cholera, and packed me off home. Mama insisted I leave.' His face grew suddenly long.

'Poor Alfred. Chickenpox.' Alice was distressed.

'I haven't got it now,' Alfred announced encouragingly, and patted her hand.

James cleared his throat at this compromising movement, determined to steer the conversation away from Alfred's frailties. 'You like these Sherlock Holmes stories then,' he said out of the blue, glancing at the *Strand Magazine* on Auguste's knee.

'Like you, isn't he?' Algernon commented.

'*Non*. I am not in the least like Mr Holmes!' Auguste replied, outraged. 'Why, Mr Holmes has never to my recollection cooked anything, or shown the least interest in true cuisine. He merely suffers the invaluable Mrs Hudson to struggle in with trays of nourishment from time to time. What kind of life is that? No, he is no true detective if he does not appreciate food.'

With a chug and billows of greyish-white smoke, the train began to move out of Victoria railway station on its journey to the sea. The die is cast, thought Auguste, as it gathered speed, the rhythm pounding inexorably in his ears. The sound had a comforting reassurance after a while, so why then did he suddenly wish with all his heart that he were safe in his kitchen in Curzon Street?

'So do you agree you can tell a murderer by his face?' Algernon continued remorselessly and maliciously, aware of Auguste's reluctance to talk on the subject.

'Everyone can tell *afterwards*. It is less easy to do so beforehand,' Auguste assured him. 'How can one take a group of people, like yourselves for instance, and say you are a murderer or might be a murderer? There is no proof, and can never be any. And without proof one cannot know.

Just as without cooking and tasting you cannot know that the recipe works.'

Emily gave a little scream. 'Like *us*, Mr Didier? You think we are murderers?'

'*Non, non,*' he said hastily. 'A group *like* you. Or like the Literary Lionisers. Any group of ordinary people in their daily lives.' Could one say of any group, he wondered, that they were ordinary? What, after all, did he know of the desires and passions, the hopes and fears of these people after they left Curzon Street at night? True, it was hard to imagine their having any at all, looking at them now. A dull enough assembly. Yet put these same people in front of food and something happened to them. Each in their own way turned into an artist. Not to be compared with himself of course, but talented, definitely talented. And if food could bring about such a change, perhaps other factors could also. Perhaps the Literary Lionisers committee too would be revealed as individuals with hopes and fears.

'There are an awful lot of undiscovered murders,' Alice was saying with some relish. 'That's what my *Harmsworth Magazine* says.' Auguste had long ago tired of the *Harmsworth Magazine*, but Alice was not to be stopped. 'There was that Mrs Francis butchered in her rooms at Peckham. And that murder in Great Coram Street—'

'They found the murderer. He was a German,' Algernon remarked incautiously.

'*Nein*, he was found innocent,' glared Heinrich, always touchy on the subject of German honour.

'And the Euston Square murders,' Algernon continued doggedly.

'London isn't safe, and that's a fact,' James put in. 'But most murderers *are* found out, aren't they, Mr Didier?'

'How can we know? Most murderers of *known* murders perhaps. But of those murders not known to be murders, the push over the clifftop, or under the train, the poison

49

dealt stealthily that kills little by little. How can we know how many there are?'

'Mrs Maybrick was found out.'

'But was she guilty?' demanded Emily, taking an unusually large part in the conversation today. 'I think it was a shame. He was an arsenic eater, you know. And she only bought the arsenic for her complexion. My grandmama used it with treacle.'

'*Pardon?*' said Auguste, startled.

'Oh, not on her *bread*, Mr Auguste,' said Emily, her face unaccountably flushing bright red. 'To kill flies.'

'Ah,' said Auguste, relieved.

'Sheep,' put in James. 'You use it for sheep. Dangerous stuff.' He relapsed into silence again, perhaps at the sight of Alice's hand stealing once more into Alfred's for comfort. He frowned. Something had to be done. 'Messy business, poison,' he said quietly, glancing at his huge capable hands.

'How would you kill, Monsieur Didier, if you had to commit a murder?' asked Algernon bluntly.

'This is a parlour game perhaps, Mr Peckham?' enquired Auguste politely. 'Death is not a game.'

But Algernon was undeterred. 'Lord Wittisham then.'

Alfred Wittisham was contemplating happily his recent evening with Beatrice Throgmorton, thinking that Alice's hand had nothing like her delicate slender trusting sensitiveness. Oh, for the touch of it. He'd do anything for her. His misery swept over him once more. But there was nothing he could do. Or was there?

'Could you commit a murder?' Algernon continued.

'Oh yes,' declared Alfred enthusiastically. 'I'd – I'd' – inspiration deserted him. 'Shoot him down like a dog,' he added. This was lame in Algernon's view.

'Mr Pegg?'

'Chloroform,' he said offhandedly.

'Rather unsporting, James,' commented Alfred reprovingly and James flushed.

'Miss Dawson?'

'I think this is a very silly game,' she gasped. 'I couldn't kill a fly.' And she shut her mouth obstinately.

'Herr Freimüller?'

'I strangle,' he said shortly. There was a short silence, while everyone tried not to look at his hands.

'Sid?'

'Set me granny's dogs on 'im.'

Alice giggled. 'I'd hypnotise my victim and tell him to jump off Battersea Bridge when I wasn't there.' Some discussion followed as to whether this was practical or not.

'And you, Mr Peckham,' asked James rather belligerently. 'You haven't said how you'd do it.'

'Oh. I couldn't murder anyone,' said Algernon smugly.

There was a concerted murmur of outrage at this betrayal. Auguste noted Algernon's successful manipulation of the group. An interesting if unlikeable young man. He also considered how strange it was that despite their previous enthusiastic discussion no one had mentioned internal poison.

'There's the sea,' shouted Emily suddenly, putting an end to this morbid discussion.

'Where?' cried Alice, craning round Alfred, then jumping up together with Auguste, Emily and Algernon crowded to the left side of the carriage, by which time the brief glimpse had long since passed.

The sight of Reculver Towers drew a deep sigh of appreciation, and animation grew. At Margate, the first general exodus from the train took place, while those remaining silently congratulated themselves on their wisdom or affluence in continuing to Broadstairs or Ramsgate. Spirits rose higher still as the train chugged steadily on to Broadstairs, a glimpse of blue-grey sea and white-tipped

51

waves drawing exclamations, with the added excitement of steamers and pleasure boats gracing the scene.

At Broadstairs railway station the group's descent was far less decorous than their ascent at Victoria. Even Heinrich was seen to set his Homburg at a definitely more jaunty angle before positively hurrying to the barrier, the more quickly to enjoy the delights of the English seaside.

Outside the railway station a line of flymen waited, less vociferous than at Margate or Ramsgate where landladies paid them to attract custom, but avaricious for custom for their ancient landaus and victorias.

As their two landaus set off for Chandos Place on the seafront where their rented house awaited them, James glowered at the sight of Alice still nestling by Alfred's side. He set Alice down as an unworthy mate for his aristocratic lordship, but feared his lordship's susceptible nature. However, he had a suspicion that Alfred was keeping something from him; that there was some other lady in his life. James had no objection to that, provided she were worthy of his hero. He only hoped that she was reciprocating his advances. Alice's hand had rested for some considerable time in his lordship's which was not a good sign.

Alice knew quite well what James was thinking and that he disliked her. This puzzled her, for she was not conscious of doing anything wrong. True, she had occasionally accompanied James to Hampstead Heath on a Sunday afternoon, and eventually had been obliged to point out that her future plans did not include him. She brooded about this. She loved Alfred now, had every intention of becoming Lady Wittisham and objected to her courting being carried out in a threesome. It was not as if she were pushing herself on Alfred. She was just there when he noticed her. Unfortunately so was James Pegg.

Alfred mused happily, jogging along in the sunshine of the seaside. Perhaps in the mellowness of the Broadstairs

52

air, Sir Thomas would change his mind. People did while they were on holiday. Sir Thomas would be here for a whole week. True, Beatrice would not be present, but perhaps that was for the good. He could concentrate on winning over Sir Thomas. If only girls didn't have fathers, he thought idly, what a jolly world it would be. Just what would he do if Sir Thomas failed to change his mind? He remembered uneasily what had last passed between them.

Heinrich was looking forward to the holiday. His Imperial Majesty the Kaiser Wilhelm II would be at Cowes. He might even get an opportunity himself to visit the island of Wight. He discarded the plan. He could not relax, for these were dangerous times. Much depended on how well His Majesty did at Cowes with his yacht *Meteor*. If well, all would be well. But if badly, it boded ill for everyone, especially for the Embassy. A cloud obscured his summer sky, but cleared quickly away as he thought of the German band that would be performing on the sands. At least he would enjoy part of this holiday. He was aware suddenly of Emily Dawson sitting by his side.

Emily's hands were clasped neatly in her lap. She was suppressing a certain excitement at coming to the seaside. If only . . . It was a long time ago, surely he wouldn't recognise her?

Algernon, too, was eager and ready for the seaside adventure, as yet with no unpleasant thoughts on his mind, save one important one, which he had already dismissed as having no relevance to Broadstairs. The thought of a banquet for the Literary Lionisers did not disturb him in the least, particularly if it meant they would be waiting on the Prince of Wales. He had his eye on his future. Old Victoria couldn't last for ever. And moreover they were to cook from Mr Soyer's recipes so at least the Prince would get some decent food. Didier wasn't bad, but he had his blind spots and the Maître Soyer was one of them.

Sid had very uncomplicated thoughts. Sid was simply looking forward to the whelk and jellied-eel stalls, the ice-cream vendors and donkey rides that his day trips to Southend had convinced him adorned every seaside pier. Not to mention some nice penny-in-the-slot machines. 'What the Butler Saw', for instance.

The landaus turned off the High Street, having passed close by the grand entrance of the Albion Hotel. At the Victoria Parade on the seafront, there was a gasp as the full glory of Broadstairs was revealed. The smell of the ocean (rather sweeter than had been usual in former years owing to the provision of new outflows further from the Thanet towns) and the noise struck them simultaneously. Sudden awareness came upon them of the dull nature of their own attire, faced with the spectacle of ladies in light foulards carrying gaily coloured parasols and gentlemen in debonair blazers and audaciously white flannels promenading on the cliffside, swinging smart new canes or sticks that sported the latest fashionable knobs. The older generation chose Victoria's portrait to adorn their knobs, the younger Ranjitsinhji. Balloons, toy windmills, buckets and spades, donkeys, beach entertainers, a line of bathing machines (no tents for stately Broadstairs) and sandcastles filled the glazed eyes of the new arrivals with impressions as vivid and gay as Mr Frith's famous portrayal of Ramsgate.

So this was Mr Dickens's Watering Place. This was the English Seaside. No wonder, thought Auguste dazedly, assisting Alice down from the landau, that Dickens had declared the place too noisy and left. And if this were Broadstairs, what would Ramsgate be like? Poor, poor Egbert.

In London, with only seven days before the Week of the Lion commenced, the committee of the Literary Lionisers were now looking forward to their 'holiday' with mixed feelings. After the unfortunate scenes at the committee meeting, not only those overheard by Auguste but several private ones that had taken place after the committee meeting had broken up in complete disarray, this was by no means the pleasurable experience it had hitherto seemed.

Samuel Pipkin was, strangely, the calmest. His plans were already laid. Thomas Throgmorton had gone too far. He would suffer for riding roughshod over Samuel Pipkin Esquire. His mind was made up. It was the mind of a John Jasper.

Angelina Langham also had plans, but they were less inflexible. She had a notion that Sir Thomas would propose to her while they were away. Where better than under the heady influence of the seaside air? And, ah, then what pleasure it would give her to decline his proposal, and even more to tell him why. What would happen then she had not yet decided, but the thought of revenge could sometimes be very sweet.

Oliver Michaels had noticed the apparently growing intimacy between Angelina and Sir Thomas with some bewilderment. Surely Angelina could not seriously be encouraging Sir Thomas? Yet it looked as if she were, in which case she was not the person he thought her. True, her last husband was much older than she was. With sudden resolution, however, he knew that whatever the reason, Sir Thomas could not be allowed to marry Angelina. He was surprised to find quite how strongly he felt about the matter.

Gwendolen Figgis-Hewett couldn't wait to get to Broadstairs. There, she was sure, she would know once and for all whether or not Sir Thomas had really meant those cruel words he had spoken to her, or whether it was merely overwork on his part combined with the unfortunate effect of the high temperature at the time. Surely no one could have meant them seriously, could they? Or perhaps, she brightened, he was deliberately concealing his devotion to her in this way, shy of declaring his real feelings. Under the passion inspired by a Broadstairs moon, ah, then she could gently coax him into confidence. But what if he once again rejected her? She shivered. Her face became quite blank as she thought just what she might do if Sir Thomas did once again reject her advances.

Lord Beddington didn't much mind whether he was in Broadstairs or London provided there was something decent to drink. And preferably to eat as well.

Sir Thomas was filled with satisfaction at the prospect of the coming week. True, he had alienated some of his support, but the vote had been taken and was irreversible. Nothing would stand in the way of his chairmanship on 23rd April next. Royalty would be present at the celebrations, perhaps even Her Majesty herself. An earldom dangled its enticing prospect before him. He had no hopes that the Prince of Wales might bestow such an honour on him, but where ladies were concerned, it might well be a different matter. Yes, with Her Majesty Queen Victoria or the Princess of Wales present, his chance might be high. Either would do nicely.

Meanwhile the passions aroused at the committee meeting would have had time to die down. Thank goodness he'd sent Beatrice out of the country for a while in case she had any more ridiculous notions about marrying that brainless young masher. He may be a baronet, but he was penniless, and, moreover, one who was given to horse racing was not what he wanted for Beatrice. Luckily Beatrice did not care for the seaside, not after what had happened to her when she was ten. She'd nearly been drowned, thanks to a damn fool of a woman. He frowned. He'd been unlucky with servants one way and another. Especially once. Still, the police had told him the man was dead. Murdered. Serve him right. A sudden inexplicable shiver ran down Sir Thomas's spine.

*   *   *

56

Inspector Egbert Rose and his wife disembarked from the *Royal Sovereign* paddle steamer at Ramsgate's East Pier. He was glad he'd taken a notion to come by sea, even if Edith had looked a little on the green side. It seemed to make it more of a holiday somehow. He liked looking out on the Thames from his Factory window, and it seemed fitting that he should sail away down it on holiday. Edith had not been so sure.

'Very pleasant,' she announced as she looked approvingly round the hotel room with the large red and blue roses on the wallpaper, its roomy mahogany wardrobe and solid bed. There was even a screen by the washing bowl. She sat down heavily on the balloon-back chair with a sigh. 'Very nice, Egbert,' she repeated.

Egbert was not listening. He had thrust up the sash window to let into the room the sounds of the street and the harbour below. Ah, here was life. Here was Holiday. Life, not Death. And somewhere, faintly — he sniffed — he could even smell the sea.

A boater- and blazer-beclad Auguste walked nonchalantly into the street. The work of unpacking and arranging was done — mostly, he noted grimly, by himself. Now he, too, could enjoy the seaside. Down on the sands opposite the house was an itinerant Punch and Judy man, his booth surrounded by children. At least he assumed this must be Punch and Judy, for it was clearly not like the marionettes of the Tuileries gardens. In a sudden lull in the overall noise around him, some words floated across to him: 'That's the way to do it.' The gentleman, he observed, appeared to be hitting the lady over the head. She collapsed. Auguste smiled wrily. Truly, he could say that murder followed him everywhere.

He looked around to get his bearings, sniffing the air appreciatively, feeling already part of this English seaside.

To the right, at the west end of the bay, was the imposing Grand Hotel on the cliffside, and before it lay gardens with a bandstand. Ah yes. He knew how important this bandstand was to seaside life.

Far to the left was the old town through which they had travelled, and at its foot lay a small harbour with a few fishing boats nestling against the old wooden pier. Even from here he could see that any fishermen on the pier would be vastly outnumbered by holidaymakers. Above the harbour on the east cliff was what must be Fort House, of which he had heard, the so-called Bleak House where Mr Dickens had stayed. A tall, gaunt building, it stood perched on its own, dominating the old town far below it. It was so high in proportion to its width that it looked an unlikely building to withstand the gales of the English Channel as they swept over the cliffs. In his beloved Fort House, Dickens had spent many holidays. What a view he would have had. But so windy. Auguste shivered at the thought. When you were born under the sun of Provence, the winds of south-east England seemed harsh indeed. Fort House had too stark a beauty for his eye, as he imagined what it must be like in winter.

With sudden determination he set out briskly for the harbour. He and Sid had worked with a will unpacking his kitchen equipment and stores and it was some time before it dawned on him that the usual eager and willing helping hands were not present. Instead, strange and unusual sounds of laughter could be heard from upstairs as his pupils sorted out their belongings and bedrooms. Then a silence fell for a brief period before bursting down the stairs came an unexpected sight.

Emily headed the column, in a bright pink dress with face to match. Heinrich followed her in check jacket and trousers that would certainly not have been tolerated in the Kaiser's presence, then Alice in a provocatively thin muslin gown with hand-embroidered roses on it; Alfred with bright red cummerbund and Panama hat; James in a blue and white striped blazer and cricketing tie, and Algernon carrying what could only be one of the new gentlemen's bathing costumes in bright green stripes over his arm. Without so much as a by your leave, this gypsy band of erstwhile eager apprentices, oblivious of Auguste's indignant face, sped out of the door and disappeared.

'Sid,' said Auguste sadly, 'it is good that some have a sense of responsibility.'

'Yus,' replied Sid, but was strangely quiet as he worked. Fifteen minutes later he tiptoed out of the door, leaving Auguste in the midst of a loving discussion of the differences between the taste of *écrevisses* and *crevettes* in a sauce.

'*Eh bien*,' remarked Auguste ruefully, when he discovered Sid's defection, 'perhaps it is that I grow old.' He placed a *bain-marie* lovingly on the table, but for once failed to invent a new sauce to cook within it. He remembered the boater, he recalled the blazer waiting upstairs. '*Non*,' he informed the *bain-marie* happily, 'I do not grow old, not yet.' And within five minutes he had emerged to greet The Seaside.

'I will,' he announced to his conscience, 'investigate the fish.' He strolled along the promenade, swinging his cane, fish rather less in his mind than the many most attractive young ladies adorning the sands. Kent, he said to himself, having recently read *The Pickwick Papers* in honour of the forthcoming weekend, is known for its apples, cherries, hops – and women. He hummed to himself, and a smile lit his face, as he crossed the bridge and walked down towards the pier.

It was an attractive corner with an old inn opposite the pier and an old clap-boarded boathouse at its entrance. Most noticeable were two figureheads, no doubt from wrecks: a Scotsman performing a Highland fling, and another apparently of a Greek god. But Auguste had no time for sightseeing. The smell of the ocean was in his nostrils, and more than that, the smell of fish. Skirting round two ample matrons and a bathchair, he made his way to the end of the pier where two fishermen were engaged in tobacco-chewing and a silent contemplation of life. They glanced up as he planted himself before them.

'Ah,' said one uninterestedly.

Auguste, however, was born in a fishing village, and this was an attitude he recognised. Cannes or Broadstairs, fishermen spoke the same basic language.

'*Bonjour, messieurs*,' he announced cordially. 'I require some fish. Much fish,' he added as this did not meet with instant reaction.

'Sprats,' announced one of the men succinctly. 'Tomorrow.'

'Lobsters,' countered Auguste.

'Outa season!' He spat.

'Not by next Saturday,' said Auguste firmly. They eyed him more carefully.

'Meanwhile,' said Auguste, seeing he was gaining ground, 'I require dory, crayfish, cod, flounders, hake, sole, crab—'

'Nah.'

'The Duke of Stockbery, whom I advise, looks for a new supplier.'

The Duke of Stockbery could fish for it himself, seemed to be their reaction. Auguste had blundered.

'Ramsgate, you wants.' They turned their backs.

'This week, *mes amis*. you will look after me. And in return, on Saturday you, and not Ramsgate, will ensure that the Prince of Wales eats well.'

Slowly they turned round.

'Ah,' remarked one. 'Nothing against Teddy, not never.'

'Ah,' added his companion. 'Broadstairs scrubs and

Margate kings, mind. Ramsgate capons, Peter's lings.' They cackled.

Disregarding this since he could make nothing of it, Auguste pressed on. '*Bon*. So it is agreed. I will come each evening and give you my requests. And you, like efficient men of Kent, will supply them in the morning.'

'Ah.' They spat in unison, and resumed their seats.

Auguste shook hands with them, raised his hat, and retired. It was a job well done. Perhaps this seaside would be *amusant* after all. His imagination began to run riot, fish of all shapes and sizes floating through his mind's eye, sauces of every hue adorning their fresh magnificence.

Chapter Four

The Imperial Hotel proudly faced the sea, halfway between its two rivals, the Albion with its Dickensian associations and the relative newcomer, the Grand Hotel, standing sentinel on the West Cliff. The Imperial, with its solid, ornate façade and a tower at either end, offered comfortable grandeur, like Broadstairs itself. It had been built in the 1860s, to take advantage of the sudden influx of visitors provided by the arrival of the London, Chatham and Dover Railway at Broadstairs. This late start in railway communication with the outside world enabled Broadstairs and the Imperial to gain from the benefits of visitors, while still maintaining their reputation for selectness. Steamers called at its noisy neighbours, Margate and Ramsgate, but Broadstairs, favoured by the discriminating, in the main slumbered peacefully on. The Imperial Hotel exuded the essence of Broadstairs: we are here in our excellence should you have need of us, but we shall not stoop to seek you out.

Nevertheless its owner was a worried man. Particularly today.

'I don't know, I'm sure, Mr Dee.' Mr Cedric Multhrop subsided into one of the comfortable armchairs in his lounge, then leapt up guiltily as though a mere hotel owner had no place to be sitting down in his guests' domain. 'Should it be the red carpet or the blue? That's what I keep asking myself. The red is more correct, but new it is not, Mr Dee.

I couldn't say it's new, but then could blue be said to be royal? That's what I ask myself.'

Auguste, or Mr Dee as he had become over the week, smiled. He was, after all, on holiday even if it was the all-important 5th August, the day of the Grand Banquet, of the arrival of the Prince of Wales. He had grown quite fond of Mr Multhrop with his many worries but, being on holiday, failed to view his 'problems' with as much anxiety as Mr Multhrop himself. Auguste had responsibilities of his own. Already early on this Saturday morning he and his pupils were beginning to prepare for the banquet in the Imperial kitchens. The hotel staff had been firmly relegated to a very small part of their own domain for the preparation of luncheon and would thereafter be merely onlookers, apart from serving the food to the hoi polloi of the guests this evening, while Auguste and his pupils served the Prince of Wales's table.

'Oh, do use the blue, Papa; it's so pretty.'

Auguste's eyes misted at the sound and sight of the lovely Araminta, Multhrop's eighteen-year-old daughter, rustling down the staircase in a delightful *froufrou* of petticoats, her large blue eyes fixed on her father, but well aware of every male in sight. Her curls bounced enchantingly as she clung to her father's arm, dimpling at Auguste. 'Do say the blue.'

'Then the blue it is, my love,' said her father fondly, as much putty in her hands as was Auguste.

This had truly been a bewitching week, Auguste reflected. On Wednesday he had escorted Alice to the Grand Theatre at Margate where they had watched *Charley's Aunt*. For himself, he did not find the piece as graceful as could be wished, but Alice seemed to find it most enjoyable and had giggled over its charms ever since. They had returned on the late theatre train, and it had been most pleasant walking down from the railway station and along the seafront so late at night; ah, to have a pretty girl by one's

64

side, and the touch of her lips on yours. Which girl, however?

He might have wooed Alice away from Alfred Wittisham had Araminta not stolen his heart. Never would he forget sitting beside her in the night air watching an open-air performance of *The Parvenue* and listening to the band at Fort House on Thursday evening. Never would he forget the walk home along the promenade afterwards when her delicate little hand, albeit gloved, stole into his. The warm night air had quite gone to his head, and had Araminta not been quite so very unattainable, doubtless other parts also would have shared his intoxication. Fortunately a decidedly unromantic evening breeze had sprung up, subduing ardour in favour of a brisk walk home. Bracing was the word for the English seaside, Auguste had decided.

'Aaah!' cried out Mr Multhrop in anguish. Leaving his cry wafting after him, he disappeared in pursuit of a housemaid who was busily removing all the clean antimacassars that had only just been placed lovingly in position for the oil-bedaubed heads that would shortly be resting on them. Perhaps even royalty's oil.

An army of minions was tidying, dusting and polishing areas that the Prince of Wales could never see, unless he were to perform acrobatics; to Auguste's eye the scene resembled the gardeners at work before the arrival of the Red Queen in Mr Carroll's amusing tale. Mrs Multhrop sped around after them, confusing matters more, Mr Multhrop sped after her and Araminta remained still, the cynosure of all eyes, smiling delightfully and of no practical help whatsoever. It was not expected of her. Auguste repressed the traitorous thought that so far as household management went, she would prove like Mr David Copperfield's 'child-wife' Dora. Some discernment she had, however, for had she not made most complimentary remarks about his *filets de sole Murat*?

65

Similar panic was reigning in the kitchens. The Imperial's staff, torn between a natural *amour propre* that a rival team had been imported to cook for the Prince of Wales and relief that they would not be responsible for royalty's displeasure (yet with the ignoble hope that they might get all the credit), watched anxiously to ensure that the incoming team was competent. The procession of raised rook and chicken pies, with their intricate decorations, that made its appearance in the kitchen raised their expectations as high as the pie coffins, as did the jellies vanishing into the larders, and sorbets into the refrigerators.

Auguste had adjusted the menu to his own standards. His frantic re-reading of Dickens had revealed numerous mentions of grog. Very well, he reasoned, then grog jelly was not too far removed from the mandate he had been given, and no one could object to the addition of a delicious fruit sorbet. Dickens must have mentioned fruit somewhere. They would at least remove the richness of the goose from frightened stomachs. In one corner of the kitchens the lobsters were awaiting their fate. At least there he had been successful. But as to oysters, no. Not till September, his new friends William and Joseph maintained. In vain Auguste pleaded that the Prince of Wales would not wait until September. William pointed out that they had their reputation to consider; French passion met British indomitability, and Auguste yielded. No oysters.

William and Joseph had glanced at each other.

'Crabs now,' Joseph said. 'You could get a nicé crab or two.'

Auguste had not observed the slow smile creeping over William's face as Joseph placed in his hand a rod with a hook on the end. He looked at it blankly.

'Dat dere's a pungar 'ook; now you get all the crabs you want, mister; us'll keep all dem furriners away.'

It had been fortunate, Auguste reflected bitterly, that no

necessity had rested on his catching pungar crabs this morning. One morning's efforts at pungar catching had proved quite enough. First there was the indignity of rolling up his trousers and removing his socks and shoes, then the endless probing of horizontal holes in the rocks to see if pungars lurked within.

'Just you tap away, Mr Auguste, and if you 'it the little feller on 'is back you'll 'ear 'is 'ollow sound like.'

It sounded simple; it was not. The hollow sound was the beginning of the game, not the end. For the 'little feller', once assaulted, retreated to the back of his hole and dug in. Battle then commenced. At the end of an hour, only one 'little feller' too young to know better had been in Auguste's possession, and William and Joseph were scarcely able to restrain their mirth. French aplomb was to the fore as Auguste handed the crab to them along with the hook, raised his new Panama hat and bade them a courteous farewell.

Now Mr Multhrop was making periodic incursions into his kitchens, moaning gently, wringing his hands, as he beheld the mountains of food everywhere. The Imperial was used to large banquets, but the added responsibility of the Prince of Wales made molehills into mountains.

'I shall be ruined, beheaded, disbarred from the Buffaloes,' he wailed.

In his self-torture he was unable to answer the simplest query, and Auguste was forced to turn to Araminta.

'Miss Multhrop, where are the *bains-marie*?'

'Oh, Mr Didier, I don't eat buns.' Araminta looked distressed. She wanted to help if she could.

Auguste closed his eyes and counted to three. Perhaps Alice would make the better wife.

Sixty-seven Literary Lionisers were descending on Broadstairs from several directions. Some were travelling direct from Cowes, most were arriving from London by railway express, and the remainder by carriage from their country houses. The committee, as if for protection against the masses, elected to follow Auguste's example and had reserved a first-class railway compartment on the 10.45 express from Victoria. Here too the atmosphere was strained. Only Sir Thomas, confident of victory and in his ability to overcome all opposition by his personal charm, was at ease. The edginess of the others only added to his opinion of his own rectitude. His starched collar, sober dark grey tweed suit, and the black bowler hat in the rack above him made no concessions to the seaside.

Oliver was annoyed that Angelina had deliberately chosen to sit next to Sir Thomas; Angelina was determined to bring Sir Thomas to book as soon as she could; Gwendolen was similarly annoyed at the sight of her rival on Sir Thomas's other side and bitterly aware that she herself was viewing considerably more of Sir Thomas's back than of his face. Broadstairs would, however, solve everything, she told herself. Samuel Pipkin was tensing himself for the coming life and death struggle this evening, when the vital decision would be made by the Prince of Wales, and Mr Thackeray would be avenged. Even Lord Beddington was on edge, hands clasped round the duck's-head handle of his walking stick. He didn't sleep a wink during the journey. He had a notion something damned odd was going to happen at Broadstairs.

'Welcome to Broadstairs,' announced Sir Thomas expansively as he stepped down from the railway carriage, flicking a practised hand towards a porter. A flood of Literary Lionisers was already pouring out of the railway station, fighting in well-bred fashion over victorias and landaus. The committee, having done their duty by their flock, were left without transport.

'Came here once,' commented Lord Beddington morosely, looking round while they were waiting for cabs to return. It was one o'clock, and he needed his lunch. 'Recognise that' – he jerked a thumb at the nearby flint-faced water tower poking its head above the railway line, the pride of its engineer, Thomas Crampton.

'Oh, a *castle*,' trilled Gwendolen. 'How romantic,' she enthused. 'No wonder Dickens loved Broadstairs so. Did he, I wonder, base Dotheboys Hall upon it?'

'The water reservoir was not built when Dickens stayed here, Gwendolen,' said Sir Thomas smoothly, smiling at Angelina.

Gwendolen flushed in shame, her arms trembling in their lace leg-o'-mutton sleeves, then steadied herself. No doubt Thomas was deliberately making her look foolish in public in order to hide his real feelings. Men were strange creatures at times. She swallowed hard and thought about this afternoon's promenade. If he did not apologise then . . .

Oliver, set-faced, assisted Angelina into the first victoria that returned. She thanked him composedly and made room for Sir Thomas by her side. Samuel glared at everyone, wishing he were in Tunbridge Wells, the decent civilised sort of place that Mr Thackeray used to visit. Lord Beddington meditated lovingly on a good luncheon, followed by an even better snooze at the Reform. It was, he noticed, distinctly less warm than it had been, with an east wind blowing as they turned into the Parade.

And in this mood of low spirits, the Week of the Lion began.

In the kitchens the Imperial's chefs were now preparing to serve a simple luncheon for the new arrivals, while preparations for the banquet continued apace. Because of the lack of space, Auguste had devised a shuttle system; as luncheon moved out in stages, so more materials for the banquet could be moved in. Heinrich, James and Alfred were poised to drag in the vegetables delivered to the tradesmen's entrance, as the soup tureens for luncheon moved out. Alice and Emily were already engaged on chopping ingredients for sage and onion stuffing.

'My grandmama says,' remarked Emily, 'that it's unlucky to use sage when it's blooming. You should never let it flower at all.' She looked disapprovingly at the cluster of purple flowers amid the handfuls of green-grey leaves.

'Your grandmama will be proved correct, Miss Dawson, if you do not watch your use of that knife,' Auguste pointed out quickly. 'You do not concentrate, Miss Dawson. Where is your mind today?'

Emily's mind was partly on the enjoyable walk she had taken with Heinrich, who had unexpectedly proved a most delightful companion during the week; partly on the bright green foulard dress she had seen on sale at Bobby's in Margate yesterday when they visited the famous menagerie at the Grand Hall by the Sea, and partly it was on the coming evening. What, if any, dangers did it hold for her?

'Emily,' said Heinrich kindly, clearing his throat, 'the kidneys have arrived. You do not pay attention.' Having begun the week convinced that Emily, after her attack on his Nesselrode pudding, was one of the stupidest females he had met, Heinrich had seven days later become quite besotted by her beauty, wit and charm. Truly, this seaside air had much to recommend it. He had almost lost interest in a reunion with the Kaiser.

Alice's mind was not on kidneys either. She had had a splendid and cultural week. Not only had Auguste taken her to see the amusing *Charley's Aunt*, but Alfred had escorted her to Ramsgate to see *Harbour Lights*. It had been great fun. And even more fun had been the fact that James Pegg had not been present; secure in his knowledge, as he thought, that Alfred was taking an extra lesson in quenelles cookery from Mr Didier. She laughed at the thought of his

70

face next morning when he realised he'd been outwitted – it wasn't hard to do.

'Lord Wittisham,' called Auguste, agonised. 'You are behind in your schedule. It is time – ' seeing covered dishes of roasts exiting from the kitchen – 'to collect the quails and mutton cutlets.'

Guiltily Alfred sped to the door.

'I'll help you, Alfred,' called Alice. 'I've finished chopping.'

James, hands covered with chicken entrails, could only watch helplessly. Perturbed, he swung the cleaver viciously, chopping fowl after fowl into pieces. He wished that Alice Fenwick could be dealt with so simply.

Algernon whistled as he worked, a habit picked up from his father, who was given to musical expression while chopping up meat. It was thus a sure sign that his thoughts were far away. They were certainly not on recipes, Mr Soyer's or Mr Didier's.

Fifteen minutes later, Auguste shot out of the kitchen entrance in search of Alfred and Alice – or – more precisely, his quails and cutlets. Surely it could not take this long to gather up a few baskets of food? As he reached the corner of Chandos Place, Sir Thomas Throgmorton was descending from a carriage in front of the Imperial, handing down Angelina with impeccable politeness and leaving young Oliver Michaels to help down Gwendolen. Auguste failed to see the hidden tensions and passions behind these simple manoeuvres; to him it only signified that the banquet had acquired a reality. The Literary Lionisers had arrived.

Past the stationary victoria came a donkey cart in which, to his relief, he saw Alfred and Alice serenely sitting side by side bearing familiar baskets. The quails and the cutlets were safe. He could relax.

'Ah,' he cried out to them. '*Mes amis*, do not delay.'

Attracted by the shout, Sir Thomas glanced first at

Auguste, then at the donkey cart. He frowned for a moment in shock.

'What the devil are you doing here?' he said slowly.

Alfred blushed. 'I − er − work here,' he announced with dignity.

Auguste listened with interest to this social interchange which clearly was transgressing barriers.

Sir Thomas looked blank. 'Work here?' He stared at him and there was a pause. 'I'll have a word with *you* later,' he said grimly, turned his back on Alfred, gave his arm to Mrs Langham and advanced into the hotel.

'Welcome, Sir Thomas.' Mr Multhrop smiled nervously. He didn't as a rule greet all his guests, but this was different. It was a rehearsal for the reception of the Prince of Wales this evening.

Sir Thomas, preoccupied, took no notice.

'Who,' demanded Auguste despairingly, as the tempo quickened in the kitchen, 'is responsible for *this*? Mr Peckham,' his eye fell on the culprit, '*you* are responsible for the mutton broth. Why do you not remember the words of Brillat Savarin: the pot must smile. Not *boil*, Mr Peckham.'

'Because the words of Maître Soyer are boil gently,' announced Algernon cheekily.

'Maître *Didier* says smile, and so we smile, Monsieur Peckham,' replied Auguste, his voice steely.

'Yes, Mr Didier.' The look in Algernon's face boded ill for somebody.

'Will His Royal Highness *like* mutton broth?' wondered Alice doubtfully. 'It *is* August.'

'This menu is not my idea,' pleaded Auguste despairingly. 'I have prepared some dishes which I know will please the Prince of Wales. The quails and devilled bones, also the mutton cutlets give him much pleasure. But this mutton

72

broth. Bah! I am told Dickens partook of it at home.' The tones of disgust indicated Auguste's reasons for dreading a wife. Suppose he were to marry only to be faced with mutton broth? 'I have therefore made a small portion of almond soup. Surely in all Mr Dickens's vast works there must be some mention of almonds, and if not,' he said firmly, 'remember that in France this dish is named hedgehog soup. I feel sure Mr Dickens must mention hedgehogs.' He looked around, but no one had views on this. 'And if he does not,' he continued, 'the Prince of Wales will not mind. It is better than mutton broth in August. *Eh bien. Les entrées.* The kidneys. Where is Mr Pegg?' He looked automatically at Alfred.

''E went to 'elp Miss Araminta with the coffee,' said Sid brightly.

'He has no business to be assisting Miss Araminta,' said Auguste crossly. 'Not when kidneys require his attention.'

'I think he's sweet on her,' volunteered Emily. 'I saw them spooning on the beach,' she added, rather wistfully.

'Our guests will be deprived of their chance of spooning this soup, unless you watch this broth, Mr Peckham,' said Auguste viciously, returning to the fray. James Pegg a rival in Araminta's affections? Impossible. 'Kindly adjust the temperature, Mr Peckham, before it boils away, and then be so good as to ask Mr Pegg if he can spare the time to rejoin us.'

Auguste busied himself checking the stuffing, unable to get to the root of his unease. Eventually he did so. His pupils were developing minds of their own, behaving out of character, no longer the dull but devoted group of enthusiasts he had taught so constructively for six months. Did the seaside do this to people? Or was it more than the influence of the Broadstairs sands?

In the lounge Lord Beddington was taking a short rest after

the exigencies of luncheon. He had made no concessions to the seaside. He was wearing a decent black cloth lounge suit, and had no intentions of changing his mode of attire. He opened an eye as a door closed with a bang. One of the cooks came in, judging by the white apron. He shut his eye again, then opened it once more, and glared. Algernon Peckham glanced at him, and there was a momentary pause before he moved on to speak to James Pegg.

Beddington closed his eyes, but this time he was not asleep. He was curious to remember where he'd seen that impudent young face before. At last he did.

There'd been a bench between them at the time.

Once luncheon was over, the afternoon began in earnest for both groups of devoted toilers. The Literary Lionisers, having commanded their maids and valets, if they had them, to unpack, or if they had not, scurried through this tedious task themselves, were gathering for the first event of the week, the promenade around Dickens's Broadstairs. Armed with their texts of the Lion's own travel guide to the town, *Our English Watering Place*, The Lionisers were arrayed in their seaside apparel, no less excited at the beginning of their week's holiday than had been Auguste's pupils. For some of them, the sands were taking precedence over the works of Mr Dickens, as they gathered to await their leader amid the potted palms in the first-floor sun lounge overlooking the Victoria Parade, the sands and the sea.

In the kitchens below, the other group of devotees, those addicted to cuisine and at the moment wondering why, were entering the most vital and concentrated period of Auguste's schedule. Everyone worked in tense silence, concentrating on their own particular task. Vegetables were being prepared; eight dozen quails were ready for the ovens; trays of mutton cutlets, to be served with caper sauce in an attempt to please the Dickensian purists (as well as the Prince of

Wales) were waiting for their moment to come. Ingredients for the lobster salads were being assembled, the kidneys being sliced for *Rognons à la Didier*, herbs were being chopped or minced to the accompaniment of the words of wisdom of Emily's grandmama.

Grave discussions between the wine waiter, Auguste and Alfred were in progress; Alfred had been detailed to serve beverages and wine to the top table this evening, at which the Prince of Wales and the committee members would dine. It had been hard to convince the Imperial's *sommelier* of the necessity for the presence of porter and ginger beer. When appealed to for her support over the ginger beer, Araminta had laughed. It was not helpful, but she looked so beautiful in her blue muslin that Auguste forgave her instantly. The need for ginger beer was agreed and put down to French eccentricity.

In the sun lounge, Sir Thomas addressed his flock. 'We shall progress along the Parade and Albion Street, up to Fort House, known as Bleak House, and thence to the pier,' he announced grandly, pointing with his Golden Jubilee cane.

'A queer old wooden pier,' quoted Gwendolen blithely, determined to be noticed in her new sailor hat.

'Quite,' said Sir Thomas shortly. He marched off at a brisk pace, leading his party of fifty or so, including two in bath-chairs intent on taking the tour, come hell or high water, the latter being most probable.

'Pitch,' bleated Gwendolen, 'the pier was covered in pitch, Mr Dickens says.' No one commented.

Uncle Mack's Broadstairs Minstrels performing on the sands, the Punch and Judy man, the donkey boys and the fruit vendors were stunned into momentary silence at the sight of this huge party moving along the seafront, like a leviathan as large as the one washed up at Fishness Point in 1574. Sir Thomas was in full flood, though his

75

performance seemed to lack its usual fortissimo, thought Oliver to himself. It was almost as if his thoughts were not wholeheartedly in it for some reason. The group came to a halt outside an old cottage on the front. 'There,' Sir Thomas announced dramatically. 'Betsy Trotwood's cottage from *David Copperfield*. Until recently assumed to be at Dover.'

'Donkeys, Janet!' trilled Gwendolen at his side.

'We shall be viewing it later in the week, by kind consent of the owner,' Sir Thomas continued, ignoring this contribution. He turned to take Angelina's arm ostentatiously, in full view of Gwendolen's watchful gaze and that of Oliver.

The mass of promenaders bulged along in the committee's wake, creating some difficulty as they turned into the narrow High Street and into Albion Street. Six Broadstairs matrons attempting to shop at Marchesi's the confectioners, two errand boys buying bloaters from Mr Goodman the fishmonger, a few afternoon revellers strolling out from the Dolphin Inn and an eager group from the Tourist Cycling Club staying at the Balmoral Bijou Hotel found themselves swept along with the crowd as they pursued their leaders down Harbour Street under the ancient York Gate (which being without specific Dickensian associations hardly received a glance). Numbers had swelled to eighty by the time the group reached the old Tartar Frigate Inn and poured onto the pier.

'The chances are a thousand to one that you might stay here for ten seasons and never see a boatman in a hurry,' quoted Sir Thomas loudly to his brood, waving a lordly hand towards William and Joe who were enjoying a quiet chew of tobacco at the end of the pier. Eighty pairs of eyes focused on them with interest, clearly thinking them Dickensian relics.

'Visitors, Bill,' said Joe slowly, barely pausing in his chew.

76

'Ah.'

'Dey says dey wants to see us 'urry.'

'Ah.'

They rose slowly and deliberately to their feet like Tweedledum and Tweedledee. 'Dat young Dickens, 'e were allus in an 'urry, weren't 'e, Bill?'

'Ah. I remembers dat,' announced William. 'Used to come tearing down 'ere 'e did. Perch on the rail there, chattin' away baht 'is books an' all. Bill, 'e used to say, I got summat in mind for you. How d'yer feel about 'Am? 'Am?'

''Am, Bill?' queried Joseph in tones of one who has asked before.

'Aye. 'Am. 'Am Peggotty. That's what I'll call yer. An' 'e did, didn't 'e, Joe?'

''E did, Bill,' agreed Joseph, with a wink only visible to his partner. ''E put yer into *David Copperfield*.'

With a gasp of pleasure, impressed with this firm evidence of Dickensian times, the crowd moved forward to inspect the relics.

In one lightning movement the two fishermen picked up two pails of stinking fish heads and flung them lovingly at the Lionisers' feet. Fifty-two grateful seagulls swooped, breaking up the ranks amid cries and squeals of distress.

'Ah,' remarked William again. They resumed their seats as the Lionisers retreated.

'I hear,' said Sir Thomas hastily by way of conversation, 'the news from Cowes was not good. The Kaiser won the Queen's Cup.'

'Shouldn't mention it to His Royal Highness, Throgmorton,' rumbled Lord Beddington. 'He was banking on *Britannia* winning.'

'The Kaiser is determined to win at everything,' observed Oliver, 'especially on the sea.'

'Damned fellow,' said Beddington surprisingly energeti

cally. 'Rules our lives now. You can't go into the Foreign Office or the club without some new story about young Willie's spies.'

'Spies?' squealed Angelina in mock alarm, clutching for protection at Sir Thomas's arm.

'They're everywhere,' grunted Lord Beddington. 'Look at that German band down there. Spies, every man jack of them, I'll be bound.'

'Not all spies for Germany are German,' pontificated Sir Thomas. 'In this modern age, they are everywhere, the enemy in our midst.'

'Not in the Literary Lionisers?' squealed Angelina.

Sir Thomas smiled patronisingly and held her arm the more tightly.

Tempers in the kitchens rose with the temperature as ovens burned and broth smiled on. Kitchen tables resounded to the sound of chopping herbs and eschalots by Emily. James was occupied on lobsters and kidneys, and Algernon, studiously avoiding meat, on vegetables. Alfred had already trussed and stuffed the geese. Only Sid whistled cheerfully throughout, fetching, carrying, soothing. 'Herr Freimüller,' Auguste shouted in sudden alarm, 'where is the prune stuffing? You have provided only the sage and onion.' But there was no sign of Freimüller.

'Here it is, Mr Didier. Just needs mixing with the pork,' came Alice's calm voice.

'Alice, you are a blessed jewel among women,' said Auguste fervently.

Alice hoped that Alfred was listening and taking due note. In fact he was not. He was wondering what Sir Thomas meant by his threat to see him later. And just what he intended to say. And what he would do in return.

Fifty people (the other thirty had disengaged themselves at

78

the first mention of Dickens) were now taking tea in the gardens of the Albion Hotel under the shelter of parasols. The weather was sultry, not sunny, today but you never knew when a lurking sun ray might attempt an assault upon the complexion.

'It is here of course that Dickens himself stayed, in a house now part of this hotel, while finishing the writing of the immortal *Nicholas Nickleby*, and on other occasions and later in the hotel itself.'

'Here we are to spend a merry night, are we not, Thomas?' shouted Gwendolen in a high penetrating voice, to the intense interest of those not quite so well acquainted with Dickens's letters. Oblivious of the equivocal nature of her remarks, Gwendolen was hoping that Angelina, with whom Sir Thomas had chosen to sit at a table for two only, would take due note of her omission of the 'sir'. It was a gauntlet flung down before her rival.

'As did Dickens himself,' announced Sir Thomas, turning round having recovered some of his composure. 'Yes, on Tuesday I believe, we shall *all* be gathered here for an evening together.' He then resumed his rapt attention to Angelina, thus leaving Gwendolen with no option but to try to think of something interesting to say to Oliver Michaels and Samuel Pipkin.

'Have you thought further on that we spoke of the other evening, Angelina?' Sir Thomas said in a low voice, throbbing in what he hoped was emotion. 'I should perhaps wait for some more romantic hour.' In fact he had fully intended to wait for a suitably moonlit warm night, but the trying events of the day had put him so out of sorts that he could stand the waiting no longer. The affirmative he knew would follow would help him in the discussion this evening with the Prince of Wales. The vote had been taken, but as Angelina would undoubtedly now regret her stance, she would make her views clear to His Royal Highness.

Besides, to appear eager for a decision would be flattering to Angelina. Would she, or wouldn't she? he murmured, leaning forward.

'How is your stomach today, Thomas?' shouted Gwendolen, determined to be heard.

Sir Thomas flinched, and turned his chair even more deliberately away from the neighbouring table. 'Well, I thank you,' he managed to say offhandedly before once again addressing his rapt attention to Angelina, albeit somewhat shaken from his confident suavity.

Angelina smiled sweetly and leaned forward herself. She spoke low and earnestly to Sir Thomas. She would *not*, was the gist of what she communicated first. The reasons why took rather longer to explain and, like her decision, was between themselves, for strain though she might, Gwendolen could not hear. Shifting her chair position slightly, she saw Sir Thomas's face pale with emotion, she saw him pick up Angelina's hand and kiss it with devotion. She saw Angelina remove it modestly, with a maidenly flush on her cheeks, or thus Gwendolen's jealous eye perceived it. Maiden indeed, she snorted to herself. Mrs Langham must be nearly thirty. Mature, as she was herself.

Unable to bear what she saw as her rival's triumph, Gwendolen turned to face the teacups again, wrapped in misery. Oliver, observing the scene with the same keen interest as had she, munched his way through a Dickensian gingerbread cake, his emotions harder to determine than those of his companion.

A few minutes later, Sir Thomas was walking slowly back to the Imperial Hotel in advance of the main party. He had made the excuse that he needed to be there to greet the Prince of Wales, but making this pronouncement, which he had previously rehearsed many times, failed to fill him with the satisfaction he had anticipated. For once, his mind was not on royalty and a possible peerage, not on Dickens, not on his incipient gastritis, not even on the blow that Angelina had dealt him. It ranged over many other matters, none of which were pleasant and some of which until he came to Broadstairs he had almost put out of his mind.

'*Attention*, ladies and gentlemen. It is time. The geese!' He looked impatiently. Where was Herr Freimüller? He had been detailed to assist Mr Pegg in placing the geese in the ovens.

Heinrich burst in at the doors, carrying two bottles, followed by Emily, somewhat flushed, holding a bunch of herbs.

'Thyme for the kidneys,' she announce nervously in excuse.

'It is not time for the kidneys,' shouted Auguste. 'It is time for the geese,' extracting his head from the oven.

'That's sage, Mr Didier,' said Emily, puzzled.

Auguste stared at her, wondering whether he was lecturing to imbeciles, and his gaze fell on Heinrich. 'This is your job, Herr Freimüller,' he announced grimly.

'I get champagne,' he said. 'I am sorry, Mr Didier. For the kidneys.'

'Forget the kidneys,' said Auguste wearily. 'The geese. They must cook. *Dépêchez-vous!*'

Heinrich did not understand French, but the meaning was clear.

Oven doors flew open. James and Heinrich placed the geese, covered in their layers of goose fat, into their ovens. The die was cast. In three hours twelve roast geese would emerge succulent, rich and juicy. Would they be eaten? Auguste would take it as a reflection on his honour if they were not, despite the unseasonable time of year. Only the Prince of Wales could refuse his goose with impunity.

How glorious seemed the morrow, Auguste thought, when he could resume his holiday; tomorrow, after supervising a light luncheon, he would escort the delectable Araminta to the band concert of the Oxfordshire and Buckinghamshire Light Infantry. There he would introduce her to Egbert and Edith. Even perhaps they would bathe. The thrill of seeing Araminta in bathing dress, even in the distance, segregated as the gentlemen were from the ladies, made his heart race. Truly there must be something strange about the seaside, when the mere sight of seeing an ankle had made his heart beat the faster. How dear Maisie, or Natalia, and certainly Emma, would laugh to see him enslaved by an ankle after their more generous gifts of person! Yet enslaved he was. He and Araminta had paddled together earlier in the week, an occupation he found most strange. But she had lifted her skirts a full six inches above the ground as she entered the water, and he was captivated. If he were a poet he would write a poem to that glimpse of bare ankle. True, Araminta had no idea of what a poached egg was, but what delight for a man to cook all his life for such an angel. This seaside air of Broadstairs was magical. Never again had he thought the love of woman could touch his heart, not after the pain of knowing Tatiana was lost to him for ever. Perhaps he should be practical and take a wife for comfort. He could marry Alice. How often had he said what a helpmeet she would be, if only Alfred Wittisham were not there. He could marry Araminta. His French practicality reluctantly came to the fore. Alice would be better.

She came in with a further two bottles of champagne and took them, blue eyes shining, to Alfred, assembling the ingredients for the *Rognons à la Didier*.

'Heinrich got the champagne for me already,' Alfred pointed out tactlessly. Alice's eyes clouded.

Poor Alice, thought Auguste, she tried so hard, but he feared his lordship did not notice her save as a friend, an attitude of which James Pegg would fully approve. He looked round. Pegg had disappeared again. Auguste promptly despatched Alfred to hunt for him. Surely, *surely* Pegg could not be in pursuit of Araminta? Jealousy flared, a red dagger in his heart.

Sir Thomas walked back to his room in the Imperial somewhat later than he had intended, though he was not destined to reach it quite yet. Out of the small sitting area at the end of the corridor Gwendolen Figgis-Hewett darted like a vixen from cover. Yet a third troublesome encounter, but perhaps the easiest to deal with.

'How could you? Faithless, faithless,' she moaned, clutching at his lapels. 'Tell me it is not true, Thomas. That you did not mean what you said to me that day.'

'My dear Gwendolen,' he cut in impatiently, disengaging her from his new blazer. 'Of course I meant it. I am extremely sorry, but I have just had a most trying time.' He forced a laugh. 'Among other matters. Mr Dickens's Datchery has come back, you might say. And as to you, we are —' remembering his diplomacy — 'we are good companions, but I haven't the least wish to remarry.'

'You're going to marry *her*!' she shrieked.

'Who?' His face darkened.

'Mrs Langham.'

'Nonsense,' he said testily. 'I cannot imagine where you got that idea.'

'You lie, you lie,' she sobbed.

'Very well then, I lie.' Finally he lost his temper. 'I am indeed to marry Mrs Langham. I consider her a model of feminine beauty and virtue, and of course I would prefer to marry her above you. Who would not?' — forgetting all about the advantages of a diplomatic approach.

The shriek that went up as she sank back on to a wicker sofa drumming her heels on the ground and yelling and shouting that she wished he were dead, and that she'd been dishonoured, made him quite alarmed. Should he depart?

Should he stay? The Prince of Wales would shortly be here, and he was not yet changed. Really, this was proving a disastrous day. He pulled the rope to summon help. It was Auguste and Alfred Wittisham who answered the call, though Samuel Pipkin, attracted by the noise, was first on the scene. He realised instantly what was happening and why.

'My dear Gwendolen,' he solicitously and hypocritically began, 'I fear this fellow has upset you.'

'Nonsense,' shouted Sir Thomas, 'and who asked you anyway?'

'My dear sir.' Samuel was shocked. 'You have upset a lady. Humiliated her.'

'Yes, yes!' shrieked Gwendolen. 'He did, he did.'

'I did not,' said Sir Thomas, cornered. 'I merely suggested, Mrs Figgis-Hewett, that you were overwrought.'

'You are no gentleman, sir,' announced Samuel loftily. 'And unfit to be chairman of our Society. Mrs Figgis-Hewett will support me on this.'

Too late Sir Thomas saw the error of his ways. 'My dear Gwendolen.' He laid a hand on her heaving shoulder.

'Unhand me, sir,' she cried, leaping up and throwing herself hysterically into Samuel's arms. Over her shoulder he gleamed triumphantly at Sir Thomas. Vengeance would be his — and Mr Thackeray's — this evening.

It was then that Auguste and Alfred arrived.

This really was the last straw. 'What the devil are you doing down here?' Sir Thomas asked wearily. 'You,' he turned to Auguste, 'see to *her*.'

Auguste obediently disengaged Gwendolen and subdued the hysterics with the aid of a swift slap, and his own comforting arm.

'Is Beatrice here, sir?' asked Alfred brightly out of nervousness, with unerring instinct heading straight for disaster.

'Miss Throgmorton is in France, sir. She is not planning to marry a cook.' He gave a scathing look at Alfred's apron.

'It's a useful occupation, sir. Practical. She'll never starve,' Alfred pointed out, rallying his defences.

Sir Thomas turned puce. 'You marry my daughter over my dead body, and that's my last word.' It was not an original word, but it made his point as far as Alfred was concerned.

Sir Thomas stalked off, maddened beyond endurance, and with only five minutes to change before the Prince of Wales arrived.

The royal yacht *Osborne* had already docked at Ramsgate and the Prince of Wales was passing Dumpton Gapway, comfortably seated in Mr Multhrop's new Panhard motorcar. He was not a happy man. There was thunder in the air, in all senses. It had been far from the capital week he had come to expect from Cowes, what with Willie winning everything in sight, having to make diplomatic speeches to his own nephew about how jolly it was to lose to him, and then just as he got time to drown his sorrows at the Yacht Club he had to come to Broadstairs. There it was now. Hadn't changed since Mama used to stay here. She'd be expecting a full report on Pierremont House and the dear little village, so quiet, so tasteful. Well, it hadn't changed much, except that it was bigger and a lot of schoolboys were apparently prancing round the sacred portals of Pierremont House. Apart from that, no change. Respectable and sober. Nothing ever happened in Broadstairs. He climbed down from the motorcar onto a bright blue carpet. Strange. Why blue? Had the driver got the right place?

Mr Multhrop bustled forward in great nervousness.

'Your Royal Highness, good-bye – er – afternoon.' He bowed so far forward he nearly butted royalty in the stomach, but the Prince of Wales had met many Multhrops

85

and greeted him courteously, leaving him pink with pleasure. He greeted Sir Thomas courteously too; he greeted every damn person lined up with similar courtesy though his private thoughts were on the likelihood of a stiff brandy and soda having been placed ready in his suite. It must be his age. Once upon a time the position of the bedroom relative to those of female guests would have been far more interesting.

The preparation of ingredients for the sauce for the kidneys was now in the capable hands of Algernon Peckham, once Auguste had extracted a promise not to follow the Soyer recipe 'by mistake'.

James had returned, but now Emily and Heinrich had vanished. Auguste sighed. People seemed to have been disappearing all the afternoon, one after another. His schedule had worked, but only because he seemed to be carrying out most of it himself. Wearily he checked the table china, the hotel staff being responsible for the less venerable Literary Lionisers. But he himself must oversee the Prince of Wales's table. He went into the huge dining room, where at last he found Alfred arranging bottles on the serving tables. His practised eye ran round the room. Pekin dinner service, silver cutlery, crystal glasses, showy white napkins, all in order. He cringed at the elaborate Dickensian menus adorning each place, but was grateful for the fact that the catastrophe of the banquet, for such he was sure it would be, would be firmly laid at Mr Dickens's door and not his own. 'The chef,' he recalled saying, 'must at all times be prepared for disaster.' *Alors*, he had done his best. Surely nothing could go wrong now?

Egbert Rose was helping the sailor-suited youngster on his right to fortify his castle. Rose's face was lobster red. He was having a wonderful time and so was Edith. He liked the harbour, Edith liked the promenades, they both liked the sands and the Pierrot shows. They had visited the theatre. They had met Auguste and seen the Margate grotto with him. That was sixpennyworth of value all right. The only thing he couldn't persuade Edith to do was to visit Boulogne for the day. Easy enough, train to Margate, down to the Jetty, and off they could go on *La Marguerite* at 9.45. But no. No France for her. She liked Ramsgate. Why come to Ramsgate if you want to go to Boulogne? was her unanswerable response.

They had been sitting on the sands all day. It was not so warm today, so Edith had stopped eyeing the bathing machines wistfully and wondering if she dared. Rose dared all right. He went down early each morning and jumped up and down in the briny, enjoying every minute of it. His habitual London expression, cagey and mournful, was never to be seen. He kept firmly away from Ramsgate police court. He was having a nice seaside holiday with the added pleasure of Auguste's presence and without that of murder.

Chapter Five

Auguste caught a brief glimpse of himself in the small mirror he had unobtrusively arranged in order that he might keep an eye on events taking place behind his back; the surreptitious addition of Mrs Marshall's abominable Coralline pepper, for example, to an imperfect sauce. It was one of the less pleasant aspects of his present occupation that the Didier School of Cuisine was constantly mentioned in the same breath as Mrs Marshall's nearby School of Cookery. He trained master chefs; Mrs Marshall trained domestic servants. There was a considerable difference.

Now he groaned. He looked every bit as ridiculous as he feared. The ultimate insult had been thrown at him: he, the Maître Auguste Didier, had been obliged, nay commanded, not only to appear in Dickensian dress but to don the unmistakable apparel of Alexis Soyer: tight white drill trousers, matching tunic, short jacket, ridiculous cummerbund, slotted into which was his own kitchen knife (no doubt for a speedy self-martyrdom after the imminent disaster of this meal) and, worse, the horror on his head.

He peeped again into the mirror, hoping the sight might have vanished. It hadn't. A wide pancake-shaped black cloth hat with a huge brim rolled back on one side adorned his dark hair. He was expected to superintend a grand banquet looking like this. Like Soyer! It was too much, even for the sake of cooking for the Prince of Wales.

'Monsieur, what are you doing?' Auguste's agonised shout was addressed to the rear end of a gentleman, whose head was in an oven apparently examining a goose at close quarters.

'Just doing my job, Mr Didier.' The Prince's detective emerged, flushed.

'You expect to find an assassin masquerading as a goose?' Auguste enquired scathingly.

'Hidden weapons,' declared the detective mysteriously.

'If an assassin were to dare to enter my kitchen,' Auguste announced in tones that made it clear that no villain would have the temerity, 'do you not think that poison would be his chosen means, rather than an arsenal of rifles hidden in a kitchen range?'

'If you knew the criminal mind like I do, Mr Didier,' began the detective loftily, but he left the sentence unfinished, belatedly recalling Auguste's reputation in criminal circles. He took advantage of the noisy arrival of Auguste's staff to beat a judicious retreat, as Auguste hurled imprecations after him, based largely on the fate that would await him should the goose come to any harm as a result of his incursions into the chef's sovereign territory.

Auguste had granted his pupils a half-hour respite in which to change into their enforced Dickensian dress, and was now confronted with all six apparently sharing some enormous joke. It was intensified when they noticed the attire of their maître. Even Algernon's expression changed from sneer to genuine laughter.

'The Maître Soyer would be proud of you, maître,' he chortled.

'I like the hat, Mr Didier,' giggled Alice, tweaking it to one side.

Auguste regarded them grimly and with foreboding. No serious attention would be paid to cuisine while his pupils were cavorting around in this outlandish dress parade.

Alfred was waving a white-stockinged leg in the air, Heinrich experimentally bending over in his black knee breeches; James was pulling at his skimpy short jacket, puffing out his chest like Beerbohm Tree as d'Artagnan, Algernon was dancing a Highland fling showing off his black slipper shoes, and Alice and Emily were swishing merrily arm in arm through the kitchen in their huge, gathered black skirts covered with large, bibbed, lacy aprons. Sid, being unlikely to be displayed to the company, had been excused Dickensian dress.

'*Attention!*' Auguste's cry came too late and a dish of ribboned cucumber, garnish for the lobster salads, landed upside down on the floor. He rushed to the rescue of the lobster mayonnaise which was teetering ominously.

'That was you,' said James accusingly and with satisfaction to Alice.

'It vas not,' rumbled Heinrich. 'Mr Peckham makes the table shake. I see this.'

'It wasn't me,' shouted Algernon. 'That's not fair.'

'It was Miss Dawson,' said Sid casually.

Pandemonium ensued as discussion took place on the onus of responsibility.

'Enough,' shouted Auguste angrily. '*Mes amis*, do you forget? What has happened to you all?' He looked at them in bewilderment as they stood, abashed. 'The Prince of Wales is coming. We have to serve a grand banquet in forty-five minutes.' At this point Mr Multhrop arrived, sensed the tension and promptly departed again. '*Enfin*,' said Auguste grimly. 'Miss Fenwick, more cucumbers. Mr Peckham, clear up this abomination.' He pointed disdainfully to the green soggy mess and broken china on the floor. 'And you,' his eyes took in the other four, 'to your tasks, if you please.' Chastened, they donned their protective aprons, and set to work in silence.

Auguste began to make his final checks. The broth was

smiling happily, still clear and unclouded. He had caught it in time. The lobster salads were temptingly ready save for the cucumber garnish; kidneys and sauce awaited his last-minute cooking; the quails and cutlets awaited their ovens, the geese were browning nicely, the *entremets*, the dessert, cheeses, the prepared savouries – Auguste's practised eye ran over them all in expert fashion. He had done this so often before. His brain told him that all would be ready in time, yet anxiety remained. One day it might not be, unless careful attention was kept. One day disaster would come. And despite all his brave words, even he could not be prepared against *all* disasters.

In a small lounge, polished and dusted five times today by the Imperial's housemaids, four committee members were awaiting the arrival of the Prince of Wales, Sir Thomas and, oddly, Gwendolen, who had inexplicably not yet arrived. Outside the door hovered Alfred, detailed by Auguste to serve drinks when royalty had arrived. He was not happy in his duties tonight. He wished anyone but he were here, for the prospect of serving Sir Thomas was not a welcome one. He wondered whether he should have taken up farming instead of cooking.

Inside the room, tense silence reigned. Angelina, for instance, was wondering why Oliver had such a furious expression on his face. 'What do you think of my costume?' she enquired politely.

Lord Beddington and Samuel Pipkin made complimentary grunts. Oliver remained obstinately silent. He glanced at her Little Nell attire, the white pantaloons peeping out from under layers of petticoats, the bright blue skirt, white shawl, and the becoming poke bonnet. She looked beautiful, but he was not going to tell her so.

'I see,' she said sweetly to Oliver, 'that you feel no need to adopt Sam Weller's cheerfulness as well as his apparel.

Oliver swept off his battered top hat in ironic acknowledgement of her sally. Oliver's sharp sensitive features and figure adapted well to Sam Weller, but tonight he wished he'd chosen anything rather than the trial scene from *The Pickwick Papers* to read. He didn't feel at all humorous. He felt as black as John Jasper, and wondered even now whether to switch to *The Mystery of Edwin Drood*. Murderous was just how he felt. He would read *Edwin Drood* rather well, he thought savagely.

'Have you seen Mrs Figgis-Hewett?' Angelina enquired anxiously of Samuel Pipkin, since Oliver was clearly in no mood to converse. 'It's unlike her to be late.'

'No, my dear lady, I regret I have not. I – er – do not think she is in the best of spirits. Perhaps she has decided not to join us,' he added innocently, hugging to himself his knowledge of the dramatic scene he had encountered. He intended to press for a re-vote and one member less of old Throgmorton's supporters would suit him nicely.

Angelina fidgeted, worried but unable to leave as the Prince of Wales was due at any moment. With sudden resolution, she opened the door to despatch Alfred in search of the missing lady, but seeing Auguste just arriving for his final check that all was in order with the drinks, she appealed to him instead. Reluctantly, he disappeared in search of the missing Lioniser.

Samuel had his own thoughts, lost in a dream of vengeance. He, too, was thinking lovingly of murder. He was dressed as Dr Marigold, the cheap-jack trader from *The Christmas Stories*, his top hat fitted out with advertisements for Dr Robinson's Purifying Pills and Soyer's Magic Stove. A large white cravat and black jacket unfortunately accentuated his Pickwickian paunch. He had reluctantly decided against John Jasper, for the good reason that there being nothing distinctive about his dress, no one would realise who he was.

93

Lord Beddington, though silent, was not for once asleep. His head was itching too much from the dreadful old grey wig. This was the last time he would don fancy dress, otherwise next year they'd have him in doublet and hose, no doubt. Scrooge indeed. That had been old Throgmorton's idea. He brooded. Could it have been a roundabout reference to that old scandal? No. Thomas was a tight old so-and-so, but even he would let it die now. Or would he?

Interesting to have seen that young sneak thief about in the hotel, Lord Beddington switched thoughts, disturbed by memories of unhappier days. If he was Multhrop he'd be watching the teaspoons. That young man was the sort to fly high, having cut his teeth, so to speak, on — what was it? Ah yes, the paste diamond jewellery of old Higginbotham's wife at Radstone Hall. He'd been lucky to get off with a year for that. Darned counsel with tears in his eyes, murmuring about stalwart butchers' sons who strayed from the path, and, after all, it was only paste. Meanwhile here was he, the magistrate, in tight breeches, dirty cravat and too tight a collar stud, dressed as Scrooge.

A sudden flurry, as of a dozen Multhrops simultaneously prostrating themselves, and the doors were flung open. Angelina sprang up, expecting Gwendolen. The others joined her. The Prince of Wales had arrived, soberly and correctly clad in formal evening attire. Behind him came Sir Thomas similarly clad. Four pairs of eyes fastened momentarily on this and absorbed the fact that they had been cheated. Sir Thomas was not dressed as Bill Sikes. They alone were in unorthodox dress.

The Prince of Wales's eyes flicked speedily over the unusual evening dress of the gathering as battered top hats were speedily removed from heads and a lady with long droopy drawers swept a curtsy. He hadn't seen anything like that since his sister Vicky left the nursery.

Oliver still raged impotently, unable to believe that he could have been so mistaken in a woman. She was to marry this mountebank, this hypocritical toad of a Sir Thomas. Samuel was convulsed with fury at this new evidence of skulduggery, resolved that no holds would be barred now. Even Lord Beddington was upset, being made to look like a damn fool before Her Majesty's son. None of them betrayed their feelings, however, as they paid obeisance to the Prince, who gravely offered his hand in turn to Mr Scrooge, Dr Marigold, Mr Weller and Miss Nell.

Alfred somewhat nervously served drinks, aware of uncomfortably tight breeches. He was wondering wildly what had happened to Auguste who had promised to be at his side when, as he fully expected, glasses of this revolting potion were flung over his head by the irate tasters.

'A Dickensian mint julep, sire,' explained Sir Thomas, as the Prince of Wales apprehensively eyed the contents of his glass.

Mint? That was to be taken with roast lamb, not adulterating his drinks. The Prince of Wales replaced it and took the punch instead. He sipped the concoction cautiously. After the first sip he was wishing some awful fate on every Lioniser in the world. He could distinctly taste cold tea. He didn't know or care whether Dickens liked this stuff, but he was damned certain he didn't. Only Throgmorton seemed to have any idea of civilised behaviour. At least he was properly dressed, not looking like something out of one of Mama's precious charades at Windsor. It then dawned on him disagreeably that not only was he in for a Dickensian banquet (although he had taken care of that problem, he remembered cheeringly) but for Dickensian readings. Suddenly, Mama's charades seemed the more appealing. Even the thought of lunch at Osborne House again tomorrow didn't seem too bad an idea, even if it did mean listening to Mama telling him how she heard nightingales in the garden at Pierremont House and how she walked all the way to Pegwell when she was twelve and ate shrimp paste at the Bellevue Tavern.

Sir Thomas coughed deferentially. 'The little matter I spoke of, sire.'

Samuel's eyes suddenly riveted on his hated rival. The Prince of Wales came to with a jolt. He hadn't been paying much attention to what Throgmorton had been talking about on the way here, but he recalled his ears had caught the unpleasant words 'casting vote', and 'your important role as president'. 'Splendid, splendid,' he had said cordially and automatically at the time. Now he felt somewhat more cautious about the matter. He was going to be responsible for something that he didn't know or care the first thing about. Could it have political repercussions? Would Mama hear about it? He looked round sharply. As he feared, all eyes were on him. This was going to be awkward, without a doubt. He'd been caught without a script.

Alfred handed him another drink, and the Prince of Wales absent-mindedly took it. He gulped. At least the disgusting taste of mint concentrated his mind. He watched warily as the little fat chap with bits of paper in his hat leapt to his feet. They were all mad, these people. Who was he meant to be? Pickwick came back to him dimly as a Dickensian character.

'I vote, sire, instead of your casting vote, we should have a re-vote when Mrs Figgis-Hewett arrives, our remaining committee member. I feel we may be able to avoid troubling you, sire.'

The Prince of Wales perked up. The chap was more sensible than he looked.

Angelina fidgeted. Where was Gwendolen? And what had happened to Mr Didier?

'Ridiculous,' shrugged Sir Thomas smoothly. 'Why should we? There is no reason. No, sire, I'm afraid the rules clearly state that once a vote is taken, it is irrefutable.'

'Then we should take a vote,' shouted Samuel, oblivious of royalty.

'We've had one,' snapped Sir Thomas.

'You need my casting vote, then?' put in the Prince of Wales, lost.

'A vote about a vote, sire,' said Samuel.

'That's what you need my vote for?' asked the Prince.

'No, sir, we haven't taken it yet,' explained Samuel.

'Then why ask for my casting vote?' asked the Prince politely.

'We need a vote,' put in Lord Beddington suddenly, deciding this was a legal matter, 'to vote whether we have another vote for which we need your casting vote.'

'I see,' said the Prince. He always thought old Beddington was quite mad, and now he knew it.

Horrorstruck, Oliver and Angelina listened to their colleagues. Had they all taken leave of their senses?

'The rules are rules.' Sir Thomas, losing patience, was pink in the face.

The Prince of Wales had rules too, and they did not include turning social evenings into bear gardens. With true diplomacy, he rose to his feet. 'I shall give my answer tonight,' he announced with deliberation. By that time he could have arranged to be called away.

But even princes cannot control every situation. Before he could move for the doors, they were flung open imperiously, revealing a wide-eyed, agonised Auguste outside. Past him into the room sailed the last member of the Literary Lionisers' committee. Gwendolen was in full Dickensian dress. She was not, however, clad in the unsuitable but respectable garb of Agnes Wickfield or even that of Betsy Trotwood. *David Copperfield* had taken second place to *Great Expectations*. There on the threshold, clad in a soiled yellow-white satin dress with a very low-cut bodice, voluminous skirt, white satin slippers and gloves, stood a shrouded figure, of whose identity there was no doubt. She stood a moment to gain her audience's complete attention, then flung back the long white veil that hid her face. She sank to her knees before the Prince of Wales. 'I, Your Royal Highness, am Miss Havisham. I seek vengeance on the monster who has betrayed me. I have been abandoned.' A long, skinny, bare arm ending in a white silk glove was thrust out towards Sir Thomas.

It must be charades, thought the Prince of Wales blindly. Why had no one told him? Either that, or he was in for a very sticky evening indeed.

Mesmerised by the scene he had witnessed, and agonised by the scene he had just had with Mrs Figgis-Hewett, when he saw her costume and vainly attempted to dissuade her, Auguste recalled his prime duty and reluctantly despatched Alfred to the dining room to prepare for the serving of wines at the Prince's table. He himself returned to the kitchens, where the heat was now making the sweat run from everyone's faces. Feverishly he checked. Yes, all seemed ready, but disasters might yet ensue. Look what had happened upstairs. It was about time now to turn his attention to the kidneys. This, his own recipe, he would entrust to no one else, though Heinrich had assembled and prepared the ingredients.

'I've nowhere to put the gravy jugs,' wailed Emily.

'Improvise, Miss Dawson,' said Auguste testily, rushing between salads and soups. A maître chef was supposed to superintend, not do everything himself. Would Soyer − no, he would not think of Soyer. His hat disturbed him too much. He shuddered at his remembrance of royalty's puzzled look when he removed this ostentatious headgear. Suppose he were to think it Auguste's own choice?

Emily improvised.

A howl. 'Not there, Miss Dawson.'

James moved swiftly into the disorder being wreaked in his carefully arranged plates, set in order of service. Alice came to help him, perhaps under the impression it was Alfred or the confusion of the moment, and earned herself a stinging rebuff, thus beginning another altercation.

'You keep your bad language to yourself, Mr Pegg,' she said, pink in the face. 'You're like your soufflés – hard.'

'My soufflés aren't hard,' he glared.

'They're not your best work,' Algernon pointed out.

'Your terrines aren't very good either,' chimed in Emily.

'Coming from you, Miss Dawson,' retorted James cornered, 'with your soggy pastry—'

'Please not to be rude to Miss Dawson,' barked Heinrich walking between them, rolling pin in hand, like Siegfried to rescue Brunhilde.

'Pegg's right,' said Algernon, delightedly egging them on. 'You and the Kaiser think you rule Europe. You keep out of it.'

'Silence.' Auguste was appalled. Where was unity? Where was the true love of cuisine that united such diverse spirits? What was happening to his happy band? Drama above and now the same below. Surely this was something more than the heat of twelve geese cooking on a summer's night?

In the enormous dining room, even the chandeliers seemed to tremble as they waited breathlessly for the arrival of the Prince of Wales. His coming displayed no jot of his inner feelings, though his heart sank at the array of knee breeches and crinolines, and at last it occurred to him that the lunatics he had met upstairs were in Dickensian dress. He glanced uneasily at his own evening attire.

The Prince politely shook hands with six Peggottys, two Betsy Trotwoods, eight Mr Pecksniffs, seven Mr Fezziwigs, eight Mrs Fezziwigs, two Doras, a couple of Little Dorrits, two Miss Flites, a villainous gentleman who announced he was the convict Magwitch, and numerous other Lionisers too nervous to announce their identities. Then he turned to seek his reward: a banquet cooked by Auguste Didier. He had been placed at the head of the table, a Solomon come to judgement, but a far from happy one.

From his vantage point through a serving hatch, Auguste watched as the assembly took their seats after a brief prayer intoned by Sir Thomas. The chairman was on the Prince's left, with Angelina opposite him and Lord Beddington next to him. Oliver was below the salt, as far as Sir Thomas was concerned, and Gwendolen had been placed next to Lord Beddington so that Sir Thomas did not have to look at her. Somehow, however, she had conspired to change places with Oliver so that she was staring triumphantly into Sir Thomas's face diagonally up the table. The woman was mad. In fact, he thought, glancing at Angelina, all women were mad. He just didn't comprehend what she had told him this afternoon.

The Prince of Wales studied his Dickensian menu with instant alarm, followed by deep misgivings. This was not what he had employed Didier for. He glanced up, saw Auguste's anguished eyes, and thought he understood. Nevertheless, he expected assistance from him.

'Mutton broth,' announced Sir Thomas proudly, as Heinrich and James, somewhat awkwardly in their knee breeches, moved round the table to serve the soup. 'You will recall, sire, Mrs Bedwin's restorative broth in *Oliver Twist*.'

The Prince of Wales looked at the bowl sharply. Twist? He was the fellow in the workhouse who wanted more, wasn't he? Well, *he* wasn't going to have any at all and that was flat. He took a large sip of his sherry and refused the soup. He was rewarded in this wise decision by Auguste's tactful appearance carrying a small dish of almond soup, which he unostentatiously placed before the Prince of Wales. 'Your own mutton broth, sire.' While everyone's attention was on Samuel Pipkin who showed ominous signs of speaking, he quickly murmured: 'It's almond soup, sire. As mentioned by Dickens to an anonymous friend.'

'Perhaps you are correct, sire,' Samuel was announcing firmly. 'Now Mrs Figgis-Hewett has joined us, there should undoubtedly be a new vote later.' He had had an opportunity of assessing Miss Havisham's feelings on the subject, not that these were hard to predict. After her outburst, she now remained silent, darting odd looks of triumph at her betrayer.

The Prince of Wales frowned. He could not recall agreeing to this at all, but as it offered a chance of avoiding his own intervention, he nodded fervently, and took some more almond soup. This Dickens had the right idea after all, no matter who his anonymous friend might be.

'Sire, alas, the rules of the club do not permit this,' said Sir Thomas. 'Not without a vote.'

'My casting vote?' queried the Prince.

'No, sire, a vote on the constitution, which can only be taken at the annual general meeting.'

Sir Thomas was not going to be swayed. With Gwendolen certain to change her vote, and as he could not rely on foolish Angelina to change hers, the situation was dangerous in the extreme. But he would not press too vehemently or he would lose the support of the Prince. It was too much on top of an already most trying day. He looked round uneasily, and Alfred stepped forward to fill his glass with white wine. Emily cleared the soup plates and Heinrich and Algernon were bringing out individual plates of lobster salad.

'Sire.' Gwendolen's voice was shrill enough to penetrate from the end of the table, quite putting the Prince off his lobster. 'I support Mr Pipkin's proposal for a vote.'

'I regret this is impossible, sire. If you recall, I showed you the rule. It is irreversible,' said Sir Thomas adamantly.

The Prince of Wales's lobster suddenly tasted of flannel. He hated everyone. He did recall the rule, he cordially disliked women who flung themselves at his feet threatening breach of promise actions, and moreover he didn't like the look of that jumped-up Pickwick there.

'I suggest we take a look at it later, and meanwhile enjoy this delicious meal.' The Prince summoned his private detective: a message was to arrive no later than 9.30 p.m. calling him urgently to Osborne. Mama was seriously ill, Alexandra was seriously ill, the boot boy's aunt was seriously ill. Anything. 'And of course,' he continued blandly to the committee, 'if I can then be of assistance, I should be delighted.' Oh, for that uncomfortable bed on his yacht that he now resolved to be aboard this very evening, before any such vote could be called. Like Mr Barkis, he intended to go out with the tide. A note in his voice that he had long cultivated indicated that the discussion was at an end. His lobster promptly improved in taste.

There was a short silence as each person cogitated on his position; Oliver and Angelina broke it, with polite murmurings of gratitude and apology for troubling him, Their politeness extended only to the Prince of Wales. They ignored each other. Oliver wondered why Angelina was not clamouring for a new vote in order to support her fiancé and decided that this was some further infamous plan on her part. Angelina wondered whether she would change sides, just to show this pompous young man what she thought of him. Sir Thomas relaxed a little. Now he had time on his side. Lord Beddington wondered what was next on the menu, Samuel squirmed with suppressed rage and this obvious sign of the Prince of Wales's inclinations. And Gwendolen smiled. She was thinking lovingly of what was to come.

The lobster plates were removed by Emily, and replaced by Alice with bowls for the entrée and plates for the remove to follow. James placed two dishes of kidneys in champagne and mushroom catsup sauce on the table while Algernon and Heinrich faced the organised maelstrom of the kitchen to gather the quails and cutlets for the remove. Auguste had added the course in the interests of the Prince of Wales; it was to be served virtually at the same time as the entrée, in defiance of the rules, in the hope it would attract less attention. The Prince glanced at Auguste, who gave an imperceptible nod. Relieved, the Prince of Wales gave his assent to a portion of kidneys handed to him by Sir Thomas. One mouthful of the sauce and he nodded appreciation. Pity they didn't award the Order of the Garter to cooks. They had a better line in diplomacy than old Chamberlain himself and certainly did more good in the world.

'This is Mrs Crupp's dish of kidneys, sir, for which she sent out to the pastrycook in *David Copperfield*. We have allowed ourselves a little licence with the sauce,' Angelina explained.

'Splendid, splendid,' was the Prince of Wales's comment. He eyed the dish thoughtfully. Normally he did not indulge in second helpings, but − no, he would resist. No he wouldn't; after all, he was off to Marienbad on the 19th. He murmured in Alice's ear. It was due to this second helping that he rejected the quail and mutton cutlets (with pickled walnuts) as Alice and Algernon, with a somewhat nervous eye on Lord Beddington, offered them.

'I don't recall quails on my menu,' commented Sir Thomas querulously.

'The remove, Sir Thomas. The *réleves*. A Dickens favourite according to his manager, Dolby,' said Oliver provocatively from his lowly position, two seats away from Sir Thomas. 'One must have a remove, must one not?'

103

'I always think it sounds like murder,' trilled Gwendolen suddenly, coming back into the conversation.

'What does?' demanded Samuel, startled from his dreams of vengeance.'

'Remove,' she answered darkly. 'Removing a source of pestilence,' and relapsed into silence again. The Prince of Wales decided not to recall the quails.

'And now for the geese,' Sir Thomas declared, as Auguste emerged from the kitchen, Soyer hat crammed on.

Goose? The Prince of Wales gazed in horror as a large, succulent goose was borne in by Heinrich to the dining-room serving table for carving by Auguste. No leaving this task to others. Goose required the most careful carving. Auguste almost laughed as he saw the expression on the Prince of Wales's face as a plateful of roast goose advanced towards him in the hands of James Pegg, followed by an endless procession, it seemed, of forcemeats, vegetables and gravies. A lift of an eyebrow, a mute appeal to Auguste, who interpreted it correctly and despatched back to the kitchen for the rejected quail and cutlets.

'With pickled walnuts, sire, as in *The Pickwick Papers*,' Angelina announced gravely. The look Sir Thomas gave her was not a pleasant one, as he defiantly took a sizeable helping of goose.

'The best goose that ever was,' approved Oliver gravely after they had finished, catching Auguste's eye as he watched anxiously from his vantage point.

Sir Thomas, however, or rather his stomach, clearly did not agree, for halfway through the *entremets*, with a few words of apology he absented himself from the table.

'It's his stomach,' explained Gwendolen to the Prince of Wales. 'He suffers greatly from gastritis.' She shot a look of triumph at her hated rival. No doubt Angelina Langham, the upstart, did not even know about Thomas's delicate stomach.

The Prince of Wales bestowed a polite eye upon her, then turned to the rather more salubrious prospect of his favourite savoury.

By the time the coffee made its appearance, Sir Thomas his re-appearance, and Alfred served the brandy, Auguste began to breathe more easily. No catastrophe had taken place. Indeed, modesty forbade him to contemplate too long what he could count a personal success. He would not swear that the Prince of Wales had enjoyed every minute, but at least he, Auguste Didier, had done what he could. The suppressed tension between members of the committee was still boiling, almost like Algernon's mutton broth; it was certainly not smiling. Sir Thomas drank several cups of coffee and refused the brandy. 'My performance, sire,' he said in a low voice, already hoarse as if from emotion. 'I am to give the first reading. Bill Sikes and the murder of Nancy. If you would forgive me yet again, I must go to change into the appropriate costume.' As if already suffering from an excess of emotion, he left.

Annoyed at the fellow leaping up and down like a jack-in-the-box, wishing that he could escape as easily, and regretful that he had not demanded his urgent message for somewhat earlier, the Prince of Wales shifted uneasily in his plush upright seat in the ballroom to which they had adjourned. He felt as if he were at one of Mama's evenings. She never invited him to the jolly ones. He had to sit out in the corridor at Windsor listening to Electrophone transmissions of some opera that went on and on before the warblers saw fit to die with some interminable aria. Mama didn't bother to invite him when she hauled over Lord George Sanger's circus two weeks ago. Oh no.

Where was old Throgmorton? He was taking a devil of a time to change. The audience was fidgeting behind him, and there was a limit to the amount of time he intended to chat to this crazy woman next to him in the soiled wedding dress and veil. He felt as if he were at yet another family wedding. Hallo, something was happening at last.

Samuel Pipkin, eagerness all over his face, had bounded up to the reading desk, arranged to look identical to that used by Dickens himself in his tours around the country. Samuel begged the company's indulgence as chairman elect to entertain them with a short piece in Sir Thomas's absence. He had not thought his chance would come so opportunely.

Entertaining it was, if unusual for a Dickens evening, for Samuel was a consummate actor. When he read from Mr Thackeray's *Book of Snobs*, choosing the 'Great City Snob' as his text, imitating the while Sir Thomas's mannerism of impatiently snapping his fingers and clasping his lapel, followed by his grave walk, hands behind back, no one had had the least doubt as to whom was meant. A ripple of suppressed laughter ran round the room. Samuel was declaiming of the 'grave, pompous and awful being' with great zest when Sir Thomas himself arrived, clad as Bill Sikes, and with murder on his own mind to judge by his face when he took in Samuel's performance. Carefully grubbied white breeches tied below the knee, open-necked shirt and spotted scarf tied untidily, lace-up boots, he struck as much awe into the onlookers as would Sikes himself. But remembering the vote to come, Sir Thomas controlled himself in his words. He, at least, was a gentleman.

He strode to the desk. 'Thank you, Mr Pipkin,' he said, drinking from the glass of water placed for his convenience. 'I look forward later to your own delightful performance of a cheap-jack. It could not fail to be excellent in your hands, and quite put Mr Thackeray in the shade.

'Now I open tonight's reading from the master's great *Oliver Twist*, the famous scene chosen by Dickens for his own readings and which led to his early death, from the violent emotion that swept over him each time he read this passage.'

The emotion seemed to have reached Sir Thomas early for his face was very pale, and he drank the remaining water before commencing his tale. His voice was even more hoarse now, with the emotion of the reading. 'The robber . . . dragged her into the middle of the room and, looking once towards the door, placed his heavy hand upon her mouth.' His own hand came round like Sikes's, and then passed over his brow. ' ". . . spare my life for the love of Heaven as I spared yours," rejoined the girl, clinging to him. "Bill, dear Bill, you cannot have the heart to kill me." '

Auguste, watching from the doorway, was fascinated, rapt as he continued his performance, the audience equally gripped.

' "The man struggled violently to release his arm." ' Sir Thomas picked up the empty glass, replaced it, continuing brokenly: ' ". . . Bill," cried the girl.' All eyes were on Sir Thomas. Even the Prince of Wales was interested. This man should have his vote, no doubt about it. He had presence. Better than old Pipsqueak. Perhaps he'd stay after all.

'. . . The housebreaker freed one arm, and grasped his pistol . . . he beat it twice, with all the force he could summon, upon the upturned face that almost touched his own.'

The effort seemed almost too much for the reader, whose voice dropped deeply, Auguste noticed uneasily.

'She staggered and fell; nearly blinded with the blood that rained down from a deep gash in her forehead; but raising herself with difficulty . . . breathed one prayer for mercy to her Maker. It was a ghastly figure to look upon.'

Sir Thomas's face was pale, paler even than those of his audience, most of whom were wondering whether this were not a little too much emotion after all that goose. 'The murderer staggering backwards to the wall and shutting out the sight with his hand, seized a heavy club and struck . . .'

It ended in a choking splutter as Sir Thomas, following

Nancy's tragic end, collapsed to his knees, clutching at and dragging over the lectern, and then falling to the floor where he lay as insensible as Nancy herself.

A burst of tentative clapping petered out and a strange unease ran round the audience as Sir Thomas failed to rise. Angelina ran forward and knelt over him.

'A doctor, we need a doctor. Is there a doctor here? And water, quickly.' She stood up.

Auguste was already at her side, feeling for a pulse.

'Thomas,' cried Gwendolen in alarm, running up. 'It's his stomach, his stomach.'

'Marigold,' cried Samuel, confusing reality in hysteria, 'I'm Dr Marigold.'

'His heart beats too rapidly,' Auguste said to Angelina in concern. Surely this was no ordinary stomach illness? Then he saw the eyes, the dilated pupils, as did Oliver Michaels peering over Auguste's shoulder.

'That's odd,' said Oliver quietly.

From the audience, a gentleman with check trousers, a huge bulbous nose and an eyepatch arrived. 'Squeers,' he announced apologetically. 'I'm a doctor. Let me see him.'

Auguste thankfully ceded his place, quietly pointing to the eyes. 'Opium?' said Oliver to him as he stood up.

'Poison of one kind or another, I fear,' said Auguste gravely. 'Look at the rash on his face — that was not there before.' He stood aside as the doctor, consulting quickly with Mr Multhrop who had arrived glassy-eyed and panic-stricken, arranged to have Sir Thomas carried to another room. Perhaps the patient had taken medicine for his stomach while he had been away from the table, and taken too much.

'Food poisoning,' said Multhrop hollowly, avoiding Auguste's eye.

'Possibly,' said the doctor noncommittally.

Auguste glanced towards the Prince of Wales deep in

conversation with Lord Beddington. Quickly his mind ran over all the awful possibilities. Food poisoning? Not with *his* food. No, this was something more serious. And this situation, albeit not poison, had happened before too. Suppose it were not an accident. Suppose—

'Sire,' he said, 'may I speak with you?'

The Prince of Wales looked up annoyed. Cooks, however good, should not interrupt his conversations.

'Sir Thomas is not very well, sire.'

'I am exceedingly sorry to hear it.' The Prince turned back.

Auguste hesitated, then plunged again. 'You will recall, sire, at Cannes a gentleman was taken ill.' The Prince's head swivelled back to him, and the royal eyes fixed on him. 'I fear somewhat the same circumstances.'

'Ah.' The Prince of Wales rose to his feet. 'If you will excuse me, Beddington, I see my detective beckoning me.'

Ten minutes later a small party, including a highly suspicious private detective, made its way out through the tradesmen's entrance, escorted by Auguste. The only other person privy to the beating of the retreat was a young kitchenmaid, who stared at her future monarch in amazement.

Auguste went slowly into the kitchens, unable to think fully of all the awful possibilities of the situation. Mr Multhrop was ordering hot water and coffee demanded by the doctor.

'I feel, Mr Multhrop,' Auguste interjected in the effort to convert unspeakable thoughts in concrete action, 'we should stop work in the kitchen.'

'You can't take time off *now*, Mr Dee,' said Mr Multhrop, horrified.

He smiled despite himself. 'No, sir, the food will need to be examined.'

Multhrop looked at him in panic, then remembered he

wasn't responsible for the food. 'Yes,' he said eagerly, 'you're right.'

The order was implemented. No further work was to be carried out, no food touched. The kitchens were to be locked.

'But what about breakfast?' wailed Mr Multhrop. 'Why lock them?' Auguste did not answer. How could he explain that something inside him, experience, foreboding, sick terror, told him this might be necessary?

Before breakfast a far worse problem than a locked kitchen hit Mr Multhrop, the Imperial and Auguste.

At 4 a.m. after a night in which thunderstorms had rumbled and broke continually, and despite Squeers' and a Broadstairs doctor's best ministrations, Sir Thomas Throgmorton died.

Squeers came out to where Mr Multhrop was sitting, wilting on a chair foreseeing the end of his hotel. 'He's dead, I'm afraid,' he said. 'Can't issue a certificate. Some highly toxic poison. Atropine, unless I'm much mistaken. Belladonna. That rash was significant, and the delirium, hallucinations.'

'An accident, perhaps?' offered Mr Multhrop hopefully.

'It would have been a large dose. Odd kind of accident. We're not talking about children eating deadly nightshade. This might be suicide or murder. I'll have to notify the police.'

'The police,' moaned Mr Multhrop, mind flitting wearily from one problem to another. 'But this is the Imperial.'

The doctor had little sympathy for the Imperial.

'Suicide seems unlikely,' reflected Auguste dully, eyes smarting with tiredness. 'He'd have had to have taken it during the meal or shortly after. A curious time to choose with the Prince of Wales present, and a reading to give.'

The doctor looked at him. Auguste was still attired

110

incongruously in his Soyer costume. 'You're the cook?'

With those three simple words, nightmare swept over Auguste. He himself had said it: suicide or murder. And if the latter, he was the cook.

The serpent was present even in this Eden of Broadstairs. Again it had slithered in on his holiday, and, worst, it was a murder in which he would be interrogated. Once again he was in the sobering presence of violent death. That it was at the seaside made it seem all the worse. His career, all that was left to him now Tatiana was gone for ever, was ruined. For ever he would be the 'cook at the Throgmorton death'. Then a small spark of comfort occurred to him.

Egbert Rose was at Ramsgate.

Chapter Six

Egbert Rose lay in bed blissfully contemplating breakfast. Kippers, kedgeree, kidneys – what a sturdy sound all these good breakfast dishes had. Not that he wanted any of them this morning. He had slept well, entirely oblivious of the thunderstorms that Edith told him somewhat reproachfully had kept her sleepless all night. Edith was already up, and had awoken him with her cries of woe when she drew back the heavy plush curtains to discover grey skies and drizzle. Would it clear in time for the band concert this afternoon? This was her main anxiety. Should she don her heavier serge walking dress or be optimistic and wear the foulard she had planned? She eyed its mauve folds wistfully.

'Which do you think, Egbert?' she enquired dolefully, uncomfortably aware that the draught coming in the window did not bode well for the foulard.

'A nice fresh herring,' he murmured, turning over and going back to sleep.

'Oh Egbert,' she snorted, banging the door behind her as she departed for the bathroom.

Rose enjoyed having breakfast at Ramsgate. In fact he was enjoying this whole holiday. He enjoyed not being known as Inspector Rose, he enjoyed the sausages from Spratling's Colonial Butchers, he enjoyed kedgeree, and most of all he enjoyed the fresh fish brought in by the landlady's schoolboy son. Fresh fish was something he didn't see a lot of in Highbury.

113

'I've finished, Egbert,' announced Edith unnecessarily, sweeping back into the room swathed in the huge purple dressing gown she had bought for decorousness lest she be passed in the corridor on the way to the bathroom. Her pink cheeks bore testimony to the scrubbing they had endured from Dr Mackenzie's Arsenical Soap (as used by Madame Patti, Ellaline Terriss, etc.).

Rose smiled. He liked seeing Edith happy. He thought a little wistfully of Provence, tried and failed to see Edith as happy in the Hôtel Paradis, and returned to savour anew the pleasures of Ramsgate. Perhaps they'd take an excursion by brake to Pegwell Village this afternoon if the concert had to be cancelled because of rain. Or perhaps it might clear up?

He jumped out of bed, contemplated his new seaside pyjamas with renewed pleasure, and prepared to enjoy the second week of his precious holiday.

Thirty minutes later, Edith clad in mauve foulard and he in grey flannels and blazer, they descended for breakfast. Edith walked first into the small dining room already crowded with boarders.

'Why, good morning, Auguste,' he heard her say in tones of mingled surprise and pleasure. He blinked. He must have heard her wrong. But no. There at a table was a clearly dejected, drooping Auguste, with large dark circles under his eyes.

Rose's first reaction was pleasure, the second unease, and the third a downright sinking feeling inside that had nothing to do with appetite.

'Would your friend like a nice hot kipper?' asked Mrs Burbanks the landlady solicitously, on the grounds that foreigners, however well they spoke English, would never understand it. 'He says not, but he don't look well to me. A nice hot cup of tea is what he needs.' She bustled out, and five minutes later Auguste was sipping from a willow-pattern cup with Edith's and Egbert's eyes on him. Coffee,

114

strong and black, was what he needed, not Mr Jackson's breakfast tea, but how could one explain that to the good English landlady?

Nevertheless, he did feel somewhat improved, and he turned to Rose. 'You must forgive me, *mon ami*, but . . .'

'In trouble, eh, Auguste?' Rose asked quietly. 'Something wrong?'

'I fear so. I fear so very much. I shall be arrested, perhaps beheaded.' His lack of sleep was contributing to an irrational but lingering fear that the Prince of Wales might also drop dead. How well *did* he know his pupils? Suppose one of them had put something nasty in the food by error − or by purpose. Even worse, suppose Heinrich Freimüller were a foreign agent, deputed to kill the Prince? If atropine it was, it was easily obtainable in extract of belladonna. Or suppose that accidentally seeds or fruit of the atropine group of plants had been included in the vegetables or herbs? He had not checked them all personally. His mind ran rampant over the terrible possibilities.

Rose raised his eyebrows and drank a cup of Mrs Burbanks' tea. The herring looked delicious but he wasn't at all sure he was going to enjoy it as much as he'd thought. 'Sure you won't have a herring, Auguste?'

Auguste shuddered. 'No. I thank you, Egbert.'

'Then you'd better tell me.'

'It is murder, I think, my friend,' he said dolefully.

Edith clucked in anxiety. Rose dropped his fork. 'Murder,' he repeated. 'Not again. How the deuce − I beg your pardon, my love − do you manage to do it, Auguste?'

'I do not know, *mon ami*, but do it I do. It is not certain, but I fear it must be. Poison, you see.'

'Ah.' Rose now understood fully the reason for the early visit. 'One of your pupils, is it?'

'*Non*. It is Sir Thomas Throgmorton, after the Grand Dickensian Banquet I told you about.'

115

Rose whistled, and the dining room assembly looked up, annoyed at being disturbed in their silence.

'After the meal for which I was responsible,' Auguste continued mournfully.

Suddenly the drizzle outside looked a lot less likely to clear up.

'Murder,' repeated Rose. 'Poison. You cooked the meal.' He sighed. 'This is where we came in, at Stockbery Towers.'

Auguste smiled faintly. 'Egbert, I am not sure. It was only five hours ago he died. But who would choose to commit suicide in the middle of a dinner sitting next to the Prince of Wales?'

The knife dropped to join its companion. 'The Prince of Wales?' echoed Rose hollowly. Suddenly this was ceasing to be solely his friend's problem. If the Prince of Wales were involved in any way, Scotland Yard would be too. Thomas Throgmorton – wasn't he some kind of banker? International banker, his memory threw up. Rose could have groaned aloud. Trust Auguste to get mixed up with it. He couldn't throw him to the wolves of his colleagues at the Factory. Suppose Twitch had an urge to flex his ambitious wings over this one?

'These kippers are very good, Auguste,' said Edith hopefully. 'Are you sure you won't join us? You need to keep your strength up.'

Auguste reached out his hand and took hers. 'Dear Edith, will you forgive me? Your holiday – and I come with tales of murder.'

'I expect Egbert will help you. Won't you, Egbert?'

He would not be seen to give way easily. He regarded Auguste morosely. 'I'm on holiday,' he pointed out.

'*Moi aussi, mon ami*,' replied Auguste dolefully.

'I suppose you'd better tell me all about it. *After* I've finished this herring.'

One hour later, Rose stood at the window of his room

looking down at the harbour scene. He had already spent much time on the hotel telephone to Scotland Yard. 'My dear,' he said at last to Edith, 'do you think you might enjoy the rest of your holiday at Broadstairs?'

The delights of the Paragon, the Baths, the Marina Pier, Ellington Park and the Leghorn hat in Lewis Hyland and Linom's window floated temptingly before her eyes. 'I'm sure I would, Egbert,' she answered loyally.

Auguste returned to Broadstairs by donkey cart, somewhat cheered, feeling he could face anything. First he should go to the hotel to see what was happening.

His ability to face anything was severely tested by Mr Multhrop, who clutched him firmly by his lapels as he entered the door, as if holding him under close arrest, an impression strengthened by the sight of a uniformed policeman standing behind him.

'I thought you had run away, Mr Dee,' cried Multhrop in relief. 'So did the police,' he added. A speculative glance from the constable at Mr Didier.

'My superiors would like to see you, sir. Very upset they were, sir, when they heard you'd gone missing.'

'I had not gone missing, Constable,' retorted Auguste with dignity. 'Is there any reason that I should not take an early stroll on the beaches like Mr Dickens himself?'

'This Mr Dickens isn't wanted on no murder enquiry. The inspector ain't asked for him.'

'Mr Dee,' Multhrop cried, tugging at the lapels for attention, 'you don't understand. The Prince of Wales has been kidnapped. He's not in his room.'

'Mr Multhrop,' Auguste said patiently, 'His Royal Highness left yesterday evening together with his staff. He – er – received an urgent message to return to his yacht. If you investigate, you will discover that his detective and valet have also vanished.'

'Had accomplices, did you?' said the constable, gratified, advancing towards Auguste and slipping an arm far from lovingly through his. 'I think you'd better see the Inspector right now.'

Auguste was promptly frogmarched into Mr Multhrop's office, Mr Multhrop trotting along behind torn between a certain loyalty to Mr Dee and relief that officialdom had taken over. Araminta, on the point of descending the stairs in a cream piqué dress, turned round and went back to her room.

'Well, well, well, Mr Didier. We've met before, haven't we?'

Auguste groaned. The nightmare seemed to be intensifying. Inspector Naseby of all people, who had clearly been looking forward to this moment. Eight years had done nothing to mellow him.

'Now where was it?' murmured the Inspector lovingly, his weaselly features cracking into the semblance of a grin. 'Ah yes, Stockbery Towers. You got off very easy that time, Didier. Never thought that justice had been done, whatever your pal at Scotland Yard maintained.' It certainly hadn't so far as he, Naseby, was concerned. Promotion at Maidstone was never to be his; instead they'd sent him back to Ramsgate, scene of his early success in capturing the notorious smuggler Rum-Bubber Bill. Unfortunately he hadn't repeated that success and Inspector he had remained, and would do so until he left the force. Ramsgate had tired of the honour of his presence and he had been sent to Sandwich, under whose jurisdiction the Broadstairs police force came. Naseby was not pleased at the way his career had gone. And here was Monsewer Auguste Didier again, within his power. 'So now you've gorn and kidnapped the Prince of Wales, after murdering a poor innocent banking gentleman,' he purred, eyes glittering.

'Inspector Naseby!' Auguste tried to keep the tremor out

118

of his voice. 'I am delighted to see you again, even if it be under such tragic circumstances. However, the Prince of Wales has not been kidnapped. I was present when he left the hotel last evening after an urgent message recalling him to Osborne House. Family illness . . .' He let his voice trail off in the hope that Naseby would not enquire further into such a delicate matter.

'Would it surprise you to know, Mr Didier, that the Prince of Wales is not at Osborne House?' said Naseby complacently. 'That no message was sent to His Royal Highness, and that Her Majesty the Queen, the Princess of Wales, the Duke of York, the Duchess of York, Her Majesty's entire household, the gardener's boy and the royal dachshund are all in perfect health?' Naseby's chest puffed up with each phrase. Promotion loomed at last. 'What have you done with him, Didier?' he hissed.

'I have done nothing,' replied Auguste, goaded. Sleepless, his fears of the night swept back reinforced. Suppose the Prince of Wales even now lay lifeless on his yacht? 'It is not surprising that he has not arrived at Osborne House yet. It is only ten thirty, and there were thunderstorms all night, which would delay him. I do not know about illness in his family. I know only he told me he had to go. I am not his private confidant, I am only a cook, remember.'

'Oh, I remember you're the cook all right. You're the Prince of Wales's own cook, aren't you? Plans to poison him go wrong, then?'

'I am *not* the Prince of Wales's cook,' said Auguste tiredly.

'Oh?' Naseby's eyes gleamed. 'Mr Multhrop thinks you are. Been a spot of lying then?'

'I do not know why Mr Multhrop thinks this. I think the Prince of Wales may have told Sir Thomas so, after he asked for my services at the banquet. It was more diplomatic to put it that way for Mr Multhrop's chef.'

'Oh ho!' Naseby's delight could not be contained. 'A

119

likely story. Sir Thomas is dead. You pretend to Mr Multhrop to be the Prince of Wales's chef in order to gain access to the kitchens in order to poison the Prince. That right?'

'Yes – no!' shouted Auguste.

Naseby stood up slowly. 'Auguste Didier, I arrest you—'

He broke off, transfixed, as the door had opened, and Egbert Rose stood on the threshold. Even had Rose been wearing his blazer and flannels and not changed into more sober attire, Naseby would still have recognised that face. It had haunted his dreams for eight years.

Not by so much as a blink did Rose betray his own surprise at seeing Naseby, whose face had turned a delicate shade of puce.

'What are you doing here? This is my case,' he almost wailed.

Rose shook his head. 'Grave international implications, Naseby. There's the Prince of Wales to consider. The Yard's handling it now.'

Naseby glared. 'I've already got the villain. There.' He jerked a finger at Auguste. 'He's confessed.'

'Has he now? Let's hear the evidence, shall we?' Rose said pensively, walking round and sitting in Naseby's seat before he could reach it. Naseby was forced to retreat to the only other chair, in a corner.

'He's admitted having been the last person to see His Royal Highness,' he said sulkily. 'He's admitted passing himself off as the Prince's chef, and when his dastardly plan to assassinate His Royal Highness by poison didn't work, he kidnapped him. Probably murdered him.'

'Where is he then?' Rose enquired. He was enjoying himself; it was like dangling bait in front of those mackerel on Captain Hawkins's *Mary Rose* fishing boat last week. Naseby wasn't much of a catch though. He'd throw him back later.

120

'He's probably—'

'*Quo corpus*, Naseby?' Rose provoked him with dim memories of schoolboy Latin. 'Where's your body?'

'That's what he's got to tell *us*,' Naseby retorted, coming back like Jem Mace.

In the event it was not going to be Auguste who gave this information but Naseby's own sergeant, who burst in with the news that the Cowes harbour master had telephoned to announce the arrival of the yacht *Osborne* with the Prince of Wales aboard.

Naseby's face fell, as Auguste's spirits rose.

'There might have been coercion,' Naseby muttered hopefully. 'Removing a witness from the scene of a murder is an important crime. Ten to one, the Prince of Wales saw him do it,' pointing at Auguste. 'Vital witness. I'll be speaking to His Royal Highness about this.'

'I do not think that you will find the Prince overjoyed to be reminded of his presence here,' said Auguste.

'I don't need advice from you, Didier. You aren't out of the wood yet. Far from it. You were the cook of this banquet. And we've got a corpse on our hands as a result. An important corpse. He must have been given the stuff in his food.'

'Or when he left the table on two occasions,' Auguste said firmly, remembering Sir Thomas's absence after the meal, which had been longer surely than it took merely to change his clothes for those of Bill Sikes. Had he felt symptoms then? Or earlier, when he first left the table? Was what they had taken to be a problem of the stomach something more deadly? Were the paleness and emotion on his face as he arrived not fury at Pipkin's performance but symptoms of poison? Or — a thought struck him — was it in the water from which he drank at the reading lectern?

'The doctor tells us that if it's the stuff he thinks it is, it can take a little while to work, especially if Sir Thomas drank coffee. Might have brought some of the stuff up while he was away from the table. Took coffee, did he?'

Auguste nodded. 'Several cups.'

Naseby smiled. A trump had been deftly played.

'Just a minute,' said Rose mildly. 'Let's take things from the beginning. How do you know it's murder not suicide, Naseby?'

'No letter,' replied Naseby scathingly. 'Important man like that wouldn't go without a note.'

He had a point there, agreed Auguste reluctantly, remembering Sir Thomas's character. 'The reading, Eg—, Inspector Rose, this was a high moment of Sir Thomas's evening. Why should he miss it? Why not take poison later instead of during the meal or the reading itself?'

'Could have had a sudden shock,' snorted Naseby, forgetting which side he was on, and unwilling to concede anything to Auguste.

'How would he obtain the poison so quickly?' Auguste asked.

Naseby leapt up from his corner seat in a temper. 'Look here, you. You're here to answer questions, not ask them. You're a suspect, not a detective, and don't you forget it. You don't go committing murders on my territory, no matter what the Yard says.'

Rose remained diplomatically silent. Uncomfortably Auguste was made aware in the gentlest way that he was indeed a suspect at this early stage. He had been the cook.

'Tell us about the banquet,' barked Naseby, aware he had scored a minor victory.

'It began with mutton broth,' said Auguste unhappily.

Egbert Rose's eyebrows rose gently.

'It is not usual in August, this I know,' fiercely, 'but I do not compose this menu. I am told what to do. It is composed of dishes that Charles Dickens liked.'

Naseby nodded knowledgeably. 'And you cooked everything yourself?' he asked comfortably.

'Ah no. There are six pupils at my school. They assist me.'

'You're still a learner, eh?' smirked Naseby.

Auguste shot him an indignant glance. 'I am the owner of a cooking school – through the generosity of the Grand Duke Igor,' he added as a throwaway, pleased at the look of fury on Naseby's face. 'My pupils accompanied me here for a fortnight's holiday during which they would acquire the art of fish cookery.' It occurred to him with a sudden pang that this was now in jeopardy.

'And how did you get into the Imperial, you and your six cooks? Ulterior motive, it seems to me.'

'We had no motive other than to enjoy our holiday,' said Auguste a little pathetically. 'The Prince of Wales discovered that I was to be at Broadstairs at this time; my cooking pleased him,' he added simply, 'and *voilà*, he asked for me to cook this banquet too. How could I say no?' he asked rhetorically, vowing next time he would do just that.

'Seems very fishy to me,' said Naseby.

'No need to make silly jokes, Naseby,' said Rose haughtily. 'This is a serious business. There's been a murder, remember.'

Naseby, who had not been aware of making a joke, glared at Auguste. This was all his fault. 'Where are these people now, Didier?'

'At the house where we are staying, I expect. Blue Horizons on Victoria Parade. I do not know. I have not been there since yesterday morning.' Weariness swept over him.

'Six potential murderers, and you don't know where they are? Is that because you know they aren't murderers, Didier? Because you did it yourself?'

'It is not,' yelped Auguste, wishing Egbert would help.

At last he did. 'It seems to me,' he announced, 'we'd

better see all these pupils together. *After* we've learnt the post-mortem results. You've sealed the kitchen, of course, Naseby? Your men stopped any clearing up, naturally.'

Naseby's face glazed over.

'I did this myself yesterday evening,' said Auguste.

Naseby glowered. 'You went in the kitchen yourself though, I'm sure,' he said viciously.

The kitchens smelled and looked terrible. Even at the best of times, a kitchen after a banquet for over seventy was hardly appetising. This time, without even the zest of being able to assess the success of his recipes from the quantities consumed or left on plates, it seemed to Auguste a sorry place indeed. The scullery was full of dirty pans and half-washed china; the larders littered with cold geese, cutlets and vegetables everywhere; the tables groaning with unappetising-looking dishes of kidneys, tureens of soup and half-eaten tarts.

Rose and Naseby gulped, for once their thoughts in accord. There were a lot of dirty dishes to sort through, one by one. Rose sighed. 'Just give us an idea where to start, Mr Didier, and we'll get a team in,' Naseby nodded fervently. 'I suppose,' continued Rose, looking around hopelessly, 'we can't say that the top table had a different menu. It wouldn't be as easy as that.'

'*Non*, Inspector, everyone had the same — oh, save for the Prince of Wales for whom I made a special soup.'

Naseby positively glowed. 'And who's to say Sir Thomas didn't eat it instead?' impressing even himself by his quickwitted thinking.

Auguste shrugged, 'Perhaps someone saw. I cannot say. You could ask the Prince of Wales — if you think he is a reliable witness,' he added ironically.

Naseby's eyes narrowed as he indicated that this would be an early priority.

'But I do not see why Sir Thomas should eat it. The Prince does not like mutton broth. He does like almond soup. Sir Thomas himself ordered the mutton broth on the menu.'

'So you say.'

'And anyone else will say,' snapped Auguste, losing patience, and earning himself a warning look from Egbert.

'Very well. Show us this broth.' They duly investigated the remains of the huge tureens of soup.

'Next was the lobster,' said Auguste, waves of tiredness sweeping over him. 'Everyone had his own salad prepared in the kitchen.'

'Where are the plates with the remains?'

Auguste took them into the scullery. 'The plates at least for the first four courses are washed as they come out of the dining room.' Rose groaned. 'But l do not see how the lobster could be poisoned. It was all prepared together, the mayonnaise mixed up with it and then the mixtures put in shells and the shells put on plates.'

'So only the person who served the lobster or put it on the plates could have poisoned it?'

Auguste agreed bleakly, but it seemed so unlikely.

'Here are the dishes for the *entremet* courses, some of those for the roast course, those for the cheese, the savouries and the desserts, the glasses and the coffee cups. Only the glasses for the roast and dessert wine, of course. The others would be washed first as a priority. And the brandy glasses are here.' Wearily he pointed out each stack. 'And there,' he said to Naseby, 'in that bin you will find the lobster shells in which each portion of salad was arranged.'

A smile was almost brought to Auguste's face at the thought of Multhrop's reaction as half the Imperial's china vanished into medical detectives' laboratories.

'Next the entrées.' Auguste indicated the large dishes of dark brown stickiness. He had been so proud of that sauce now so stale and unappetising. Truly the creations of one

125

day are the rubbish of the next. 'And the remove, the quails and cutlets.'

'Could anyone tell which quail and cutlet would be served to Sir Thomas?'

'Or the Prince of Wales?' put in Naseby indefatigably.

'Or the Prince of Wales,' repeated Rose. It was after all possible – if they had a madman among them.

'The cutlets yes, certainly, since the Prince rejected them first time round, and asked for them later,' dredging up memories from the depths of his mind. 'But Sir Thomas – I suppose only the person who served them could be sure.'

'And who was that?'

'I really can't recall,' said Auguste. 'Somewhere there is a list.'

'Wouldn't be you, by any chance?' enquired Naseby sourly.

Auguste did not bother to reply. 'The geese,' he said shortly. 'The vegetables,' leading the way into the huge meat larder. '*Voilà*, Inspector Naseby, here you will find the cabbage steamed with cocaine, the potatoes mashed with morphine, the parsnips baked with pilocarpine.'

'Know a lot about poisons, do you, Mr Didier?' put in Naseby suavely.

Auguste flushed red.

'Go home and get some sleep, Mr Didier, that's my advice,' said Rose kindly. It was clearly an order, and Auguste obeyed it.

He walked slowly into Blue Horizons, longing for sleep, knowing that he had first to face six anxious faces. In fact it was only five. Algernon Peckham in a display of bravado had chosen to walk to Kingsgate. His companions sat round the kitchen table, the remains of an inadequate breakfast in front of them. This was the room where only last week they had eagerly discussed the merits of anchovy (protagonist

126

Auguste) versus red wine sauce for fillets of John Dory; whether sole on prawn mousse covered with aspic (Alice's invention) brought out the true flavours of the fish, or smothered them; whether mussels were preferable simply cooked in white wine or whether, as Emily contended, with cream and sorrel sauce added. Her grandmama, it appeared, had a recipe.

'Vot is happening?' demanded Heinrich heavily. They had all returned after the closing of the kitchen.

'I'm afraid that Sir Thomas is dead,' said Auguste sombrely.

'Have a cup of coffee, Mr Didier,' said Alice practically, handing him a cup. He took it gratefully.

'Will that mean they have to talk to us, Mr Didier?' whispered Emily after a pause. Heinrich moved closer to her.

'A formality,' said Auguste reassuringly. 'Naturally the police will wish to make enquiries. We cooked and served the meal that Sir Thomas had recently eaten; it is true he could have taken the poison afterwards, however, or when he was away from the table during the *entremets*. He suffered from a weak stomach. Perhaps he took too much medicine.'

Their faces began to brighten, but in spite of his words Auguste could not share their optimism. Stomach medicines would not contain sufficient belladonna, if belladonna it was.

'Anyone could have dropped poison into his food,' objected James stolidly. 'It's not fair we should be blamed. It could have been anyone passing by the serving table, or in the kitchens, or sitting near Sir Thomas—'

'The Prince of Wales, perhaps?' suggested Auguste drily.

'You don't think the poison was intended for him, do you, Mr Didier?' asked Alice, with horrorstricken face.

'I do not know, I do not know, *mes enfants*.' Auguste covered his face with his hands. There was immediate and

127

respectful silence. The maître *did not know*. This had never happened before. Alfred broke it.

'Suicide, I expect.'

'Bills,' mumbled Heinrich to general puzzlement. 'He could have been taking bills.'

'He had a weak stomach,' pointed out Emily in support of this theory.

Auguste uncovered his face. 'We must continue our holiday − ' the word struck a curious note − 'as best we can. I am glad to say my friend Inspector Rose of the Yard will investigate. This means it will be done quickly − and there will be no mistakes,' he said reassuringly. 'After all,' he concluded, rising to his feet, 'why on earth should any of you choose to murder Sir Thomas? No, it is a formality only.' He half-stumbled out of the room up to his bed and blessed, blessed sleep, where his dreams were a mixture of lobsters with evil intent towards the Prince of Wales, of Charles Dickens teaching him how to catch a pungar, and of Araminta, receding further and further into a boiling sea of mutton broth.

In the kitchen, without his restraining presence, discussion broke out animatedly. Only Alfred did not join in. He was uncomfortably aware that Auguste was wrong. One at least of their number had every reason to wish Sir Thomas dead.

Huddled in one corner of the first-floor sun lounge, the remains of the committee of Literary Lionisers were holding an emergency meeting before facing their sundry charges. Three couples had already been seen leaving the hotel with baggage. News of Sir Thomas's death had hit them hard in different ways.

Samuel Pipkin tried to keep excitement from his voice; in truth he was as shocked as any of them at the reality of what in his mind he had longed for. That Throgmorton had died by poison was hard enough for them to take in, when

all had assumed sudden acute stomach illness. Accident –
the mushrooms, the lobster. Food poisoning. Only later did
Oliver Michaels come back with the sobering news that the
hotel was strangely full of policemen, that there was no
breakfast to be had save for coffee and muffins, without
a trek to the Albion Hotel, and moreover there was thought
to be something odd about Sir Thomas's death which no
one would specify.

'Suicide!' had been their doubtful diagnosis.

Gwendolen was clad in her dark blue serge travelling dress,
this being the nearest to mourning she could manage. A
sleepless night had convinced her that in the event of
Thomas's death her role was forlorn fiancée.

'Nonsense,' she cried. 'Suicide? Out of the question.
Why? When we were happily betrothed?'

Her listeners agreed, suicide was unlikely given Sir
Thomas's character, but there agreement stopped.

'Happy!' snarled Samuel. 'Forgive me, dear lady, but that
did not appear to be the case last night.'

'Fiancée?' Oliver blurted out. 'But Angelina was engaged
to him.'

Angelina turned a cold eye on him.

'We were affianced, Mr Michaels. I feel I should know
my own situation best,' said Gwendolen tartly. 'Dear
Thomas and I were on the point of announcing our
engagement. And have you never heard of lovers' tiffs, Mr
Pipkin?' Grandly. 'Ah, do you think,' her face blanched,
'that he poisoned himself because of our quarrel? Over *me*?'
The word ended in a wail, and Angelina ran to her to try
to forestall a further attack of hysteria.

'Thomas, Thomas,' Gwendolen moaned quietly to herself,
and made no further bid for the limelight.

'What we have to do,' said Samuel, taking advantage of
her exit from the ring, 'and I take it no one objects if I now
chair this committee,' he added off-handedly, 'is to decide

129

whether the Week of the Lion should continue or be cancelled.'

'I fear we have to make a quick decision,' said Oliver ironically, looking out of the window and seeing a departing victoria. News had travelled fast.

'We have no choice ourselves,' Angelina pointed out. 'We have to stay. I have no doubt the police will need to ask us questions.'

Samuel paled slightly. 'But surely — how could we be thought responsible, if the food or wine were poisoned?'

'Quite easily,' said Oliver blithely. 'It would have been possible for one of us to have poisoned his food, perhaps. He was hardly a popular man with any of us.'

'He was with me,' moaned Gwendolen.

'With you, of course,' he agreed gently. 'Forgive me.' But everyone was uncomfortably aware of last night's scene. 'It seems to me more likely he may have taken too much medicine when he left the table yesterday,' he continued slowly.

'Yes, yes, his weak stomach,' said Gwendolen eagerly.

'But we can't be sure it wasn't murder — yet. If it's confirmed, our Lionisers will begin disappearing very rapidly.'

There was a gasp at this public utterance of the forbidden word.

Lord Beddington was somewhat disgruntled. He had offered his services to this Scotland Yard fellow in his role as a magistrate, only to have them refused. 'Damn cheek,' he told his colleagues. It was a sign of their anxiety that no one noticed this strong language despite the presence of ladies. 'Anyway, he wants everyone to stay. All seventy of them.'

'In that case,' said Oliver, 'we've no choice. We'll have to carry on with the Week of the Lion tour if only to give these good people something to do. *And* ourselves,' he added.

Samuel glared at him. He was going to have this young Snodgrass off his committee in double quick time. 'This was precisely the point I was going to make, Michaels. I put it to the committee.' He looked round, somewhat disappointed his first resolution met no opposition.

'This afternoon we were – are – due for a walk to Ramsgate.' Everyone looked outside to the still overcast sky. 'We shall decide after luncheon,' Samuel announced firmly.

Walking down the Promenade to the Albion Hotel for luncheon, with Samuel striding ahead like Stonewall Jackson, and Gwendolen having found an apparent soul mate in Lord Beddington, Oliver found himself forced to walk next to Angelina.

'So Sir Thomas had two fiancées,' he said politely. 'Please accept my sincere condolences.'

She glared at him. 'Oh, Oliver,' she said, pushing her parasol open vigorously, 'don't be so foolish. You can't really believe I was engaged to Sir Thomas, can you?'

He displayed complete surprise. 'Why not? He told me you were. Mrs Figgis-Hewett told me yesterday you were. I saw you leaning together very intimately yesterday afternoon; he was kissing your hand.'

'Having one's hand kissed does not, so far as I know, oblige one to marry a man,' she answered shortly.

'Then why didn't you disillusion me?' he demanded angrily. 'It was cruel of you.'

She stopped abruptly by the gate to the Albion's gardens, whirled on him, snapping her parasol shut again: 'Because I was annoyed with you that you could even think such a thing. And why should I assume you'd be interested anyway?'

'You know—' He broke off. Did she know? Of course she did. She was avoiding the issue. 'Then why were you deliberately setting your cap at Sir Thomas all the while? I watched you, Angelina.'

131

'I had my reasons,' she said, after a pause.

'Is that all you're going to say?' he demanded.

'Yes.' She put her nose high in the air and stalked up the garden. He followed her, troubled.

Marginally refreshed, Auguste made his way back to the Imperial Hotel late that afternoon. In the Victoria Gardens, the Oxfordshire and Buckinghamshire Light Infantry band were regaling their audience with tunes from *The Shop Girl*, promenaders were risking the doubtful weather and adorning the seafront in their Sunday afternoon best. Tomorrow was Bank Holiday Monday, the highlight of the holiday for all but the most upper and select of classes, and this weekend was a kind of holiday rehearsal for it, albeit muted in respect for the Sabbath.

Auguste was thankful when he turned into the doorway of the hotel, the sight of other temptations removed from him. There were few guests to be seen. The reason for that, he was to discover, was that Mr Multhrop had made speedy arrangements with the Albion and Grand Hotels to serve luncheon, his own kitchens being *hors de combat*.

Araminta, a vision in grey, came forward somewhat reluctantly to greet Auguste. 'Papa says you may be a murderer,' was her ingenuous opening gambit.

Auguste suppressed a moment's irritation with his beloved, but not his uncharitable thoughts towards Mr Multhrop.

'No, *chérie*,' he explained kindly, 'I am not a murderer. It is merely that they wish to question me, for I had responsibility for the food last night. It is possible but by no means certain,' he added firmly, 'that the poison was taken by Sir Thomas during the meal.'

'Like the Borgias,' breathed Araminta, in a rare display of erudition.

'Precisely,' said Auguste, trying to see Gwendolen Figgis-Hewett in the role of Lucrezia Borgia.

132

'All the same,' said Araminta thoughtfully, 'Papa says I'm not to see you again till it's over, and you're either arrested or cleared. I would have liked to,' she added wistfully. 'Oh, Auguste, you *will* get cleared, won't you?' Her lovely eyes brimmed over until he almost forgave the disloyalty.

Mr Multhrop rushed into the foyer like the White Rabbit, saw them and tried to edge away, but Auguste caught him.

'Mr Dee, you know how it is,' he said, smiling appealingly.'

'*Non*, Mr Multhrop, I do not know how it is. I have asked my friend from Scotland Yard to help. Now would I do that if I were guilty? He is in charge.'

Multhrop thought for a moment. 'No,' he said doubtfully, then brightened. 'They've had a lot of cases of bribery at Scotland Yard, haven't they?'

Auguste looked him in the eye. 'I will inform Inspector Rose that you fear he and his department are as corrupt as that of Chief Inspectors Clarke, Druscovich and Palmer.'

Mr Multhrop's eyes bulged. 'Please don't bother,' he said nervously, envisaging himself carried off for criminal libel. Or was it slander? 'I'm sure any friend of yours . . .' His voice trailed off unhappily.

'*Bon*. Then Araminta may accompany me to the sands.'

'I suppose so,' clearly weighing up the chances of Auguste's swimming underwater to the women's bathing machine section and drowning his beloved daughter. But there, one had to take some chances in life.

'Come for your turn on the gridiron, Auguste?' Rose, complete with baggage and Edith, had returned to take up new quarters in the Imperial Hotel.

'Inspector Egbert Rose and Mrs Rose, Mr Multhrop,' said Auguste feebly. 'Multhrop is the Imperial's owner, Inspector. And this is Miss Multhrop, Edith, Egbert.'

Araminta was clearly impressed.

Edith looked around her. It wasn't as cosy as Mrs Burbanks' guest house or even as Highbury. But it was certainly very nice. Quite grand in fact. It might not be Ramsgate, but Broadstairs might prove to be quite enjoyable after all. She would have something to tell the Highbury Ladies' Circle at any rate.

Chapter Seven

Egbert Rose woke up to grey skies over Broadstairs, cheered up as he realised he was on holiday, and then remembered that he was not. With a regretful look at Edith still slumbering at his side in the huge mahogany bed, he swung his feet down to face the day.

One hour later, after a breakfast that reminded him of his French experience in its meagreness, and made worse by the perpetual drone of Mr Multhrop's stream of nervous apologies to each new arrival, he was ready to greet Auguste and his flock.

Yesterday afternoon he and Naseby, with Auguste hovering in the background, had crawled over Sir Thomas's suite of rooms and interrogated every single member of the Imperial's staff on duty the previous evening. A terrified housemaid, eyed sternly by Mr Multhrop, admitted to seeing Sir Thomas in his room during the course of the evening.

' 'E came in when I was turning down 'is bed,' she volunteered, curtsying to Rose in fright, somewhat muddled between his ranking and that of the Prince of Wales. 'About half past eight it was,' she added, impressed by her own powers of recollection. ' 'E went into the bathroom, and I went. Then I saw 'e'd gone, so I comes back to finish orf. And then 'e comes in again. Says 'e 'as to change his clothes. Back in the bathroom, so I turns down the bed, and goes.' She wasn't going to leave this time, however; having got over her initial fright, curiosity made her follow the detectives into the large bathroom, with clawfoot bath standing proudly mid-floor and a matching rose and violet embossed pedestal water closet.

'Fond of his medicine, wasn't he?' commented Rose as he opened the cabinet in the bathroom where a row of bottles and jars indicated Sir Thomas's concern for his health. 'Wasn't leaving anything to chance. Homoeopathic, patent, the lot. Ipecacuanha, tincture of hellebore viridis, Nux vomica, Dr J. Johnson's Pills, Blair's Gout Pills, Dr Grinrod's Remedy for Spasms, Cockles' Anti-bilious pills − oh, and Mexican Hair Renewer − Dixon's Rhubarb and Tartar Emetic, and Ward's Red Pills. Made of antimony and dragon's blood, they say.' He grunted. 'Dragon's blood,' he repeated disgustedly.

' 'E was making funny noises,' the maid offered importantly, and, pleased at the instant attention this won her, added, 'Like when me ma's 'aving another.' Naseby and Rose inspected the sanitary ware closely, but if Sir Thomas had indeed been sick, then there were no traces left.

'You're sure of this, girl?' barked Naseby. 'Sure that's what the noise was? A retch.'

The housemaid clearly took this as a side comment to Rose on her character. 'I'm an 'onest girl, sir,' she pointed out, affronted. 'This is what I 'eard. Listen.'

The sounds that followed from her would have qualified her to audition for Mr Dickens's Infant Phenomenon.

'All right, that's enough,' said Rose hastily. 'But that noise needn't have been a retch − could have been all sorts of things.' He cast a scathing eye at the rows of bottles. 'He did suffer from gastritis, we know that.'

Naseby had positively glowed with satisfaction at the revelations of this budding Sarah Bernhardt. 'Seems to put it squarely on the meal to me, Rose. Too much of a coincidence for Sir Thomas to feel ill and then to be poisoned

136

after that. Doesn't look too good for our mutual friend, does it?' He was almost jovial.

'Didn't know you were a Dickens enthusiast, Naseby.'

Naseby looked blank and then dismissed this as more evidence of London eccentricity.

Fortunately this morning Rose had contrived to rid himself of Naseby's services. He wanted to be able to draw his own conclusions, without Naseby's helpful commentary.

The once proud members of the Auguste Didier School of Cuisine looked a doleful group as they followed Auguste. Bringing up the rear was Sid, but even he was subdued this morning. Their attire was a mixture of the sombre and seaside wear. Gone were the frivolous hats and bright blazers. Seaside wear seemed inappropriate, yet they could not see that they had reason to mourn the passing of Sir Thomas Throgmorton. A certain resentment was becoming evident among them, which the sight of the desolate kitchen enhanced. On Saturday night, they had worked hard on their holiday for the sake of the Prince of Wales, and this was all the thanks they got. Here they were, objects of suspicion to be interrogated by the police, and not even noticed by the one or two newspaper men who had arrived at the hotel.

The death of Sir Thomas Throgmorton after a sudden illness was worth a paragraph in view of his role of international banker. The coincidental presence of the Prince of Wales in Broadstairs for a brief private visit to a friend on the same evening converted it into a two-paragraph story. Three newspaper men with nothing else to report, since the Transvaal crisis was deemed beyond their capability, were despatched to Broadstairs to try to rootle out any facts that might justify a further paragraph. Apart from the fact that the breakfast was bad and the service worse and that one or two police constables appeared to be taking their holidays in the hotel, they had picked up nothing of interest.

Rose firmly closed the door as he heard Mr Multhrop's

anxious voice coming distinctly nearer to the now unlocked kitchens. He had clearly discovered the fact that the dining room too was locked against him. The empty dishes, china, and uneaten food had been taken away for examination, so the sight and smell were somewhat more palatable than they had been the day before.

Auguste braced himself to sound casual: '*Alors, mes amis*, Inspector Rose wishes us to perform a play for him. We will show him course by course just what happened on Saturday evening – as far as we were concerned. Dish by dish, course by course, you will each re-enact your roles.'

'But there aren't any dishes,' pointed out Emily matter-of-factly.

'In pantomime, Miss Dawson,' Auguste explained gently. 'And then, *voilà*, Inspector Rose will get to the bottom of the mystery and we can enjoy our holiday.'

Even Auguste felt his voice lacked conviction, and his pupils to judge from their faces were similarly unconvinced. Scotland Yard meant serious trouble, and though this thin-faced lugubrious-looking man might seem mild at first, there was a quiet, controlled purposefulness about him that made holidays seem a long way away.

Rose glanced at the menu with which Auguste had supplied him. 'We'll start with the soup,' he said encouragingly. 'Mrs Dickens's mutton broth. Who prepared that?'

Algernon cleared his throat and spoke a little more shrilly than he had intended. 'Me. But everyone had soup,' he added defensively. 'There can't have been anything added to it.'

'The Prince of Wales didn't have the broth,' said James zealously, a believer in accuracy.

'Does that make him the murderer?' whispered Alice in an aside to Alfred.

Auguste, overhearing, frowned at this frivolity. Murder,

138

as he had reason to know all too well, was a serious business.

'Who served it?' repeated Rose, and as no one spoke, picked on the most nervous-looking individual. 'Lord Wittisham?'

'I was outside serving drinks. Isn't that right, Mr Didier?' he almost bleated. He was aware that everyone was looking at him, and it was clear what they were thinking. He was the only person to serve drinks. He and no one else could have adulterated the wine. 'I couldn't . . . It would have been seen.'

'Not in the red wine,' Algernon pointed out, as if conscientiously.

'So who served the soup?' repeated Rose patiently.

'Me,' said Heinrich grudgingly.

'And me,' volunteered James. 'Heinrich and I were with each other all the time. We'd have seen if one of us had tipped something into the soup.'

'Show me,' said Rose, shortly.

Self-consciously they took the tureens from the kitchens into the dining room, placed them on the trolley, and took it round an empty table. It was evident that without three hands James Pegg could not have infiltrated poison into the soup bowl.

'The people next to Sir Thomas could have added something,' suggested Alice helpfully.

Rose glanced at the table plan: 'Lord Beddington, miss, or the Prince of Wales?'

'Oh.' Alice subsided.

Rose stared at the table, imagining it full of people, talking – but surely not blind. 'Think it possible for anyone to add poison to a dish intended for Sir Thomas, Mr Didier?'

'Only Lord Beddington,' said Auguste. 'Mrs Langham would have to reach across the table, surely impossible. Unless there was some incident that diverted and concentrated the general attention, but I noticed nothing.

139

Did you?' He looked round the group, but there was no sign of any reaction.

'Very well. Clear away for the next course,' said Rose. He hadn't expected anything definite to emerge, but it was useful background. Emily Dawson cleared imaginary soup bowls.

'I prepared the lobster salad,' said Alice bravely. 'I put all the ingredients together and put them on individual plates, but lots of people helped get the lobster out of their shells, and Alfred made the mayonnaise. Sid helped me carry them to that table ready for serving. Miss Dawson did the garnish,' she explained in a rush.

'She did it twice,' pointed out Algernon officiously. 'It fell on the floor, if you remember, Emily. You did a fresh lot at the last moment.'

Emily went pink, reflecting that if she'd had charge of this youth in his formative years, things might have been different. 'What if I did?' she cried, near to tears. 'How do you poison cucumber ribbons and why should I anyway?' No one answered.

'Very well, serve the salads.'

Heinrich and Algernon once more moved imaginary plates from an empty table, staggered under their load into the dining room and served another empty table.

'Perhaps Sir Thomas ate a bad lobster,' offered Sid brightly. 'I remember my gran ate a bad winkle once.'

'It was all mixed up,' said Algernon who seemed to be appointing himself *ad hoc* detective.

Rose tried to suppress the memory of all those smelly shells now being analysed. 'Which of you gave Sir Thomas his salad?' he enquired casually.

Algernon and Heinrich glanced at each other. 'He did,' said Algernon, just as Heinrich came in with 'Herr Peckham.' Rose made no comment.

'I cleared the dishes,' Emily said shrilly, defensive of

140

Heinrich. 'I'm sure he ate it all. He wouldn't if he didn't like it.'

'You cleared the dishes of every course?'

'Yes, she did,' said Alice, 'and I laid them. Except the lobster of course.'

'The tureens, now,' said Auguste.

'More soup?'

'No, the entrée.'

Rose began to feel he was back in the maze at Stockbery, but doggedly continued making notes. He'd work this jigsaw puzzle out later. 'Kidneys,' he said, consulting the menu. 'Mrs Crupp's.'

'They were my concern, Inspector,' said Auguste proudly. 'Not Mrs Crupp's kidneys, but kidneys *à la Didier*. The ingredients were gathered together for me by Lord Wittisham, the kidneys themselves prepared by Mr Pegg, and I attended to the final cooking and preparation of the sauce.' There was a certain defiance in his tone. How could his beautiful champagne-based sauce be indicted for murder? He went to the hob, and mixed vigorously. Behind him stood Sid, holding an imaginary tureen. 'Herr Freimüller served it,' said Auguste.

'No, I not do that. Mr Pegg do it,' Heinrich said hurriedly.

'Why was that?' Rose looked at Pegg blandly.

'I suppose Heinrich was too busy,' said James uneasily. Then seeing this was inadequate, continued, 'He was ready to take the removes from the ovens, so I took the kidneys in. I put two dishes on His Royal Highness's table and Sid took the rest through to the other kitchen.'

'Yes. I takes the lot in there for the lower orders,' said Sid. 'Hallow me, Inspector to present yer with me movements on the evening in question.' He ran vigorously to and fro between the two kitchens.

'It was all cooked together, Inspector, but that for the high table was placed there,' Auguste explained, pointing

141

to a corner table, 'and the rest was carried into the other kitchen, which is usually used for the preparation of food and storage. There it was collected and served by the Imperial's own staff to the rest of the guests.'

'Could any of them have come into this kitchen?' asked Rose.

'No, Inspector,' Auguste replied. 'We would most certainly have noticed. I had forbidden it,' he added unhappily.

'So, Mr Pegg, you placed these kidneys on the table, and they served themselves, right? In two tureens. Who dished them out? Did you notice?'

There was a speedy consultation. Alfred, in the best position to see, thought it was the Prince of Wales. Auguste considered this unlikely. His own impression was that Sir Thomas had served his end of the table. Algernon voted for Lord Beddington. Rose sighed. So much for witnesses.

'I go to fetch with Herr Peckham the quail and cutlets,' Heinrich declared grandly, if dolefully. He could see fingers of suspicion approaching nearer every minute. If only the Kaiser had not beaten *Britannia* at Cowes. Sometimes, disloyally, he wondered if the Kaiser were not a little too enthusiastic about the honour of Germany.

'They were my idea, Inspector, in case, as proved to be so, the Prince did not like goose. And Dickens does mention both, I am told,' Auguste added anxiously in case Rose too should look down upon this departure from the true Dickensian menu.

'I see. Tell me how you served these removes, Mr Freimüller.'

'I take quails, Peckham take cutlets. I go to the Prince of Vales first. He refuse it. Then to Mrs Langham and to Mrs Figgis-Hewett. They refused them too. Then Sir Thomas. I do not remember if Sir Thomas had quail,' he said unhappily. 'Always I ask myself this, but I cannot answer myself.'

'The poison isn't too likely to have been in a quail,' Rose said soothingly. 'Easier to put in a sauce or gravy.' Auguste stiffened.

'Anyway,' said Emily stoutly in mistaken loyalty, 'only Heinrich could be certain that Sir Thomas would receive the poisoned quail.'

Heinrich looked at her doubtfully. 'I do not poison quail,' he said definitely.

For the first time Auguste began to feel a tinge of fear with this relentless questioning. He had been so certain that his food could not be tampered with. Had he been wrong?

'Goose,' announced Rose. 'It says here Bob Cratchit's goose.'

Auguste paled. Goose had haunted his dreams for ten days. It would be the last straw if the bird had been poisoned. Memories of the Prince of Wales's detective emerging from the oven came back and he wondered wildly whether some abstruse method of murder had been performed before his very eyes. True, it seemed a curious way of implanting poison but— He pulled himself back to sanity. 'The goose for the high table was taken into the dining room for carving, together with the vegetables,' he explained.

'We all helped serve the goose,' said James, 'except Alfred.' Heinrich admitted to carrying in the bird, Auguste to carving, James and Algernon to transporting the results, Alice and Emily to transporting vegetables, sauces, forcemeats and gravy.

'Just a minute,' Rose interposed sharply. 'These sauces. Were they served or put on the table?'

'On the table for guests to help themselves, so it wouldn't be possible to make sure that Sir Thomas's portion was poisoned, would it? Not by us, anyway.' Emily almost clapped.

'Who served Sir Thomas's goose?' He'd nearly said cooked.

143

There was a silence. James and Algernon glanced at each other. Nothing was said. Auguste came to the rescue. 'Inspector, this is the problem. Anything tampered with in the kitchen could not be guaranteed to reach Sir Thomas unless the poisoner served it himself. And then it would have to be an individual dish — the lobster, the remove or the coffee or wine.' He went doggedly on, ignoring feeble expostulations from Alfred and Heinrich. 'Or else the server would have to add poison at the last moment — surely very risky. Otherwise it was added at the table — or to the glass of water he drank at the lectern. Or something he took in his room.' His trump cards.

'When we get the report from the laboratory, we'll know a bit more,' Rose said noncommittally.

'I didn't serve him,' said James suddenly, since this, to his mind, put him out of the running for the culprit. Algernon and Heinrich stared at him.

'It wasn't me,' said Algernon simply. 'I served the old gentleman next to him.'

'The Prince of Wales?' asked Rose.

Heinrich was as horrified as if the Kaiser himself had been insulted. Algernon merely grinned. 'Other side.'

'Lord Beddington.'

'No, *I* served him,' said James quickly. They glared at each other, neither budged their position. Rose quietly made a note.

Inexorably Rose moved on through the *entremets* and coffee, sending eight people scurrying in all directions as he masterminded the performance, the objects of which were far from clear to Auguste.

'And the drinks, Lord Wittisham,' concluded Rose. 'You served all Sir Thomas's wine? And the drinks beforehand?'

'I watched him much of the time, Inspector,' said Auguste, an anxious sheepdog watching Alfred's eyes glaze over.

'I'm sure, Mr Didier. Just covering all possibilities.'

'No one would poison wine,' stated Alfred categorically, presumably on the basis that this would be an ungentlemanly act. Food was a different matter.

'It wasn't the wine, it was the salmon, eh?' said Rose.

'Lobster, Inspector Rose,' said Alice helpfully.

'Beg your pardon, miss. Just a quotation from Mr Pickwick.' It was one of Mrs Rose's favourite books. 'Any of you met Sir Thomas before?' he continued smoothly.

'He was at the dinner we cooked for them and the Prince at Gwynne's,' said Emily. Alfred was suddenly extremely grateful that none of his colleagues knew of Beatrice Throgmorton's place in his life. But problems were about to arise.

'Ah yes, so he was,' said Rose easily. He had an idea at least some of the party were keeping something back. 'Miss Throgmorton will be here at lunchtime. She'll want to meet you, I'm sure.' Quite why Sir Thomas's daughter should be keen to make the acquaintance of some kitchen staff he did not explain. It was enough to get a reaction though.

Seven subdued people left the Imperial Hotel to walk back to Blue Horizons. Preoccupied, they failed to notice that something had changed about Broadstairs. The weather might be dull, it might be drizzling, but Broadstairs promenade had changed almost beyond recognition. Where selectness and restraint had reigned, boisterousness and laughter had taken their place. Fashionable rose-pinks and muted blue dresses had given way to garish reds, bright yellows topped with sailor hats or boaters with matching ribbons. The sands were crowded with these strange bright parrots, accompanied by young gentlemen with unorthodox headgear and unbuttoned waistcoats. Itinerant vendors buzzed everywhere, ignoring all Pier and Harbour Commission rules. More parrots were lined up along the shore, skirts hitched to their knees, paddling and screaming in the chilly water. Brakeloads and omnibuses were arriving on Victoria Parade full of fresh supplies, and swarming down the High Street towards their mecca was the first cheap, fast trainload of 'Arrys and 'Arriets in search of entertainment.

The downcast Didier School of Cuisine personnel stared in disbelief. They had completely forgotten it was Bank Holiday Monday. All the more dispirited as they entered Blue Horizons, they discovered that somehow Joe's dabs, bought with enthusiasm this morning to prepare for luncheon, failed to seem so attractive. Each one of their prospective cooks was preoccupied.

Heinrich was thinking over all the implications of the last hour, and what he would do if he were correct. He was concerned he would be locked in an English jail, and wondered if he should seek Embassy asylum. It would be most unfair if he should suffer for the Kaiser's unpopularity. In any case, the Kaiser was a most charming man, much misunderstood. Emily was just scared. Alice walked hand in hand with Alfred, though it was obvious his thoughts were not with her. Where were they? Panic began to seize her. What could he be worrying about? Alfred's thoughts were fixed in fact on Beatrice Throgmorton, and the unpleasant scene that had taken place three weeks ago. Algernon was trying to judge what danger, if any, he was in. James was trying slowly to work something out in his mind. And nearly all of them were conscious that they had not told Inspector Rose the whole truth.

Mr Multhrop at least was happy. His kitchens and dining room were open once more and he was bustling about, as jolly as Mr Fezziwig, envisaging happy hordes of merry luncheon-takers. Not, he trusted, Harrys and Harriets, as the popular press termed them. Rose steered Auguste firmly clear, and into the office. So happy was Mr

Multhrop that he failed to resent the purloining of his room.

'*Now*,' Rose said, once they were settled. 'Tell me about them, Auguste. Who's the German?'

'Heinrich Freimüller, from the German Embassy,' began Auguste awkwardly, feeling torn between two loyalties. 'The Embassy wishes to raise the standard of its present cuisine.' His expression suggested this would not take much doing. 'He is a good chef. His pastry has the makings of a *vrai maître*. It is true that his mastery of patisserie—'

'Not food, Auguste. Tell me about *him*,' said Rose patiently.

'My friend, I *do* tell you about him. As the chef is, so is the man.'

A grin passed on Rose's face. 'Have it your own way. Political chap, is he?'

'No,' said Auguste doubtfully. 'I have never heard him speak of politics.' Suddenly he wondered why. 'Yet he is most loyal to his country, as Mr Pegg is to his. James Pegg is the solid Englishman. He wishes to advance his cooking career. He is sound, very sound, but in my opinion lacks the extra something that can create a maître chef. With meat, however, he has a great affinity. His father is a veterinary surgeon, and he himself assisted his father for a year or two and then became a groom. Now he wishes to be a chef.'

'Cures them, coaxes them and cooks them, eh?' said Rose. 'Curious mixture, ain't it?'

'He is a practical man. There are animals to be saved. He does it. There are those to be cooked. He does that too. In one respect is he noteworthy. In his devotion to Lord Wittisham.'

'One of *them*, is he?'

'I do not think so. Indeed,' remembering Araminta bitterly, 'I am sure. He sees himself as a protector. He is proud of their friendship.'

147

'And what about Wittisham? Can't get used to the idea of a lord hard at work, getting his hands dirty.'

Auguste smiled. 'Ah, Lord Wittisham too is a simple man, as is Pegg. But he works differently in cuisine. When he creates a dish he begins and carries on until instinctively he knows the dish has reached perfection. Nothing is left undone, nothing left to chance. There are not many dishes he creates so, but those he does create are truly magnificent. In the rest he is merely mundane. And as for his private life, I do not think it is James Pegg he desires. I think he is beloved by Alice Fenwick, but does not see her devotion. One day he will, and proceed to create from her the perfect dish of a wife and peeress.'

'And this Alice?'

'Alice Fenwick. She too wishes a career, like Rosa Lewis, like Emma Pryde. She is the daughter of an officer in the army, but I think now alone in the world and with little money. She is determined to succeed, and she is thorough. Nothing will be omitted, where Alice is concerned.' He smiled. 'She spreads a warmth and comfort in her cookery and spreads this warm cocoon around her, drawing you in. It is the desire of her life that Lord Wittisham realises her love. She would make him a good wife,' he added wistfully, looking into his own bleak future.

'And the other lady?'

'Emily Dawson. Ah, Miss Dawson is interesting. A governess who decided to make a change. She had a windfall of money and decided to have a new career. She is a deft cook with many interesting touches to her work. Her desserts, her confectionery, her sauces are magical, though the rest of her work remains only average. But yes, she has something or I would not have taken her. I am training her so that she can cook for royalty,' Auguste declared grandly.

'And the young cock of the walk?'

Auguste smiled. 'Our Mr Peckham? Mr Algernon

Peckham I find difficult, since he is, unfortunately, an admirer of Soyer.' Tones of disgust. 'I cannot claim I *know* Mr Peckham. Yet of all of them I think that he is the nearest to possessing genius. He wishes to be a chef to travel the great country houses of Europe.'

'Nothing if not ambitious.'

'Very. His father was a butcher, I discovered.'

'Another affinity to meat, eh?'

'*Non.* Or at least Mr Peckham pretends to have none. Give him game, fish, vegetables, *entremets*, patisserie, and he is superb. Give him meat and the results are a *vin ordinaire.*'

Rose nodded. 'And Sid?'

'I do not see what Sid could have to do with this affair,' said Auguste, illogically shocked. 'He was helping in the kitchen all the time fetching and carrying. He is – well he is Sid.' He shrugged helplessly.

'I see,' said Rose, who did. Eleven years on the Ratcliff Highway beat had taught him about Sids. And on the whole they didn't go around poisoning roast geese. 'But he was in the kitchen.'

'Not in the dining room, though. Sid came to me,' admitted Auguste, as though honour-bound to disclose all relevant information, 'on the recommendation of Mr Higgins.'

'Did he now,' said Rose, highly amused at this resurgence into their affairs of the biggest fence in London. 'Well, if Mr Multhrop's teaspoons or Mrs Figgis-Hewett's jewellery vanishes, we'll know where to look.'

'Sid is not like that,' said Auguste indignantly.

'Interested in cuisine, is he?'

'No but—'

'Why does he work for you then?'

'He – I suppose he likes me,' said Auguste inadequately.

Rose looked at him kindly. 'We'll never make a policeman out of you, Auguste.'

'Sir Thomas was not a popular man, Inspector,' declared Oliver, not looking at Angelina. The five committee members of the Literary Lionisers were subdued; they had talked about the horrors of Saturday night incessantly the day before. Now, in the face of formal interrogation, they were restrained and cautious. All but one.

'He was, he was. I loved him,' moaned Gwendolen defiantly. Then Auguste's presence in the small lounge caught her attention. 'What's this fellow doing here?' she shouted, puffing out her hastily improvised dark veil which rose and fell with each indignant gasp. 'He's a waiter.'

'Mr Didier is here at my request, madam. He was overseeing the banquet and had Sir Thomas under his surveillance nearly all the time. It is possible he may have observed something you were not in a position to see,' Rose explained diplomatically.

'It's also possible he poisoned poor old Thomas,' rumbled Lord Beddington. 'Don't forget that.'

Auguste went pink. 'Sir, I did not know him.'

'Dammit, I remember you at Gwynne's,' said Samuel Pipkin indignantly. 'Of course you did.'

'That is true, sir. It is also true that I disagreed with his choice of menu, but that is hardly cause for murder.' This man was not to know that it very nearly was, by Auguste's reckoning.

'You might have been paid to assassinate him,' went on Samuel objectively. 'He was an international banker. Lots of people might have wanted to kill him.' He skirted over the small matter that he was one of them.

'I think you can take it from me,' said Rose firmly, 'that Mr Didier did not murder Sir Thomas,' earning himself a look of gratitude from Auguste. 'Now, Mrs Figgis-Hewett, I gather that you had a disagreement with Sir Thomas. You were threatening to bring a breach of promise action, or so you announced on Saturday evening.'

'A misunderstanding on my part,' she cried wildly, glaring at Auguste. 'Sir Thomas would have apologised. We had been affianced for some weeks.'

'He proposed to me that afternoon,' put in Angelina apologetically. 'Forgive me, Gwendolen, but if this is a murder case—'

'Murder,' shrieked the lady, overlooking the relevance of Angelina's provoking statement. 'No, no. Sudden illness. Accident.'

'Spontaneous combustion you'll suggest next,' snorted Samuel. 'Like Mr Krook, eh!'

Gwendolen started to scream at this hard-heartedness, but suddenly stopped again as Auguste rose to come to her aid. She remembered Saturday's ministrations all too clearly.

'I make no secret,' said Samuel suddenly, who had obviously been considering doing just that, 'that I disliked the fellow. But if we all murdered for little things like that . . . ' He forced a laugh.

'What were these little things, sir?' Rose enquired politely.

'A slight disagreement over club rules,' said Samuel airily. 'Sir Thomas was rather, ah, dogmatic. He was claiming that next year his chairmanship would last a day longer than set down in the rules. Quite ridiculous of course. Everyone agreed with me.'

'I didn't,' pointed out Lord Beddington. 'Seemed to me old Throgmorton had a point. Rules are rules. As a magistrate I see it as my duty to enforce them.'

'A day doesn't seem to matter much,' observed Rose.

'It would have meant, Inspector,' explained Angelina, 'that Sir Thomas would still be chairman when the next Year of the Lion began. Next year our Lion is William Shakespeare and as the 23rd April, the day in question, is his birthday, important celebrations will be held, as 1900 is such a special year. Sir Thomas, who set great store on his cultural activities,' trying to keep the sarcasm from her voice, 'considered he would be the best chairman for such an important event.'

'You agreed with him, madam.'

'Not over his interpretation of the rules, no,' said Angelina.

Samuel, picking up an unintentional slight that she considered Throgmorton a better chairman, bristled.

'There was a vote,' explained Oliver. Samuel stopped bristling and shifted uneasily. 'We were divided. The Prince of Wales was to give his casting vote later on that evening.'

'And Sir Thomas expected to gain it?'

'Yes,' said Angelina. 'It seemed probable,' not looking at Samuel.

'And who would be the next year's chairman otherwise?' asked Rose, guessing the answer.

'Me,' announced Samuel, less happily than he might otherwise have done.

Rose reflected, and changed the subject. 'Now if you'd tell me what happened at the dinner.'

'Slight discussion took place, Inspector,' Oliver said, taking the bull by its humiliating horns, 'on the matter of the Prince of Wales's casting vote.'

'But you still expected Sir Thomas to win? He would have no reason for suicide?'

'None at all, not on that issue anyway. He had won his point over there not being a re-vote.' Samuel glared at him.

'Re-vote?'

'We considered whether to vote again on the issue. It was thought that some people might have changed their views. It was then proposed we should have a vote about a vote.'

Rose was now convinced that all clubs and societies were mad. Processions at Plum's in St James's Square, now votes about votes. He could take a fair guess how much the Prince of Wales had enjoyed the evening.

152

'We were happy,' put in Gwendolen feebly, following her own thoughts.

'You did say you wished to change your vote to agree with me, Gwendolen,' said Samuel meanly.

'You misunderstood,' she snapped testily. 'Never would I have voted against dear Thomas. Never.'

'Anything else happen at this dinner? Did Sir Thomas seem normal to you?'

'He was not himself!' shouted Gwendolen. 'He was worried about me.'

They ignored her.

'He was rather quiet,' said Angelina doubtfully.

'She wasn't his fiancée, I was.' Gwendolen was outraged, having mulled over Angelina's earlier words.

'I was not engaged to Sir Thomas, Inspector,' said Angelina patiently.

'You was,' retorted Gwendolen, grammar deserting her as well as her fiction about her own relationship with the dead man.

'No,' replied Angelina, gently. 'You only thought I was. He did ask me to marry him, but I rejected his proposal.'

'How could you turn Thomas down?' asked Gwendolen, amazement coming before affront.

'Would he have taken this rejection hard enough to commit suicide, Mrs Langham?' asked Rose quietly.

Angelina looked suddenly shaken. 'I hardly think so, Inspector,' she said stiffly. She remained very pale, puzzling Oliver greatly.

'What I need to know now is, what Sir Thomas ate and drank.'

'What we all ate of course,' said Lord Beddington. 'All this Dickens stuff.' Really these Scotland Yard chaps were dense. No wonder he had his work cut out on the bench.

'But did he reject any courses? Soup for instance. Or lobster salad.'

153

'He took both,' said Angelina.

'The kidneys?'

'Sir Thomas served me,' said Angelina, trying to recollect. 'Then the Prince of Wales, Lord Beddington and himself. I remember, because he said afterwards he hadn't liked them.'

Auguste stiffened. Not *like* them? A sauce *à la Didier*?

'Quail and cutlets?'

'I think – yes, he omitted them. He felt,' said Angelina, with a quizzical look at Auguste, 'that they had not been specified on the menu.'

'But he ate the goose?'

'Indeed he ate the goose. And all the forcemeats,' said Angelina. 'I can't remember after that, except that he drank several cups of coffee, and some wine and some water after he returned to the table. I remember all the glasses lined up.'

'I saw him with a strawberry in his mouth,' said Gwendolen. With the memory of this fetching scene, she subsided.

'Thank you, ladies and gentlemen. I take it you'll all be staying on.' There was no question mark in Rose's voice.

'We will never desert Mr Micawber,' said Oliver gravely.

Rose shot a look at him. 'Thank you, Mr Michaels.' He paused on his way out of the room. 'By the way, I understand there was a glass of water on the lectern, and Sir Thomas drank from it.'

'I drank from it too. It wasn't poisoned,' said Samuel instantly. 'Look at me.'

No one did. It was patently clear to all that Samuel Pipkin could have poisoned the water after he had drunk from it, if indeed he had drunk from it at all. No one could recall his doing so.

The Imperial's chef, at last let loose in his own kitchen, was making up for lost honour. Luncheon was produced in double-quick time, a light snack of herrings à la Broadstairs, pies and salads. Strangely, very few people attended the luncheon.

Three who did were Edith and Egbert Rose and Auguste, almost forcibly pushed in by a desperate Mr Multhrop. 'Someone's got to be seen eating here,' he hissed. 'Oh me oh my!'

'One thing, Egbert, troubles me,' said Auguste, frowning at the herring. This chef could do with a Fish Fortnight at the Auguste Didier School of Cuisine. 'I do not think my pupils were strictly accurate about not meeting Sir Thomas before. One at least had. Lord Wittisham and Miss Fenwick had been to collect some food — the quails I believe — and were passing in a donkey cart as Sir Thomas arrived. Sir Thomas shouted to him, 'What are *you* doing here?' and Lord Wittisham replied that he worked here. I am sure they did not like each other.'

Edith looked from one to the other. 'You men,' she said fondly, taking another mouthful of Broadstairs trifle, 'you see mysteries everywhere.' Edith had spent the morning touring Broadstairs. There was not a lot to tour in the inclement weather, though the Bohemia concert party was marked down for a visit, and the bandstand too held promise, though with all these people about, she doubted she would hear the music. Egbert had said Broadstairs was a quiet, elegant place compared with Ramsgate. So far she had little reason to believe him. However, she had met a very nice lady from Pinner who said why didn't she come along with the Lionisers' visit to Fort House that afternoon. Dickens used to stay there apparently, and Edith liked Dickens. At least, she liked *The Pickwick Papers*, which her father used to read to her after Sunday School as a treat. She had some nice prints on her wall at home too.

Mr Multhrop's luncheon room suddenly acquired another visitor, albeit a non-eating one, as Inspector Naseby rushed

155

in. 'What's going on?' he asked vehemently. 'I went to Blue Horizons. Cook's skipped it, and the others said they'd already talked to you.' He saw Auguste and turned purple. 'You not locked up yet? I got a message,' he said meaningfully, 'it was this afternoon.'

'Did you? Must have been some sort of misunderstanding,' said Rose. 'My case, Naseby.'

'You can't do it alone,' announced Naseby.

'You're right there, Naseby.' Naseby looked smug. 'I must send for Twitch,' added Rose thoughtfully.

Edith pinned her best hat from Bobby's carefully onto her hair. It was after all Bank Holiday Monday. She felt confident it would not dare to rain; it was her holiday after all. Descending to the foyer in search of the Lionisers, she saw a sturdy well-dressed girl in black turning away from the reception desk. Mr Multhrop was hurrying up to her.

'Miss Throgmorton?' Mr Multhrop bustled forward, but someone forestalled him with a glad cry.

Alfred, returning home after a kitchen luncheon with his colleagues, had seen the love of his life. He hurtled forward. 'I say, Beatrice. How wonderful to see you.' He seized her hands in his, and mindful of her enthusiastic response to his advances a few weeks ago, took her in her arms and planted a kiss on her cheek. In his enthusiasm, and being no lover of Sir Thomas, he quite forgot to offer her his condolences.

'I don't think this is right, Alfred,' said Beatrice firmly, removing cheek and hands.

A sentiment with which Alice Fenwick, watching this tender reunion, was in full agreement.

Only the thought of Araminta could cheer Auguste this afternoon. Not even the invention of a new timbale had succeeded. A murder, and he wasn't even allowed to play

156

detective. He was a suspect, at least until the analyst's reports had cleared him. Truly, Broadstairs seemed a bleak place. It grew much brighter when Araminta floated down the stairs, a vision in pale blue foulard with feathery hat to match, her curls peeping out beneath. He looked doubtfully at the rain-filled skies. The day was overcast; the sun was struggling to emerge, but so far not succeeding. There was even a mist over the sands. No doubt Mr Turner would have found it attractive to paint, but he, Auguste Didier, did not. Not when he had looked forward to a brief glimpse of Araminta jumping up and down in the sea in a bathing dress.

'You will risk going out like this?' he enquired.

Her large eyes opened in surprise. 'Papa says it's all right so long as there are other people around.'

'I did not mean risk with *me*,' he answered, annoyed, 'but it is trying to rain and your dress is not covered.'

She smiled beatifically. 'It won't rain,' she said in assurance. It wouldn't dare. 'Where are we going?'

'I have to buy some cod,' he announced. Indeed he was looking forward to this discussion with William and Joe.

Araminta wrinkled up her nose. 'I think *I'd* like to see Punch and Judy,' she announced.

William and Joe and their entire consignment of cod vanished in the desire to please Araminta.

The Punch and Judy booth was far from crowded, due to the overwhelming preference of the day excursionists for Pierrots, Uncle Mack and the Bohemia concert party. Indeed in the twenty chairs hopefully placed before it, only six were occupied; two by Auguste and Araminta, two by a disgruntled nursemaid and a purposeful-looking six-year-old female charge, and two small boys who sat innocently near the stand, dangling their legs from their chairs.

The curtains were drawn back to the sound of a hurdy-gurdy. A despairing showman, whom Araminta announced to Auguste's mystification was called The Professor, cursed

157

the weather and his audience of six. This was not the way to do it.

'Mr Punch,' he began forlornly. 'Where are you?'

A long-nosed Punchinello puppet popped his head up on the stand, clad in a red costume and nightcap with a bell on the end. 'I'm here!' he shrieked in a falsetto voice.

Araminta laughed and clapped her hands.

'I've got a big stick,' mentioned Punch confidingly to his audience, as Judy appeared with her baby.

'This is a romance?' Auguste enquired, puzzled, remembering what he had seen before when the lady puppet was attacked and hoping there would be no repetition. 'Like the Sleeping Beauty?'

Araminta giggled, whether at him or at Punch hitting the baby over the head he wasn't sure; the baby collapsed in a heap over the side of the stand.

'That's the way to do it,' Punch informed his audience.

Auguste glanced anxiously at the children. This was surely strong meat for them? The little girl, however, appeared to be roaring her approval as Punch proceeded to batter his wife and lay her by the baby's side. Next a policeman puppet arrived carrying a gallows. A shiver ran up Auguste's spine. One of the small boys was busy throwing nuts at Punch in an effort to help justice.

'Shall I kill him too?' enquired Punch.

'Yes,' shouted the younger members of the audience.

Auguste watched horrified as Punch manoeuvred the policeman into hanging himself. 'The morals of this story are not good.' He shook his head.

Araminta looked puzzled.

'He is an evil man, this Punch,' explained Auguste.

'It's only a play,' said Araminta, holding his hand to comfort him. 'Don't worry about it. It's not real.'

'As Sir Thomas's death was real,' said Auguste gravely. 'Araminta, you were around that day. Did you see anyone talking to Sir Thomas at all, who might have upset him?'

She did not seem to hear him. Mr Punch was about to murder a crocodile with his big stick, since the reptile for some unknown reason had stolen his sausages. Mr Punch should be grateful, thought Auguste, if they were English sausages.

'Kill him!' shouted out Araminta loudly.

'What did you say?' enquired Punch.

'Kill him!' advised four voices. Auguste and the governess abstained.

The crocodile corpse joined the others. 'That's the way to do it,' said Araminta pleased, as all the puppets came to life again for a curtain call. She squeezed Auguste's hand and he quite forgot to repeat his question.

The Literary Lionisers, or those who had survived the damp morning walk to Ramsgate along the sands (in the steps of the great Dickens on his walk with Hans Christian Andersen), were equally divided as to those who wished no more to do with the Imperial, Broadstairs or indeed the Lionisers, those to whom the sudden disappearance of their leader was an added bonus, and those who were determined not to miss what they had already paid for. The latter two groups, just over thirty in all, were walking purposefully towards Fort House, the object of the afternoon programme. Faced with the sight of the excursionists arriving in the morning, they had not hesitated. They, too, regardless of the loss of their leader, were intent on being suitably dressed for Bank Holiday. Boaters, with judicious hat retainers in view of the fickle wind, parasols, and Y and N Diagonal seam corsets for easier walking (as well as for bicycling) were speedily pulled into service.

Samuel Pipkin was in a most difficult position. In order to assume his new role as leader of the party, his dislike of Dickens had to be muted, to put it mildly. How far should his conversion go? Could a few allusions be made to Thackeray? he wondered wistfully; on the whole, he thought not. Gwendolen, still clad in dark blue, was indefatigably marching with the party next to a most sympathetic lady. She told her that it had been suggested to her that she should remain behind to rest, but she did not consider her darling Thomas would have approved of this.

Edith Rose fully agreed.

Angelina walked along the cobbled path to the house, revelling in the damp air blowing in her face. Oliver marched grimly along behind her. A strong breeze caught the upstanding feathered plumes of her hat and blew it off. Pointing out the value of hat pins, Oliver fielded it and returned it to her with a bow. She took it. She thanked him stiffly. He caught her eye. She laughed.

Lord Beddington stomped along in silence. Why did this fellow Dickens want to live on the top of a hill? These writers were strange folk. Next year he'd try a travellers' group instead. After all, committees were much the same anywhere. Didn't matter about the subject.

Behind them twenty-eight rank and file Lionisers exclaimed and marvelled at the quaint harbour beneath them, their thoughts torn between Dickens and murder. Some of them indeed were under the impression that Sir Thomas's disappearance from the scene was some kind of re-enactment of *The Mystery of Edwin Drood*. Would he reappear perhaps like Edwin Drood himself might have done if Mr Dickens had been spared long enough to conclude it?

As the party arrived at the small front door of the house, some puffing from the climb, Samuel held up his hand impressively. 'On top of a breezy hill on the road to Kingsgate,' he began to quote in low deferential tone, 'a cornfield between it and the sea.' He coughed importantly. 'Ladies and gentlemen, Fort House, known to Bradstonians, as those who live in Broadstairs are called, as Bleak House.

owner, studied the illustrious visitors' book, looked round the study with Mr Luke Fildes' picture of the Empty Chair in their mind's eye, and had seen the chalet where Dickens wrote his last words before his death, they were drained of emotion, and it was fortunate that Rochester Castle provided exercise without undue stress.

Lord Beddington was not appreciating the day to its fullest, despite the fact that for some unknown reason it had seemed a good idea to buy a Panama hat. What should he do about that young scoundrel? Could it or could it not have a bearing on this present case of murder? He alone of all the Lionisers was unmoved by illusions of great men. He'd been forty when Dickens died in 1870, quite old enough to know that, whatever the fuss made over him, Dickens's private life was hardly on a par with Queen Victoria's. Not that he'd anything against that. After all, Dickens had had the decency to keep it to himself, not go telling the world about it. Beddington had lived long enough to know that very few people were quite what the public considered them. Including old Throgmorton and, he supposed with some surprise, himself.

Gwendolen sitting next to him did not object to his silence. She was wondering whether Angelina could possibly be cast as Sir Thomas's Mr Datchery. No, that was too fanciful. He knew she was coming and, besides, whatever motive could Angelina have for murder? Regretfully, Gwendolen dismissed the notion.

Egbert Rose had talked to many bereaved ladies; he talked to them quietly, straightforwardly, compassionately. But he had never met one quite like this. Beatrice Throgmorton was a large lady, although not yet twenty-one. Her eyes in her otherwise bovine face were intelligent, her manner brisk. She had spent the time since her arrival making calm arrangements for the transfer of her father's body to their

Buckinghamshire home after the inquest tomorrow, and was now apparently set on clearing up this murder before she left.

'There's a lady here who says,' she began without preliminaries, 'she's my father's fiancée. Is this correct, would you know?'

'I think, miss, it may be a figment of the lady's imagination. Treat her gently, miss, but not too seriously.'

Beatrice looked uncomprehending. 'I don't intend to treat her at all, Inspector. I wondered if she had poisoned him, that is all.'

'She seems to have felt herself slighted,' said Rose cautiously. He would leave well alone and omit the part about Miss Havisham. 'But that's not to say she'd commit murder.'

'Someone did,' pointed out Beatrice. 'Who else disliked him enough?'

'That's what I need to know from you, miss.' Rose was beginning to feel like one of his own suspects under relentless interrogation. 'Your father thought he recognised someone here in the hotel.'

'Lord Wittisham,' said Beatrice promptly. 'They disliked each other. Lord Wittisham believes that I wish to marry him. He proposed. My father overheard and, without consulting me or waiting to hear my reply, forbade him the house. Lord Wittisham made strong objections. My father was far from pleased. I do not come of age until I am twenty-five and my father's consent was needed for me to marry. There is also the question of a great deal of money. Mine. I did not, and do not, in fact intend to marry Lord Wittisham, but I disliked my father's approach, so I informed Lord Wittisham I would consider the matter. I intended,' for the first time Rose saw the beginnings of emotion, 'to teach my father a lesson.'

'And have you told Lord Wittisham yet?'

'No,' said Beatrice composedly. 'I suppose I ought to.'

176

'You don't think he took his revenge on your father, do you? It would solve his problem nicely, or so he would have thought.'

She stared. 'Can you see Alfred doing anything like that?' Her tone implied she might think the more of him if he did.

Rose thought of the vacuous young man, and silently agreed. Then he remembered Wittisham was one of Emma Pryde's protégés and that Emma was not known for encouraging entirely vacuous young men. There must be more to him than Beatrice thought.

'Have there been attempts on your father's life before?'

'He never mentioned any,' she said, reflecting. 'In fact rather the contrary.'

'*What?*'

She almost smiled. 'It does sound strange, I admit. My father told me that when he was young he got in a fight with someone and nearly killed him, and that the man swore vengeance. They fought over a girl, I understand. Not my mother. Father was what you might call a rake. I think,' she added thoughtfully, 'that I take after him.'

Rose glanced at her large, cumbrous figure and wondered anew about the passions of men and women. 'The Lionisers are having an evening at the Albion Hotel tonight, and not only will they be there but all the people who cooked and served your father's dinner that evening. I'd like to be sure there's no one there whom you recognise from the past. Would you come?'

She rose to her feet. 'My father was murdered, Inspector. I consider it my duty to help in any way I can. I should – ' she hesitated – 'explain that I was not close to my father. My mother died when I was fifteen, but I was brought up by a series of incompetent governesses and I saw little of either parent. My mother was always ill, my father often away or working. By the time I was out of the schoolroom, I had lost my need for a parent. Nevertheless, I shall help.

177

I believe in justice,' she said firmly. 'Oh yes, I believe in justice.'

' "Magnificent ruin," quoted Mr Augustus Snodgrass,' Samuel Pipkin proclaimed. The Literary Lionisers gazed up at the most splendid Norman keep in England. 'Magnificent,' repeated Samuel in his own person, ducking one of the numerous pigeons that had proprietary rights in the pink dianthus-covered walls. Samuel had now read all passages from the Lion's work relevant to Rochester Castle, and enumerated every single friend that Dickens had brought there, as far as could be traced.

Oliver and Angelina were inspecting a Jubilee memorial put up twelve years ago commemorating 'fifty years of ever-broadening commerce, fifty years of ever-brightening science, fifty years of ever-widening empire!' It could not last, Oliver thought. Next year would see the dawn of the twentieth century. Would it continue to see expansion? Would the Empire go on for ever? He didn't like this new war in South Africa. It boded no good for the opening of the new century. But he dismissed such gloomy thoughts as he followed Angelina in full-skirted blue walking dress up the stairs to the top of the keep, and duly admired the magnificent view.

'Glorious pile,' quoted Angelina. Samuel again produced *The Pickwick Papers*, after a short cough to draw everyone's attention. Unobtrusively Angelina and Oliver crept back down the stairs.

'Snodgrass,' Oliver remarked, picking up Angela's quotation, when at last they reached the safety of the gardens far below, 'do not let me be baulked in this matter – do *not* obtain the assistance of several stalwart Lionisers to carry me prostrate back to Broadstairs, do not listen to me when I say never, never again shall I visit a sight connected to the late great Mr Charles Dickens. I say do *not*.'

'Mr Snodgrass,' answered Angelina solemnly, seizing Oliver's hand enthusiastically, 'not for *worlds*.'

'A thrill passed over Mr Winkle's face,' concluded Oliver hollowly.

Angelina laughed. 'You are an idiot, Oliver. What did you join for if you don't like literary sights?'

'For you, dearest Angelina. Now it can be told.' He smote his breast, and fell on one knee.

'Nonsense. You didn't even know me then.'

'I see nothing but the truth will do,' he said ruefully, rising to his feet again. 'Young man flattered – young up-and-coming playwright joins committee of literary lions – young man speedily discovers his mistake – apart from lovely young lady, jolly boring – stuck with it – what to do? Brazen it out? Shoot myself?' Reverting from Mr Jingle to Oliver Michaels, he added, 'Six months have proved to me that the passions of Lions are as nothing compared with those of Lionisers.'

'Not always,' she replied, laughing. 'Look at Dickens and Thackeray. Look at Speke and Burton. Look at Gilbert and Sullivan—'

'Look at Harald Langham and Thomas Throgmorton,' interposed Oliver quietly.

Taken by surprise, she could not answer for a moment and then said angrily, 'If you knew, why didn't you say something before?'

He shrugged. 'It was none of my business until—'

'Until Sir Thomas died and you thought I might have a motive for murder?' she finished sweetly.

'I was going to say until I fell in love with you,' he answered mildly.

'Oh, Oliver.' The Literary Lionisers descending from the keep were horrified at the sight of elegant Mrs Langham clasped in the arms of another committee member, ten were jealous, and the rest averted their eyes.

179

'Oliver,' Angelina said presently, 'I have to explain. You don't really think I'm a murderess, do you? A Mrs Maybrick?'

'Are you?'

'No.'

He grinned and released her except for one hand, of which he kept tight hold. 'Now tell me,' he commanded.

'My husband was a very good poet, as you know, but he was unlucky, one of those people who are always in the wrong place at the wrong time in his career. And then towards the end of his life when he was already ill, he had one last hope to cling to. He was excellently placed to be the next Poet Laureate when the position fell vacant in ninety-six. But he was too proud to plead at the right doors. He wasn't close to the Queen. Sir Thomas Throgmorton was. Sir Thomas had quarrelled with my husband over some business matter and persuaded the powers that be that my husband was no fit person to hold the position, whatever the quality of his poetry. It was given to Alfred Austin instead. Harald died three months later, I believe of a broken heart. I suppose it was childish of me, but I vowed to break Sir Thomas's, if I could. So I got involved with the Lionisers to do just that.' She tried to smile. 'Vain of me, was it not?'

'No.'

'So I took my petty revenge. But he got his by being murdered.' She shook, and Oliver drew her to him, holding her very close, his memory of Angelina assisting Sir Thomas to serve out the dish of kidneys entirely obliterated.

James Pegg should have been a happy man, for he was with Alfred and unaccompanied by Alice. Indeed, she did not accompany them on this stroll along the Western Esplanade to the Dumpton Gap even in their thoughts. Alfred's thoughts were elsewhere. 'Isn't she a stunner?' he asked James rhetorically. Despite his outdated slang, James

180

understood him, and agreed, though not in the same sense as Alfred. Beatrice Throgmorton would stun anybody, in James's view.

'Alfred,' he said, plucking up courage, 'did you really threaten to kill Sir Thomas?'

'I may have done.' Alfred looked sullen. 'They can't really suspect me though, can they?' pleadingly, as though James could protect him.

'They might. Sir Thomas did have a quarrel with someone in the hotel before dinner. But it couldn't have been you though, could it?'

'No,' said Alfred shortly, and changed the subject.

James walked back to Broadstairs alone, for Alfred had decided to continue to Ramsgate to purchase a new boater in honour of his forthcoming engagement to Beatrice. James stuck his hands in his pockets moodily as he went back into Blue Horizons trying to think carefully about what he'd overheard that Saturday afternoon, and how he could turn it to his advantage. On his way up the stairs, however, he was once again an unwitting eavesdropper.

'It was a perfectly innocent meeting, I assure you.' The unmistakable voice of Algernon Peckham.

'No one 'as an innocent meeting with old 'Iggins. Gorblimey, even the beer thinks twice before going into the Seamen's Rest. You're up to summat, ain't you? What you doin' 'ere? Got plans involving Mr Didier, 'ave yer?' Sid was getting aggressive.

The answer was lost but it must have reassured Sid, for he sounded somewhat mollified. 'What yer do is yer own business, but one sign that things ain't right and I'm orf to Monsieur Didier — and the perlice. An' that ain't me usual practice.'

The door opened suddenly and a furious Algernon emerged to find James leaning over the stair rail listening quietly.

* * *

181

Emily and Heinrich were strolling along the Eastern Esplanade towards Kingsgate. Emily wore her new cream linen skirt and jacket, with a biscuit-coloured Leghorn hat. She was as happy as possible in the circumstances. She was safe now, though she had new anxieties. She glanced at Heinrich. There seemed to be a sudden restraint between them, or was it her imagination?

'Have you ever been married, Heinrich?' There, it was out.

'*Nein*.'

'Oh.'

'In my job,' he explained, 'it is difficult.'

'What *is* your job exactly?'

'I am Embassy cook. You have to travel, live in the Embassy. It is no place for a wife.' Emily was suddenly even less happy. 'I wanted to marry once, very much. It was not possible. I have never wanted to again.' This wasn't true. All last week he had been happier than for thirty years; he was in love, overwhelmed with the charms of Emily Dawson and the outrageous hope that she might return his affection and become his wife.

She tried timidly: 'I am alone too.'

He patted her hand. 'You should not go through life alone, Miss Dawson,' he said absent-mindedly. 'It is not good.'

Emily was in full agreement. But 'Miss Dawson' he'd called her. It had been Emily all last week.

'Heinrich, are you worried about anything?'

'*Nein*, Miss Emily, *nein*.' His voice was hearty yet the answer did not convince her.

'You haven't seemed the same since – since it happened,' she plunged.

'I do not think any of us be the same,' said Heinrich, frowning. 'Murder is not a usual thing.'

'I still think it was an accident,' said Emily. 'Accidents

182

do happen—' She shivered, a sudden memory seizing her.

'And even if it vas not, ve have no need to vorry,' he said firmly.

'Atropine is confirmed, and far too much to have been a slight slip of the deadly nightshade. The analyst was quite excited,' said Rose to Auguste in Mr Multhrop's requisitioned office. Auguste had lingered hopefully in the foyer hoping Araminta might appear. She did not. 'It's a funny thing about atropine,' Rose went on. 'He said it had hardly ever been used intentionally to murder people in Europe, though it's being used all the time out East for helping relatives on to the next world. He's come back with a report on the rest of the china and food too. The later courses are all clear, though one or two hadn't much left on them to analyse. But that's my theory thrown out of court, that the later courses were to blame. Provided Emily and Alice aren't acting together, the coffee's clear – unless something was added at table.'

'Unlikely,' observed Auguste, 'since he had already felt ill.'

'So it comes back to the alcohol, probably the brandy, and Lord Wittisham.'

'I did notice that the level of my brandy was considerably reduced,' admitted Auguste, 'but perhaps my memory is at fault.'

'First time you've ever admitted *that* possibility, Auguste.'

'You are right, my friend. My memory is not at fault.'

'So everything comes back to our Lord Wittisham. The time gap is right, he had the opportunity and he had a good motive: with Sir Thomas out of the way, he could get the girl and her money. It must have seemed a heaven-sent opportunity with Mrs Figgis-Hewett shouting about breach of promise – if heaven-sent is the word,' added Rose hastily, 'and our Mr Pipkin shouting about his rights.'

183

'How did Lord Wittisham happen to have atropine with him, if it was done on the spur of the moment?'

Rose frowned. 'Perhaps he planned it. He knew Throgmorton was going to be here, didn't he? You told them, you said.'

'Yes,' said Auguste unhappily.

'Well, then,' pointed out Rose reassuringly, 'you gave them five days' warning to get their poison ready, plus another seven days down here.'

'But you do not just march into a druggist's and demand atropine,' objected Auguste.

'No, but this form of atropine is used by one group of people apart from chemists. Those who are in contact with horses.'

'Veterinary surgeons?'

'Horse trainers, owners, anyone with a stables. Like Wittisham, no doubt. Grooms, of course.'

'Grooms,' echoed Auguste with a sudden and sickening thought. 'But James Pegg was a groom, *and* his father is a veterinary surgeon. And, Egbert,' thinking back, 'do you not remember he mentioned the bitterness of atropine. How did he know that? We, I am sure, did not mention it.'

'There you are then, Wittisham could get the poison through Pegg even if he had no access himself. Unless, of course,' he added, 'Mr Pegg had a motive himself.'

The landlord of the Albion Hotel was as happy as Mr Multhrop was doleful. He had been doing excellent business from the Lionisers, so good that he was beneficent enough to feel sorry for poor old Cedric. 'Send them along to me,' he had said cheerily. What, after all, could be more suitable for the Lionisers than the hotel within whose walls Dickens spent so much time, and where he had completed *Nicholas Nickleby*, the Albion 'where we had that merry night two years ago', he wrote to his friend Forster, an occasion made the merrier by indulgence in the landlord's 'excellent hollands'.

The present landlord was all too eager to keep up his predecessor's reputation in the matter of hollands, and was only too delighted to dispense it to as many Lionisers who requested it. Since it was a beverage blessed by the great Dickens, it was perceived by the Lionisers as an entirely suitable drink for the ladies, and by the time Rose and Auguste arrived, another merry night was well in progress. Gin, however, whether the Dutch variety or no, was beginning to have distressing results on the ladies in particular, who nevertheless persisted in their belief that it was all right because Mr Dickens had said so.

There had been anxious consultations among the committee as to the propriety of attending a 'merry night' with Sir Thomas dead. On balance they decided to attend, in the interests of the group, a decision endorsed by Rose who was anxious to see both groups of his suspects together in an informal setting. Not to mention Beatrice Throgmorton.

Huddled together in the large lounge as if for protection against the monster they had unwittingly unleashed by their programme, the members of the committee were fully aware of the literally sobering fact that Scotland Yard was on its way. They were somewhat taken aback, however, when its representative arrived not only with the chef, but with an assortment of eight other people, one or two of whom were faintly familiar, though unidentifiable save by Angelina, who had been best placed on Saturday evening to recognise the 'waiters' at the banquet.

Angelina had cheered up considerably, having rid herself of the burden of guilt she was carrying. Oliver had reassured her that Sir Thomas could not possibly have committed suicide through anguish at her rejection and she was now prepared to enjoy the rest of the week immensely, even if

185

it did involve a murder investigation. It was a shocking thing, no doubt, but compared with her future, which suddenly seemed to hold out enticing prospects of a new and exciting life, it had retreated into the background.

The eighth stranger to most of the Lionisers was Beatrice Throgmorton, dressed superbly and hugely in black, her quick eye running speedily around the assembled company. Alfred started to his feet, but his glad cry of welcome was cut short when Beatrice inclined her stately head in his direction and moved off to sit sandwiched between Auguste Didier and Egbert Rose.

The landlord, anxious to please, pushed glasses of hollands before the newcomers. They all took it for white wine and discovered their mistake. Beatrice blinked and continued to sip, Auguste and Rose choked.

'This,' said Auguste carefully, 'is not a common drink in France: I was not brought up to it.'

'Hollands, sir,' said the landlord reproachfully, 'Dickens liked it.'

Auguste glared. What Dickens liked was the last thing he wished to have lying in, or rather on, his stomach. His stomach was as finely tuned an instrument as was his palate. It had no need of being scorched. Irreparable damage might be done to one of the main tools of his trade.

'What is that woman to you, Alfred?' asked Alice hurt, remembering yesterday's encounter.

'That's Miss Beatrice Throgmorton,' replied James, delighted to impart bad news. 'Alfred's fiancée.'

'Fiancée!' Alice went pale and looked down into her hollands.

'I'm a lucky chap,' said Alfred smiling.

Alice said nothing, but her hands tightened round her glass.

'Is there anyone here you recognise, Miss Throgmorton?' Rose asked her in a low voice.

186

Beatrice looked round carefully once more and named a few Lionisers.

'Besides those. In these two small groups of people here.'

'Mrs Langham,' she said. 'Lord Beddington. He often used to come to the house.'

'Anyone else?'

Beatrice drank her hollands steadily. She frowned. 'It's so difficult,' she said after a while. 'You see people out of context, years later, you try to judge by a hazy memory – I'm just not sure. There's something familiar about one, perhaps – oh, I know *him*.' She pointed at Algernon Peckham, who was merrier than Auguste had ever seen him, teasing Emily to Heinrich's disapproval. 'He was working in the gardens at the château when I was staying in France, and I discovered he was English. Everyone thought he was Italian. He disappeared after the burglary.'

'Burglary?' said Rose sharply, a dim distant bell ringing in his mind.

'The Countess de la Ferté's famous necklace that belonged to Madame de Pompadour was stolen.'

'Was it now,' said Rose, already moving purposefully towards a telephone. When Twitch came. there were a few things he could bring with him.

Gwendolen had had a distressing day and was making up for it with several glasses of this delightfully spicy lemonade. Unfortunately the lemonade was beginning to wreak its awful revenge in several ways, one of which could not be ignored. With a regretful look at her glass, and a warning glance at Lord Beddington should he tamper with its contents while she was gone – she had observed his hand stealing towards it already – she rose to make her way upstairs to the ladies' retiring room. She passed Egbert Rose. She stopped in front of him, leaning forward confidentially and giving him the full benefit of the satin décolletage.

187

'Datchery,' she announced. 'He said he'd met Datchery.'

'Who, ma'am?' asked Rose, bewildered.

She blinked. This man was supposed to be at Scotland Yard. 'Sir Thomas,' she answered indignantly. 'My fiancé,' glaring at Beatrice.

'He'd met who?'

'A character in *The Mystery of Edwin Drood*, Inspector,' explained Beatrice kindly. 'A mysterious person who comes along to solve the mystery after the disappearance of Edwin Drood himself.'

'And did he, miss?'

'No, because Dickens did not finish the book. He died.'

'He was murdered,' said Gwendolen definitely.

Samuel Pipkin giggled. 'Oh come, my dear lady, he died a natural death.'

'Who?' asked Rose, startled.

'Dickens,' said Samuel.

'Thomas,' said Gwendolen.

'Where does Datchery come in?' asked Rose impatiently.

Angelina leaned forward to explain, leaving Gwendolen to slip away (almost literally) to resume her mission. She was back within minutes, pale in the face.

'He's there!' she shrieked. 'In the ladies' retiring room!'

'Who?' Rose leapt up.

'Datchery.' She had some difficulty enunciating the name.

'But who is it, ma'am? Sir Thomas didn't say who Datchery was.'

'No, no,' she began to laugh hysterically. 'This is the *real* Mr Datchery. He's in Dickensian dress with a long beard, but he's a young man really, sitting there in the ladies' retiring room drinking hollands and writing—'

'Oh!' The landlord looked up cunningly. 'That's not Mr Datchery, ma'am. That's Mr Dickens.'

'Dickens?' cried Angelina.

'Well, his ghost at any rate.'

'Ghost?' said Rose and Auguste in unison. They had no liking for ghosts since their previous experience.

'Sometimes he sits in here, sometimes upstairs, sometimes in the ladies' retiring room. It all depends what he's writing at the time.'

'Why did he write his books in the ladies' retiring room?' enquired Auguste. This Dickens was a most curious man.

The landlord regarded him pityingly. 'I can see you don't know your Dickens, sir. Or Broadstairs. It wasn't a ladies' retiring room when he was here. Part of the time he stayed in what's now our hotel; it wasn't even part of the hotel but a private house. We've expanded, sir. Expanded very much.' His chest followed suit. 'It's not everyone can see him, of course. You're very privileged, madam.'

Gwendolen did not agree. She fainted.

The female Lionisers left the rest of their hollands untouched and began to think in terms of returning to the hotel. The ladies' retiring room remained unused.

Passing through the foyer on a last check before retiring, Mr Multhrop found himself engulfed in a merry throng of post-hollands revellers, intent on beginning a new party. His reactions were mixed. While he welcomed this new-found enthusiasm for Broadstairs after the gloomy events of the past few days, this rowdy pink-faced band, hardly recognisable as the distinguished gathering of Literary Lionisers, was not to his taste. Outside the hotel he would have attributed such behaviour to day excursionist 'Arrys and 'Arriets and called the police. As it was, he was forced to his usual obsequious tolerance. Summoning a bleary-eyed waiter to serve further alcoholic beverages, he beat a strategic retreat, to the raucous sound of upraised voices trilling 'Mid pleasures and gin-palaces . . . there's no place like home.' And that was where he devoutly wished them.

The inhabitants of Blue Horizons were making quieter arrivals home, one by one.

Alfred had inveigled Beatrice to take a stroll along the pier to gaze at the stars; he was in exalted mood, and felt daring enough to ask her for her answer. The kilted Scots figurehead loomed above them, his feet busily executing all the steps of a neat Highland fling when Alfred glanced up.

'I'm afraid not, Alfred,' was Beatrice's reply.

He stared at her bemusedly. 'What?' he said eventually and feebly.

'No, Alfred,' she said. 'I do not wish to marry you.'

'The shock of your father's death. You need more time.'

'It's nothing to do with the shock of my father's death. I do not wish to marry you. I never have.'

'But—' His mouth fell open like one of William and Joe's larger fishy wares. Then he perceived the truth. 'You think me a murderer,' he cried.

'Don't be silly, Alfred,' Beatrice snapped impatiently. 'You're not a murderer.' Yet his expression as he looked at her and the strength with which he seized her arm made her uncomfortably aware of their isolated position. She wrenched her arm away, conscious of fear. What did she *know* of him after all? Alcohol can disguise, but sometimes reveal the true man. She turned, and abandoning dignity, hitched up her skirts and ran.

Heinrich, reeling after several glasses of schnapps, held carefully on to Emily's arm; whether for her protection or his, he did not question. Enthused by physical contact with his beloved, he suggested a stroll in the Victoria Gardens; Emily, unusually flushed, and equally enthused, agreed.

By the time they reached the bandstand he was even more enthused with the charms of Miss Dawson. Not since Greta all those years ago had a woman seemed to him so desirable.

190

Hollands had blotted out all inhibitions and worries. 'Emily,' he said huskily. 'Emily.'

'Yes, Heinrich?' she breathed.

But he was incapable of saying more, and instead seized her in a bearlike hug, heedless of her cry that he was squashing her. Enthusiasm was all very well, thought Emily, but surely this agony was not the romance she had dreamed of. She struggled ineffectively and he released her, but not because of her struggles. Like Gwendolen before him, the hollands had caught up with him. Muttering incomprehensibly, he made for some bushes where he disappeared from Emily's view. He did not return. He could not, for he was lying recumbent and unconscious on the carefully tended garden.

Emily waited, disappointed, rejected – and angry. When he had not reappeared after fifteen minutes, convinced she had been abandoned, she set off home alone.

Alice, too, was alone. She had seen Alfred disappearing with Beatrice Throgmorton and walked quickly back along the promenade. She took a walk up to the West Cliff before returning to Blue Horizons, overwhelmed in misery. What was she to do now?

Algernon Peckham was alone. He had had the fright of his life seeing that woman in the hotel. What the dickens, so to speak, was he to do? So he had been a gardener at the Château de la Ferté. That proved nothing, did it? There was no proof that it was he who had taken the necklace.

Naturally, he would say, he had disappeared from the château; he was scared they'd pin the crime on him because he'd done stir – time. Yes, that was the way to handle it. All the same, there were other problems to be thought about.

James Pegg wandered home alone. He too had seen Alfred departing with Beatrice, but unlike Alice he had followed them, and had been witness to Alfred's humiliating rejection.

191

He did not rush to console Alfred, however. He had a lot to think about, and he preferred to do it slowly and alone.

Auguste did not walk home alone to Blue Horizons. He had the exciting company of Sid. Sid was keeping a close eye on Mr Didier; not that he thought anyone would try to poison *him*, but you never knew, when the likes of Peckham were around.

When they returned, they found Alice in the kitchen. She was crying. Man to man, Sid and Auguste exchanged glances. Auguste nodded, Sid disappeared.

'They're engaged,' she wailed as soon as Sid had closed the door. 'He's led me on.'

'Are you sure, Alice?' he asked cautiously, uncertain what he could say if she was sure.

She nodded and burst into a fresh flood of tears. 'I feel so *silly*. He doesn't even notice me. He doesn't even think of me as a *woman*.'

'*Chérie*.' He knelt down by her chair and drew her to him. She was warm in his arms, and he felt Lord Wittisham was foolish indeed.

'Oh, Mr Didier.' She raised her tear-stained face to his and it seemed quite natural to place his lips on hers, and since she seemed to welcome it, he kept them there. For some time. It occurred to him forcibly that he would have no objection at all to extending this romantic episode further. Much further. But an irritating and inopportune appearance of honour made him hesitate to benefit from her rejection by Alfred at least for tonight. He ordered conscience to remove itself immediately, but it did not. Regretfully he kissed her forehead, extracted himself from her embrace and sent her on her way to a virtuous bed.

Once in his own, he dreamed again of Tatiana, but she was far away from Broadstairs.

Chapter Nine

The night of the hollands had left in its wake the day of the doldrums at Blue Horizons. There were bright spots for Auguste, however. The sun was shining, and an early morning trip to the pier had produced some unusually good mackerel.

Being on breakfast duty, Alice and Emily were the first two pupils down to breakfast. Heinrich was next, entering the kitchen bleary-eyed. Emily ignored him and he slumped down in a chair, trying to catch her eye. It refused to be caught. She had been deserted. He had left her mid-kiss and come home. Did he dislike the smell of her southernwood hair wash or her home-made lavender perfume? She wondered what Grandmama would have advised in all the circumstances.

Few of Auguste's pupils seemed inclined to mackerel for breakfast. In fact Auguste and Sid were the only volunteers and even Auguste had second thoughts as he smelt them on the gridiron. Black coffee was much favoured however. So was silence. Sid was the exception, whistling happily about daring young men on flying trapezes, the sound throbbing through Alice's headache and giving Emily very uncharitable thoughts.

Algernon and James came in together, requesting thin toast, and black coffee. Alice fulfilled the orders, then sat down as far as she could from Alfred who had just arrived. Emily could serve him. Alice, slightly pink, glanced at

Auguste, and continued to avoid Alfred's eyes which were fixed on her beseechingly.

Alfred had had a dark night of the soul. He had seen how entirely wrong it had been for him to have assumed that Beatrice Throgmorton would look twice at him. In any case, upon reflection, did he really want her now he compared her sturdy body and overpowering nature with Alice's pliable warmth? He stole covert glances at her across the table. True, she was not blue-blooded, but she was an officer's daughter and therefore fit for a gentleman. He was suddenly and belatedly delightfully aware of her adoration, of her devotion, of her light hand with the pastry, and even at breakfast time he could contemplate with pleasure how jolly nice it would be to kiss her. He gazed at her ardently. When she required more coffee he leapt up, determined to prove his newfound love and to take the opportunity the task afforded of sitting by her side. James watched aghast, toast suspended halfway to his mouth; the rest of the table observed the manoeuvre with interest, and Alice felt surprise then delight. Auguste, patronisingly benevolent, glowed with virtue at his sexual restraint.

As yet the sunshine could not be enjoyed for this morning the inquest was to take place. Once again the world of the sands and holidays was left far behind as the Auguste Didier School of Cuisine and the committee members of the Literary Lionisers, together with such other Lionisers as could squeeze into the room allotted to them in police headquarters, were once again taken back over the events of last Saturday night. The three uninterested pressmen from the Imperial attended. After this, they could no longer, they supposed, justify a prolonged holiday in Broadstairs; it would be back to Fleet Street. They took desultory notes throughout the succession of witnesses that took the stand, They were profoundly bored. Until it came to the verdict: murder.

Sergeant Stitch, formally attired in dark lounge suit, stiff collar, bowler hat and umbrella, walked out of the railway station, prepared to show Broadstairs how things should really be done. To this end, he had not even considered packing anything that could remotely be considered seaside wear, and as a result suppressed a pang of envy when his cab turned along the Victoria Parade and his eyes beheld a scene that reminded him irresistibly of his annual holiday at Margate, fortunately yet to come.

'Scotland Yard,' he informed Mr Multhrop severely, taking him for the doorman as he marched through the doors of the Imperial Hotel.

'Ah, Stitch.' Rose looked up from a Naseby-dominated desk as Mr Multhrop speedily opened the door and almost pushed the sergeant in. Better be a butler than have policemen littering up his foyer. As far as Rose was concerned, even Stitch made a welcome diversion from Naseby. Better the devil you know. His brain seemed to seize up when Naseby was around, whereas Stitch sharpened it, like a whetstone. Edith was right. Albert, she had remarked − Rose hadn't known Twitch even had a Christian name − is like pummy stone, whereas Naseby (who had had a definite smirk on his face when he saw her new hat) is like Irritating Plaster, he causes irruptions.

'Seen your room yet?' Rose enquired politely.

'No, sir. Eager to begin work, sir.'

'No sea view,' said Rose absently. 'Thought you might get distracted.'

Stitch gulped. 'Quite right, sir,' thinking lovingly of what he would do when he was promoted Inspector. The only problem was that Rose would then be Chief Inspector unless some awful fate overtook him . . . Stitch's nose had twitched eagerly as he took in the size of the Imperial. It was going to be another of those cases with coronets that Rose was

195

so good at. And this time he, and not that chef, would be at Rose's right hand. Usually he got palmed off with the Mile End Road, stabbings in Chinatown, Lascars, opium dens — you name it, Stitch was on the case. Master Didier got Mayfair, he thought incorrectly and unjustly.

'Here's my report, sir. Results of my enquiries.'

'Pertaining to this case?' breathed Naseby, eyes gleaming.

'Just so, Naseby,' said Rose blandly, eyes skimming quickly through pages of Stitch's careful copperplate handwriting.

'I looked up reports from the Continental police as requested, sir.' Virtue oozed out of Stitch. 'You were right,' no harm in giving justice where it was (for once) due, 'the thief of the Château de la Ferté case was believed to be English. Jobbing gardener, by name Augustus Poplar.'

'Alias Algernon Peckham,' said Rose. 'Only a few miles in it.'

'What, sir?' Twitch did not follow the reasoning.

'Anything on Poplar in our files?'

'No, sir, not in the Metropolitan area.'

'Keep trying. Look under Peckham. Now, Throgmorton,' Rose said, returning to the report. Stitch had been working hard, Rose granted him that. Like a mole was Twitch — blind, but a good digger. Rose whistled. Naseby tried hard to read over his shoulder. Stitch stood stolidly to attention.

'Born in 1845. Widower, one daughter. Studied London School of Economics, Heidelberg, Sorbonne, Vienna, Foreign department of Masterman's Bank 1870–83, President 1883 to date. Adviser to Treasury and Foreign and Colonial Offices.'

'That's the formal information, sir. It gets more interesting.'

'You seem quite excited, Stitch,' Rose commented drily.

'Must be the sea air.' Stitch ran a finger round his collar.

'Rumours that he had profited from the Barings Crisis

196

of 1890.' Rose frowned. Wasn't that the time when the Bank of England stepped in to avoid the whole City suffering? 'Interesting, but I don't see how it can affect this case. Still, you never know.'

'And we were in touch with him twice at the Yard, sir,' Stitch burst forth, eager to display the fruits of his research. 'Once when the Yard needed advice over a fraud case, and once over a theft!'

'Theft again eh?' said Rose studying the report.

'Big one sir. Twenty thousand pounds in bearer bonds. Cashed abroad.'

'When?'

'About ten years ago, sir. The villain was never caught.'

'Peckham would have been about fourteen. Pity,' observed Rose regretfully. What would he do about that young man and the necklace? He rather thought he'd let him stew for a while; with the murder investigation on, he couldn't get far − or he'd be a fool to try, and Peckham was no fool.

'Oh, there was no doubt who stole them, sir. His groom.'

'Groom?' echoed Rose. 'Name?'

'I didn't bring it, sir.' Stitch's face was crestfallen.

'Back to the Yard, Stitch. I want everything on that case.'

'But I've only just got here,' bleated Stitch.

Rose paused. An evil look came into his eye. The sun was shining. It was holiday time, he reflected wistfully, wondering where Edith was. He relented. 'Get them on the telephone then.'

'The crime's ten years old, sir,' Stitch pointed out. 'Is it that urgent?'

Rose sighed. 'Ever heard of cumulative probabilities, Stitch?'

Stitch hadn't.

'There's an advertisement I read in here,' said Rose, tapping the local newspaper, 'for Mother Seigel's Syrup.

This learned advertisement suggests that, just like in the Bertillon system, when you get a lot of small pieces of evidence grouped together, it can add up to be something prodigious in the way of proof. And I'm hearing the word "groom" one too many times for it to be coincidence. So after you've heard from the Factory, Stitch, we'll — ' the 'we' did not include Naseby — 'be having a word with Mr James Pegg.'

Beatrice Throgmorton saw no point in delaying her departure. The inquest was over. She had duly registered the death of her father at the Council Offices that afternoon and the funeral had now speedily to be carried out in Buckinghamshire. She paid her account at the Imperial Hotel, and with her maid staggering under six hatboxes, followed by a small procession of luggage borne by sturdy footmen, she climbed into a victoria to depart for the railway station. Her cab had no sooner left the Imperial than Egbert Rose tore out of his office, ran to the reception desk to enquire Miss Throgmorton's whereabouts and, being told, continued this headlong rush out of the hotel, hotly pursued by Stitch and Naseby.

There were no victorias conveniently passing, and Rose was forced to commandeer a passing donkey cart, much to the amazement of its young driver, especially when a bowler-hatted Stitch leapt in after him.

'Follow that victoria,' Rose commanded.

' 'Ere, no more!' yelled the boy, seeing Naseby about to follow suit.

'Scotland Yard, laddie. Hurry,' said Stitch grimly. The boy cast one horrified look at the bowler-hatted majesty and communicated his message to the donkey. With a jerk they were off. When he left his home this morning he had not expected to be carrying Lestrade of the Yard and Sherlock Holmes, and was by no means certain he was ready for this responsibility.

Looking by chance out of his kitchen window, Auguste was amazed to see a donkey cart with Egbert Rose and – yes – Stitch driving past. He blinked. Was this a late hallucinatory effect of the hollands? Seeing Naseby in hot pursuit running on foot after the cart almost convinced him it was. The donkey turned into the High Street, negotiating without enthusiasm the usual morning traffic jams in its odd corners and narrow width.

No Miss Betsy Trotwood leapt out to bar the way to their donkey, but a large van delivering beer to the Prince Albert public house did. A second delivery van by their side, full of interesting-looking vegetables, proved another hazard; the donkey was unwilling to move from these Elysian fields. By the time it had been persuaded onwards the victoria was out of sight. When they reached the railway station it was already plying for new hire and the sound of an engine gathering up steam could be heard. They raced onto the platform, followed a minute or two later by a panting Naseby, only to see the railway train, now bearing Miss Throgmorton, steaming slowly away, enveloping them in white smoke.

'That's that,' said Rose gloomily. 'We won't be able to reach the lady until we can telephone tonight.'

''Ere, where are your platform tickets?' demanded the ticket collector.

'Scotland Yard,' Stitch informed him loftily.

'Platform tickets,' retorted the ticket collector.

'You know me, my man,' said Naseby angrily. 'Inspector Naseby, Sandwich police.'

'Yes, I do.' A happy look came to his face. 'That'll be thruppence,' he said firmly.

'We want to hasten the discovery of Sir Thomas's murderer. Mr Didier, just in case the police think it's me,' Angelina declared honestly.

She and Oliver were sitting side by side in the small parlour at Blue Horizons, having arrived unannounced while the Auguste Didier School of Cuisine was in session in the kitchen. Auguste had persuaded his pupils that, having missed a lesson this morning owing to the inquest, this afternoon would prove an ideal time to instruct them on the magnificence of the St Pierre or John Dory. With regretful eyes on the sunshine outside, they had reluctantly yielded, though not as reluctantly as Auguste had yielded to Angelina's entreaties to be allowed to interrupt the lesson.

'It is brave of you to come,' he observed, his mind still in the kitchen where his unsupervised pupils were no doubt ruining the John Dory.

'Oliver persuaded me,' admitted Angelina. 'He felt it foolish for me to do otherwise. We may be able to help. We could investigate,' she said hopefully, remembering 'Lady Molly of Scotland Yard'. 'We can talk to our fellow committee members in a way that you can't and not even the police can.'

'And why come to me, not go to see Inspector Rose?'

'My friend Lady Jane told me you were a sort of Watson to—' She stopped abruptly as she saw the look of outrage on Auguste's face. 'I mean a Sherlock, of course. How foolish of me.'

Auguste smiled weakly, then laughed at himself for his vanity. 'I am honoured even to be thought Inspector Rose's Watson,' he said. 'I try not to be as foolish as the doctor, and not to blunder in where the Inspector wishes to go quietly. Yet there are no places I can go, things I can observe that, as a policeman, he cannot. So perhaps this is true of you also. And now, Mr Michaels, I wish to ask you one question. Where did you obtain that delightful snake-buckle belt?'

*   *   *

200

'*Alors, mes enfants*, how is our St Pierre?'

No one replied with glad tidings of a perfect dinner about to be served. Indeed only Algernon, Emily and Heinrich were present. The latter two did not appear to be speaking to each other, and Sid and Algernon were prowling round each other like lean and hungry panthers waiting for an opportunity to strike. James, Alice and Alfred hurried in guiltily a few minutes later, glaring at each other for being thrust into proximity, the former carrying bread and milk for dinner, and the latter clutching a treasure trove of samphire as a peace offering.

'I know you wanted to try it, Mr Didier,' he said.

'Where did you get it, Alfred?' enquired Alice anxiously. 'You didn't go clambering over the cliffs, did you?'

'No,' said Alfred shortly. He had no wish to confess that he had visited Madame Mantela, a lady palmist in Margate, in order to discover what his future might hold, the results of which had been far from reassuring.

But not even the prospect of experimenting with cooking samphire raised a sense of oppression that evening; such conversations as were half-heartedly begun petered out.

'Tomorrow afternoon, *mes amis*. I see Inspector Rose again, and then perhaps he will have news for us so that we can resume our holiday,' Auguste said optimistically. He did not believe it. But seven pairs of eyes fastened on him at this news, each with their separate thoughts.

Charles Dickens seemed to have stayed in a remarkable number of houses in Broadstairs, the Lionisers were beginning to feel, looking at their itinerary on Thursday morning. They seemed destined to study every single house exhaustively. It was perhaps only in the last ten years that Broadstairs had fully come to realise what treasure trove lay buried in its midst, and plaques began enthusiastically to sprout everywhere. Aged residents were suddenly objects of pilgrimage from such far-off places as America, and soon there were few people over sixty who did not have some hastily dusted-down anecdote, remembered, borrowed or adjusted, ready for eager visitors. The Lionisers somewhat mystified them, since they were perversely not content with the usual stories, but demanded to know dates, times and exact locations and had an annoying habit of checking these against vast volumes of Letters and Lives. Why books should know better than them was puzzling to Bradstonians, but they were anxious to please their visitors so did their best to comply.

The first call this Thursday morning was the very first house that Mr Dickens had rented on his very first never-to-be-forgotten visit to the village in 1837, No. 12 High Street. From this tiny house had flowed some at least of the immortal words that the world had come to know as *The Pickwick Papers*. Now thirty-five intrepid Lionisers were gazing at the outside of the small single-fronted cottage with its tiny parlour overlooking the street. The owner's wife looked nervously out at the throng from behind her lace curtains. 'Here,' began Samuel Pipkin loudly, 'Mr Dickens spent August and September 1837. Here he found inspiration—'

'And pears,' interjected Gwendolen, who had been reading her guide books. 'There's an old pear tree in the garden.'

'Thank you, Mrs Figgis-Hewett,' said Samuel crossly; he proceeded with his speech, only to be interrupted again by the owner's wife who hesitantly opened the door, a less than enthusiastic expression on her face. It was agreed that only ten people should tramp round the tiny cottage at a time; the remainder were forced to mingle with the morning shoppers and then to walk on to the old St Mary's Chapel, which once had held the shrine of Our Lady of Bradstow and to which passing ships would lower their sails in honour. But it had nothing to do with Mr Dickens, the Lionisers thought, impatient to be on their way.

202

Lord Beddington was gazing hopefully into Randalls, the bookmakers. True, Goodwood was over, but betting went on, thank goodness. The Charing Races were on this afternoon. He was debating between a horse called the Prince of Wales and an outsider called Pretty Polly. He decided on the latter, for once on impulse, not form. The Prince of Wales could hardly be said to be a good luck symbol at the moment.

'Who do you think killed Sir Thomas, Lord Beddington?' Angelina's voice made him jump and he forgot all about Pretty Polly, and all about his chances of sneaking away from the Canterbury trip tomorrow to see the second day of the Kent versus Australia match. Dickens was all very well, but cricket was better. Faced with such a direct question, and from Mrs Langham, he felt obliged to reply. He could not take refuge in a timely snooze.

'Plenty of people would like to have done,' he said, more forthcoming than she expected. 'Nothing against him myself,' he added hastily, 'but lots of rumours. Heard of the Barings Crisis?'

'Yes,' said Angelina doubtfully. It was a long time ago and her head had been full of balls and parties, not City uproars, when she was twenty-one.

'Nine years ago, nearly. Barings nearly went down for over twenty million. That would have punched a few holes in the City's sang-froid, I can tell you.' He contemplated this thought for a moment. 'The Government refused to intervene. Governor of the Bank of England stepped in. Organised a seven-million guarantee. Cracked the whip in the City. No banks to call in loans. Crisis averted, City settles down. Baring's now stronger than ever.'

'Thomas involved?' asked Angelina, inadvertently falling into his Mr Jingle-like speech.

'One bank refused to comply with the Bank of England

and threatened to call in its brokers' loans. Bank of England not pleased. Told him so. Changed his mind rapidly. Rumour has it Throgmorton's bank did same thing – didn't get found out. Did very nicely out of it, too.' He didn't add that he had too, and Throgmorton knew it.

'Do you think anyone here knew of that?'

'I did,' rumbled Beddington virtuously. 'My firm had one of the loans called in. It made me wary of Throgmorton – but it doesn't make me a murderer nine years later.'

'Oh, I didn't mean to imply—'

'Yes, you did.' A rare smile crossed his face. 'You should try Pipkin. Try saying diamonds to him. Australian diamonds.' He positively chuckled.

'You don't think, by any chance,' said Angelina, taking advantage of his obvious and inexplicable good humour, and noting the untraditional and definitely garish silk handkerchief in his pocket, 'that the poison was intended for you? Sir Thomas did not drink from your glass for any reason?'

Lord Beddington looked dumbfounded. 'Me? No one would want to murder *me*, madam.'

'There's no one who bears you a grudge?'

'Good heavens, no.' He was almost hurt. 'Except that young rascal of course. Can't remember his name. One of the waiters. Ah, called after a tree. Poplar. That's it. Came up before me on the bench once. Gave him a stiff sentence in a House of Correction to teach him better ways. I could tell he was a wrong 'un. Had a quick hand with the safe and an even quicker eye to the jewels. I had a notion we'd be hearing more of him. And, see, I was right!' he concluded triumphantly.

'But his being here is coincidence, surely? He had no reason to kill Sir Thomas, did he?'

'You tell me, my dear.' Glancing over his shoulder, he

disappeared quickly into the bookmakers'. Pipkin was advancing to summon the next party.

Indefatigably the Lionisers prowled their way along Albion Street and surged up the narrow Fort Road, but this time they stopped before they got to Fort House. Their prey this morning was Lawn House, lying just below it on the hillside. Here Dickens stayed for his holiday one year, baulked of being able to rent Fort House as he desired. 'A small villa between the hill and the cornfield,' quoted Samuel rapturously. He had almost forgotten his previous dislike of Dickens, carried away by the opportunities for rhetoric that the Great Man was so unexpectedly granting him.

The owner opened the door and almost closed it again. He was used to groups of two or three respectful Americans, not prides of culture-hungry Lionisers.

Gwendolen was clad in dark grey and was wearing the hat she had just purchased from the Iduns Brothers Bazaar. This was not her usual choice of milliner, but it possessed the only dark-coloured hat in Broadstairs apparently. She had decided not to attend the funeral, believing now that dignified restraint was her best role. She had become rather confused as to what had actually happened between Thomas and herself. She was, however, quite astute enough to realise the purport of all Oliver Michaels' carefully thought-out questions.

'You mean, could I have administered poison to Sir Thomas? The idea is absurd,' she announced loftily. 'And, moreover, highly objectionable. I loved him. Besides, when could I have done it?' she asked, more practically.

Oliver had his own ideas on this, which he could hardly put to Mrs Figgis-Hewett; they involved her dramatic appearance before the dinner began when he had worked out she could have added something to Sir Thomas's drink in the confusion.

'No, my dear young man,' she smiled, assuming she had won her point, 'if you seek a villain, look no further!' Her finger shot out; it pointed to Samuel Pipkin.

Samuel was moving determinedly into position before the last house of the morning, the private dwelling on the seafront where Mary Strong had chased away donkeys from the grassland in front of her cottage, thus inspiring Dickens to create Miss Betsy Trotwood in *David Copperfield*, though he tactfully set her residence in Dover.

'Donkeys, Janet,' Gwendolen trilled again, but the will to fight had left her, and she easily ceded place of honour to Samuel. He marched victorious into the parlour where David Copperfield himself had sat. And Charles Dickens too no doubt. It was notable that Samuel had made no mention of Thackeray for over forty-eight hours.

Angelina had worried how best to approach Mr Pipkin tactfully, but Oliver had no such social qualms.

'Diamonds,' he announced thoughtfully as Samuel emerged from the parlour into Nuckell's Place. Samuel jumped, distracted from his next address on the beauty of the old Assembly Rooms. But he was no easy target. He was not to be swayed from duty. An eye on Gwendolen, he ostentatiously produced his copy of *Our Watering Place* and began to read.

' "This is a bleak chamber in our watering place which is yet called the Assembly Rooms and understood to be available on hire for balls or concerts, and, some few seasons since, an ancient gentleman came down who said that he had danced there in bygone ages with the Honourable Miss Peepy, well known to have been the Beauty of her day and the cruel occasion of innumerable duels." Ah,' Samuel commented, eyes now anywhere but on Gwendolen 'how cruel is age, how poignantly Mr Dickens portrays it and how recognisable even today is Miss Peepy.' Polite cough.

'I am not a Miss Peepy,' shouted Gwendolen, more infuriated than wounded. Angelina hurried to her in concern, but she shook her arm off. 'I have been silent' (this was news to the Lionisers) 'but my lips shall be sealed no longer. Ask him about his diamond ventures in Australia and poor Thomas.'

Samuel turned red, then white. 'I have nothing to say,' he said and stomped off.

Gwendolen, thoroughly upset by the morning's events but mindful of her appointment for dinner that evening, decided to slip into Mr Horrell's, in order to purchase some of his advertised Special Skin Soap, In the doorway she met the subject of her dinner appointment himself. Lord Beddington, mindful of the same appointment, was rather optimistically emerging from the shop with a bottle of Lockyers Sulphur Hair-restorer, and six tablets of Amiral soap ('Removes Burden of Corpulency').

Auguste was singing an old song of Provence as he worked, then changed countries and song to 'My Love is Like a Red, Red Rose'. Araminta was in his mind. He was content. He had spent much time on the pier with William and Joe and had returned to find his pupils assembled, eager to learn for once. They had all been hard at work ever since. He was cooking; murder was, for the moment at any rate, not in his thoughts, the sun was at last shining in the way it should do on a seaside holiday, and there were still three more days of holiday to go. Three days of Araminta. Moreover, to complete his joy, William and Joe, as if taking pity on him, had produced some delicious Dover sole and some more delicious John Dory with the promise of other delights to come. Perhaps for tomorrow he would prepare a true *aioli de morue*. No, he would not. Why should they eat salt fish, when William and Joe commanded the seas? Yesterday he had taught the class about the wonders of John

Dory. Today they would enjoy a *Saint Pierre au gratin* for luncheon with a true *salade niçoise*. Tonight the sole. What should—

He never came to a conclusion for Angelina and Oliver came at just the wrong moment, just as the fish required the hand of the maître. Once again, he left the pupils to superintend the luncheon and departed into the small parlour to hear their story. Really, detective work was all very well, but not when it interfered with *cuisine*.

'So you see, Mr Pipkin did have a real motive,' said Angelina excitedly. 'Lord Beddington explained that five or six years ago the Australian banking organisation broke down altogether and nobody stepped in to save it. Many people were ruined. Mr Pipkin had been advised to put his money into diamond mining and it was handled through this Australian bank. He lost nearly all his money. His adviser had been Thomas Throgmorton. Beddington thinks Pipkin thinks,' concluded Angelina confusedly, 'that Sir Thomas did it on purpose because he disliked Pipkin.'

'But when could Mr Pipkin have given the poison to Sir Thomas?' asked Auguste reasonably. 'He was at the far end of the table; he had no opportunity.'

'He could have done it beforehand when we met for drinks and everyone's attention was on Mrs Figgis-Hewett,' said Angelina, albeit with a feeling of disloyalty to a fellow female.

'This is possible,' admitted Auguste, 'but doubtful. And does it not make the time problem even worse? Sir Thomas drank a lot of coffee, and as this is often given as an enema in atropine poisoning cases, it might have led to his being sick, perhaps even delayed the onset of symptoms. Yet I feel it is unlikely to have delayed it so long.'

'So you don't give us full marks, Mr Didier.' Oliver was disappointed.

'You carry out excellent research,' said Auguste

208

diplomatically. 'But now it is for me, the analyst, to take over. We must sort out these ingredients and consider their relevance to the final dish.'

He puzzled about it when they had left. Two things occurred to him: firstly, that they were extremely anxious to divert attention away from Mrs Langham, which was natural enough. The second was the stirrings of a memory in his mind.

He returned thoughtfully to the *Saint Pierre au gratin*, only to discover that matters had not progressed well in his absence. He passed Sid and Algernon on the stairs having a heated argument, which stopped abruptly as he appeared. Alfred was nowhere to be seen, Emily and Heinrich were bickering over the mayonnaise, and James Pegg and Alice were silently working together on a salad.

At luncheon there was an odd restlessness among his pupils, which Auguste attributed to excitement at seeing what a true *salade niçoise* should taste like. Alice explained the real reason: 'We're all going bathing, Mr Didier. Why don't you come? Miss Multhrop will be there,' she teased.

Yes, why didn't he?

'That would be most pleasant,' he said, gratified. 'I have to visit Inspector Rose at three-thirty, but there is time to bathe as well.'

As if in anticipation of the coming treat, relations had thawed between the pupils. Alice now sat next to Alfred, Heinrich next to Emily, Algernon was chatting to Sid. Only James remained as abstracted as he had all day yesterday. In the evening Auguste had found him wandering around on his own. Auguste glanced at him curiously. Perhaps it was love of Araminta or perhaps, glancing at Alfred, it was pique that his lordship had reverted to Alice. Perhaps James still secretly adored Alice?

There was a scramble to finish luncheon, and due regard was not paid in Auguste's view to the seriousness of the John

209

Dory as a fish. The usual critique was reserved for the evening, in view of the common abstraction. Coffee was taken amid a rush to wash up the dishes, and at last, at two o'clock, they were free.

'It's too nice an afternoon to spend inside listening to a lecture,' announced a Lioniser suddenly.

Mr Multhrop groaned. 'No, no, the sun will hurt your complexion, dear madam. It is bad to take too much sun.' He had a splendid tea arranged and could see his profits disappearing yet further.

But it was too late. The idea had borne fruit. Yesterday had been the group's first taste of real sunshine and comparative warmth and it had fired their enthusiasm. There was a sudden rebellion – or, rather, a retreat. Faced with a lecture on 'Dickens's Use of Language in *Hard Times*' or the delights of the Broadstairs sands, the Lionisers did not hesitate. They were going to break out of their self-imposed cage. Bathing, which before leaving London had been deemed suitable only for the lower classes, suddenly seemed a most adventurous and desirable way of spending an afternoon. Bathing dresses had been surreptitiously acquired, those provided in the machines, Araminta had assured them, being definitely not suitable for ladies and gentlemen of their status. Being now the proud possessors of these shocking and daring items, they were determined to try them out.

'After all, bathing is a Dickensian-approved activity,' pointed out one person, anxious to appease her conscience. 'He did write to that American professor that Boz "disappears and presently emerges from a bathing machine, and may be seen – a kind of salmon-coloured porpoise – splashing about in the ocean".'

'He bathed naked as was the custom, madam, for both men and women,' pointed out Oliver wickedly and

210

grandly. 'We must do the same, to be true to the Master.'

'Oh!' cried the good lady, shocked, flustered and titillated.

'He doesn't mean it,' soothed Angelina.

'Don't I?' muttered Oliver, seizing her hand.

The attendant of the bathing machines was overwhelmed by the sudden rush for service as first the Lionisers' committee, then Auguste Didier and his retinue arrived, with the rest of the Lionisers in hot pursuit. The latter were forced to repair to the waiting area where they enviously sipped ginger beer while waiting their turn and watching the old horses pull the machines into the water, one after another.

Auguste and Sid had made the mistake of sharing a machine. Since the machine began to move towards the water as soon as they were inside, changing in its damp, smelly and restricted confines was none too easy, despite the lure of their newly acquired bathing costumes. Auguste wondered if his blue one-piece button-to-neck stockinette costume were not too daring with its knee-length shorts and short sleeves. What would happen when this material got wet? He was rather glad that Araminta would be some way removed from him, and reflected that cold water might be no bad thing. Sid had chosen plain black drawers, constructed from his granny's old skirt.

One by one, the men descended, Heinrich in demure body-concealing maroon jersey, Alfred in rakish red and white striped drawers with plain red jersey top, James in black stockinette, and Algernon in garish green stripes. Oliver was dashing in blue serge, Samuel Pipkin pumpkin-like in large enveloping flannel; Lord Beddington rivalled Sid in black drawers, though it is doubtful whether they were made from his grandmother's skirt.

The men's eyes automatically swivelled left to the women's section at a tasteful thirty yards' distance. Heinrich felt possessively protective as he recognised Emily's head in a mob cap, the rest of her splashing up and down in grey serge

211

knickers, tunic and blouse and black stockings. Alice, more sporty, boasted navy blue knickerbockers and striped jersey, without stockings, and serviceable yellow jaconet bathing cap.

'They're looking at us!' screamed Emily, promptly disappearing from view underwater; Alice waved to Alfred and promptly followed her example, as a scream came from behind. Gwendolen Figgis-Hewett had stepped out of her machine into three feet of water. All eyes were on her in a bright red cretonne two-piece and Normandy satin hat with wide frill. Gwendolen did like to be beside the seaside. She jumped up and down experimentally in the briny, took a step further full of confidence, then further and further still. Forgetting all about her need to keep one foot on the ground and splashing wildly, she announced she was swimming, and then shrieked. She was out of her depth.

'Help!' Her hand was thrust up.

Gentlemen dithered. Was it a greater crime to let her drown or to cross the great divide to the women's section to rescue her? Fortunately they were not called upon for the supreme test, however, for Alice scooped her up from behind and tried to propel her into safer water. It was not easy for Gwendolen seemed hysterical and determined to avoid arrest. Emily, swimming vigorously, came to assist her, and together they managed to reach shallow water, where Gwendolen promptly denied she had been in danger. The men resumed their bobbing about.

'Angelina!' shouted Oliver as he caught sight of her trim figure clad in pink cotton. She did not hear him and vigorously continued splashing. The sea was a mass of foam with so many bodies stirring it up, and some of the men ventured further out to try their skills at swimming. Of them, only Alfred, Auguste and James were adept. The rest bobbed up and down at chin height, or remained by the bathing-machine steps.

Auguste found himself caught up in the general excitement

and cursed his heavy waterlogged costume. In his childhood swimming at Cannes there had been no need for these ridiculous costumes. There was no great excitement about swimming either. One swam because one had to. But then there were no Aramintas at Cannes. She was a vision of loveliness with her curls peeping out from her mob cap — and oh, those beautiful arms emerging from the short sleeves of her blouse. He wondered what would happen if he swam to her underwater and surprised her, and decided he would probably be imprisoned by Naseby for rape.

He was the first to emerge from the water, partly because he had an appointment with Rose, partly because he could see Araminta leaving. True, he had told James Pegg he would be available to discuss a problem with him after bathing, but now that must wait until he had seen Rose. He had certainly not drawn James's attention to Araminta's departure — or his own.

Hastily he dried himself on the thin towel and clambered into clothes that stuck to every inch of his damp body. Pulling on his socks and shoes, he opened the door to realise that, since Sid was still in the water, so was the bathing machine. He had three feet of shallow water to cross — and there was Araminta floating across the sands. Hastily he whipped off shoes and socks and prepared to paddle.

'You're too early, Auguste,' Rose said sourly. It was all too clear Auguste had been out enjoying the pleasures of Broadstairs, one of which was just disappearing up the main staircase, folding up her parasol. 'Twitch hasn't heard from the Factory yet.'

'About what, *mon ami*?'

Rose told him. 'Grooms,' he said. 'Amazing. James Pegg. But I still don't see *how* he could have done it.'

Auguste looked unhappy. One of *his* pupils? It reflected

on his honour. He could not, would not believe it. *'Mon ami*, I have an idea,' he announced.

Three minutes later they were in the still-locked room lately occupied by Sir Thomas Throgmorton. Auguste marched to the bathroom. 'In here,' he said. 'I think – yes.' His memory had not played him false. There it was in the cabinet amid the long row of bottles.

'Grinrod's Remedy for Spasms,' said Rose. 'You think he took some? How does that help us?'

'Because this remedy, Egbert, contains *morphine.*'

'So?'

'Your analyst's report about atropine stated that morphine is sometimes a treatment. Suppose he took it thinking that his malaise stemmed from his gastric trouble? What with the coffee, it would help to slow down the symptoms even further. He was drinking a great deal, he felt ill – pain, burning, hoarseness. But the full force of the poison was staved off for a while. Atropine affects different people in different ways, if you recall. This would make it possible that the poison *was* administered earlier in the meal. The soup, the salad even.'

Rose considered. 'It's *possible*. I'll say that. So our thesis is he was Throgmorton's groom. Runs off with the money, comes back to this country thinking he's safe after ten years, changes his name perhaps, then you announce *he'll* be waiting on Sir Thomas down here. Daren't risk being seen and so he makes his plans. Yes, as soon as I hear from the Factory, we'd better have a word with Mr James Pegg.'

Sergeant Stitch came marching into the bathroom, to find Egbert Rose. He did not for the moment notice Auguste. When he did, his cup of woe was full. Naseby would have sympathised.

The rest of the revellers emerged dripping from the brine. Their clothes felt damp, corsets defied fastening by chilling

214

fingers, socks and stockings were recalcitrant, the bathing attendant was shouting impatiently. One by one they emerged down the steps onto the sands, glowing. They had bathed. They were ready to enjoy the fruits of victory, and to listen to Uncle Mack's Broadstairs Minstrels.

One bathing machine, however, had remained in the water. So had its occupant.

Chapter Ten

Picking his way around the fishing nets, Auguste leant over the rail of the pier towards his native France as if by so doing he could distance himself a little from yesterday's tragedy. There was no escaping the fact that, short of being kidnapped, James Pegg had tragically drowned. It still seemed impossible to believe that he would not once more come marching into the kitchens in Lord Wittisham's wake.

Auguste was conscious that he had manufactured an excuse to come down to the pier early this Friday morning in order to get away from the sombre atmosphere in Blue Horizons. Even fish failed to hold allure for him this morning and he was almost relieved to find that William and Joe were for once not at their usual station at the end of the pier. He gazed out across the sea, and went over yesterday's events once more. The tide had been going out, which made accident more likely, and indeed how could anyone have murdered Pegg so publicly? Yet reason told him that where murder had so recently occurred, accident would be a strange coincidence.

Rose had been accompanied by Naseby on his visit to Blue Horizons yesterday evening; Naseby had scarcely concealed his glee as regards the effects of the ramifications of James Pegg's disappearance on Auguste. 'Bad business,' he'd said to Rose, rubbing his hands briskly. 'Bad for our friend.'

He would have been surprised to know with what feeling Auguste shared that view. He blamed himself bitterly for not having waited for Pegg at the bathing machines. By then he might already have been dead of course, but there was no way of knowing. Auguste felt responsible since Pegg was one of his flock. And suppose it were murder? Once again he would be a suspect. Suppose someone had held James's head underwater until he drowned? But surely only an excellent swimmer could have done that? With sinking heart, Auguste realised that he was one of the few strong swimmers there.

Rose's lean body had reclined, deceptively relaxed, in the shabby armchair at Blue Horizons. 'Any of you recall him talking about going anywhere? Any of you near him in the water?' he threw out casually, sipping a cup of Auguste's camomile tea. First time he'd ever drunk it, although Auguste was keen enough to hand it out at times of crisis. He wouldn't be repeating the experience.

'No, and we were in the women's section,' pointed out Emily, setting clear demarcation lines. 'Me and Alice,' to get it entirely straight.

Rose smiled at her. 'Thank you, Miss Dawson. Did you notice Mr Pegg at all?'

Two vigorous shakes of the head from Emily and Alice.

'Mr Didier?'

'He could swim well,' said Auguste, rushing to get his ordeal over. 'He was swimming next to me out into the deeper water.'

'You didn't see him getting into difficulties, calling at all.' It was a statement, not a question.

'No. There was a lot happening. People were splashing and shouting. There was much noise,' he explained unhappily, as though this carefree behaviour were in some way disrespectful to the dead.

'Anyone know if he has family? I'll need his home address.'

'I will give it to you, Inspector.' Alfred stirred feebly from his dejection. 'He has a father,' he managed to say. 'Also a sister. He – he spoke to me of them.' Alice held his hand comfortingly.

'We'll need them here for the inquest – that's when we find the body, of course.'

'Inquest?' queried Heinrich with foreboding. 'But he has probably drowned.'

'Sudden death. There has to be an inquest in this country,' said Rose briskly, 'to decide whether it's accident, suicide – or murder. Just like there was on Sir Thomas.'

Everyone glanced quickly round at his neighbours, but there seemed little surprise at the introduction of the word murder.

'You don't think,' said Emily, a hopeful note in her tone, 'that he could have killed himself?'

'Had he reason to?'

'He didn't like me,' said Alice rather plaintively, 'or, rather, he didn't like me being friendly with Alfred, but I don't think he'd kill himself over it. Why should he?'

'He was very quiet recently. He obviously had something on his mind,' said Algernon offhandedly.

'Did he talk to any of you about any problems he might have had? Personal ones?'

'Only those to do with cooking,' said Emily helpfully. 'And I don't think he'd kill himself over a soufflé. He wasn't as dedicated as Mr Didier.'

Rose caught Auguste's eyes and looked hastily away. Odd how in the middle of something as serious as a death investigation, it was easier, not harder, to laugh. Some kind of antidote perhaps.

'I looked in his room,' Alfred was saying. 'There wasn't any last letter to me, or anyone else. But I know he wouldn't go without saying goodbye.'

'I think you'll find he's been murdered all right,' Algernon stated.

219

'How could anyone murder him?' asked Emily stoutly. 'He was a big man. If Heinrich had tried to kill him, he could have easily resisted. No, he's just decided to go off somewhere.'

'Emily, I cannot swim,' Heinrich reminded her sharply.

Auguste smiled to himself. Emily was about as much help as Araminta in a crisis.

'Who swam out with him besides Mr Didier?' enquired Rose.

'Mr Michaels came a little way out, I think,' said Auguste.

'Alfred, you swam out,' Algernon reminded him helpfully.

'I may have done,' he muttered, 'but I didn't see James. I wish I had. The — um — ladies were shouting.' His face was consumed with renewed unhappiness.

'No use looking at me, Inspector, I wuz 'anging on to the machine. Keep yer feet on the ground. That's the best way to swim,' offered Sid virtuously.

'Where were you, Mr Peckham?' asked Rose, not losing sight of the fact that helpful as he was about others, he was somewhat circumspect about his own movements.

'I can't remember,' Algernon responded. 'But look at me. Is it likely I could have drowned James Pegg?' They appraised his slight figure and remembered James's. It was unlikely in the extreme. Algernon looked triumphant. 'No, Inspector, old Pegg's just slipped off to watch cricket. Couldn't stand any more fish.'

Auguste Didier fixed him with a baleful eye. Algernon ignored it.

'Pegg?' Samuel Pipkin was asking one hour later, after Rose and Auguste had walked slowly to the Imperial, averting their eyes from the gleaming dark ocean.

'One of the waiters here last Saturday, sir,' replied Rose. 'A large stocky man, about thirty. Dark.'

'I don't notice waiters,' said Samuel.

'I remember him,' said Gwendolen suddenly. 'He was the young man served us the entrée. I remember his hands. Big strong hands.' There was a wistful note in her voice. The late Mr Figgis-Hewett had not been conspicuous for physique.

'Do any of you remember seeing him in the water? He was a good swimmer, I believe. Mr Didier informs me, for instance, that you swam a little way, Mr Michaels.'

'Do you?' enquired Oliver of Auguste with interest. 'If you say so, then no doubt I did. I was aware there were several of us, but I really did not have my mind—' He stopped. He could hardly say that he was too intent on trying to catch a glimpse of Angelina even if it was only her eye. This poor fellow Pegg was dead, after all. 'Inspector, I suppose he couldn't have been your murderer, could he? Perhaps he took this way out?'

'Technically it's possible, Mr Michaels. He might have managed to slip something in the entrée, but for the life of me I can't see how. Yet it's an odd way to commit suicide in the middle of a group of people. He left no note either and that's not usual.'

'Perhaps he couldn't write,' said Gwendolen brightly. She had been reading too many Dickens novels, thought Rose. Hadn't she heard of Forster's Education Act?

'I saw him,' rumbled Lord Beddington unexpectedly. 'I was standing in the water by the machines and saw this big chap swim out.' He remembered the moment vividly. Those damned drawers of his were waterlogged, and he couldn't move anywhere.

'Anything more?'

'Lost sight of him. Mrs Figgis-Hewett screamed and we all turned towards the sound. Remember thinking he might have gone to help her.'

'Did he, Mrs Figgis-Hewett?'

'No,' she said, outraged. 'He was a *man*. Anyway, I didn't need help, as I told the young person who seized hold of me.'

'Mr Pipkin, did you see anything?'

'No,' he replied shortly. 'I remained in the shallows.' He could hardly add that he had been thinking about Dickens and his glorious passages in *David Copperfield* of the East Anglian coast and Mr Peggotty.

'This,' said Rose as they had left the Lioniser, 'doesn't look good for your pupils, Auguste.'

'It could be one of the Lionisers,' said Auguste desperately. 'Perhaps James was blackmailing one of them, over knowledge of the murder of Sir Thomas.'

'Unlikely. Especially as the Lionisers' last safe chance of murder would have been at the drinks gathering beforehand. Pegg was not present then.'

'But he may have known *something*,' insisted Auguste, unwilling to face the fact that one of his group could have slaughtered a colleague.

'It's possible, yes. We'll go over his room in the morning,' Rose conceded. 'You've locked it?'

Auguste nodded. 'It may not be blackmail,' he offered suddenly. 'I don't see him as a blackmailer. Perhaps he saw or knew something he did not understand, and wished to seek an explanation before he came to us. That seems more like James.'

'Never mind the character, stick to the alleybi,' quoted Rose suddenly. 'There, that's your Dickens for you. *The Pickwick Papers*. Pickwick didn't have a corpse on his hands though,' he added morosely.

'Neither do we – yet,' Auguste pointed out. 'At least,' he amended, thinking of Sir Thomas, 'we don't have James Pegg's body.'

At this moment Araminta whisked across the foyer. With a jolt, Auguste realised that not only had she been present but that, even worse, she might well not yet have heard of the tragedy. He hurried to her, concerned.

'Araminta, you have heard the news of your friend Mr Pegg?' He held her hands.

'Mr Pegg?' She looked bewildered and gently he explained.

'Oh dear,' she said inadequately. 'I don't think I can help you,' she added doubtfully, extending her full charm on Rose who was hovering behind Auguste.

'You saw nothing of him while he was in the water?'

'I was with the other ladies,' she pointed out.

'And your eyes did not stray towards the gentlemen?' asked Auguste a little wistfully.

'No. Why should they?' she enquired. Then: 'Oh, poor Mr Pegg.' She hesitated. 'It might have been a cow that trampled him.'

They stared at her blankly.

'People often take their animals down there to bathe. Horses and cattle. Even elephants from the circus. But now I remember,' she smiled her lovely smile – 'the Pier and Harbour Commission have forbidden it after one o'clock. Papa told me so. So that's all right, isn't t?' She seemed somewhat anxious on this point. 'There, I've solved your case.'

Such was her charm that Auguste fervently thanked her. Happy that she had been of assistance, she passed on her way like Robert Browning's Pippa. It was only when he saw Rose's wry smile that it dawned on Auguste that she had said not a word about Pegg and her relationship to him. Fleetingly he wondered if anyone could be that artless, but he pushed the uncharitable thought away.

'What authority do you have,' snarled Naseby, 'for allowing a principal suspect to be present?'

'Mine,' said Rose wearily, no stomach for the fight. 'Have a word with the Commissioner if you wish.'

Auguste was paying no attention to Naseby. As he had

223

returned from the pier, his attention had been drawn to the small group on the sands. He recognised Egbert and he knew there could be only one reason for his presence. Unwillingly, legs like lead, he went to join him. Now at his feet was the body of James Pegg, wearing only half of his bathing costume, one shoe missing, skin wrinkled and pale. Auguste felt momentarily sick, then an overwhelming emotion. What an end to hopes, to a life. No more would James Pegg cook delicious venison, or pheasants. No more game pies. Auguste had never felt *close* to Pegg, but that was immaterial. He was dead, and pointlessly dead – unless of course he was Sir Thomas's murderer. Yet somehow, looking at the lifeless body, Auguste could not believe it.

'Broadstairs won't like this,' the doctor announced after the body had been borne away for post-mortem. 'Not on their sands. Good job it happened early.'

'Pegg would be pleased not to have caused too much of a disturbance,' said Rose sarcastically.

The doctor glanced at him. 'Job getting on top of you, is it?' he remarked kindly.

'He could be right,' Rose commented to Auguste after doctor, body and Naseby had departed for police headquarters. 'There's something even nastier about murder when everyone else is enjoying themselves in the sun. First, it doesn't seem real, and then when it does, the sun makes it all the worse.'

'If James was the killer of Sir Thomas—'

'You know as well as I do he wasn't, Auguste. And this wasn't an accident either.'

'But how could it be murder? It would require two people at least to hold him down and that would be noticed.'

Rose disliked modern forms of communication, but telegrams were hardly the most expressive means of obtaining information. He failed to reach Miss Throgmorton

224

by telephone on Wednesday or Thursday; now the funeral was over, surely she would be at home. Clearing his throat, he once again took off the telephone receiver in Multhrop's office and Beatrice Throgmorton's voice came over stridently.

'Your father had a groom,' yelled Rose — it was a long way to Buckinghamshire.

'He had many grooms,' replied Beatrice. 'I hear you quite well, Inspector.' Her own voice was nearly as loud as his.

'About ten years ago. One who stole money in bonds from your father.'

A pause. 'I think I recall the matter.'

'Could it have been James Pegg?'

A long pause. 'Who?'

Rose groaned. 'James Pegg,' he yelled louder.

'I do not recall the name, but—'

'Lord Wittisham's friend. Tall, thirtyish, dark, stockily built, squarish face and rather close-set eyes.'

She cast her mind back. 'It could have been, Inspector. I cannot remember. I do recall the man was dark and tall, or so he seemed to a ten-year-old girl. I regret I do not keep a photographic record of grooms.'

'But it could have been him?'

'Oh yes, Inspector, it could have been.'

'It could have been,' repeated Rose disgustedly to Auguste as he hung up the receiver with relief. 'We'll have to go on working on it. You're very quiet,' he said, glaring at him.

'I have to tell you something, Egbert, that has been uncomfortably on my mind. I left the bathing earlier than the others, to see you. I left with — ' he hesitated — 'Miss Multhrop. I had announced my intention beforehand and James said he would accompany me. I assumed he wished to speak to *me* not you. I think now I was wrong and that it was you he wished to give some information to. I did not tell him when I left, however, because — ' he plunged —

225

'because I thought he was jealous of the partiality Miss Araminta showed me.'

Jealous? It was clear to him now that Pegg had information about the murder. Why, oh why did he not see that earlier?

'I think he was probably dead by then, Auguste. It would have made no difference,' Rose said comfortingly. 'The interesting thing to me is why our friend Wittisham didn't notice his absence.'

Gratefully, Auguste seized this stick of comfort, but all the same he continued to blame himself as he walked back to Blue Horizons. Perhaps things would look clearer in the morning.

Sergeant Stitch descended to a more leisurely breakfast than his duties at Scotland Yard allowed for, unaware of the developments he was missing on the sands. Having consumed a large dish of kedgeree and several muffins, he repaired, mortified, to Mr Multhrop's office to contact the Factory. There he caught Multhrop skulking pathetically in his old domain. Stitch eyed him sternly.

'The Yard's requisitioned this office,' he pointed out unnecessarily. 'Official business.' His tones suggested it was now as sacrosanct as any embassy on foreign soil.

'Just looking for some papers, Inspector,' stuttered Mr Multhrop.

Stitch looked on him more kindly as he ushered him out. When Rose and Auguste entered the office fifteen minutes later, he looked almost human.

'I've spoken to the Factory, sir. I regret our theory is invalid.'

Rose raised his eyebrows at the 'our'. Twitch did not notice. 'The chap who stole Sir Thomas's bonds is dead. Died in France three years ago.'

Rose grunted. It had fitted so well. Too well, perhaps.

A pity, but at least they knew where they were.

Auguste's first reaction was pleasure. He could not see Pegg as a thief. It was a vindication of his school. The school already possessed one pupil with criminal tendencies, Algernon Peckham; another would have thrown serious doubts on Auguste's judgement of character.

'He *must* have known something about Sir Thomas's death,' said Rose almost angrily. 'That's why he wanted to walk back here with you. Why couldn't the fool have told you earlier?'

'He was very quiet yesterday at luncheon, almost listless as we went to the beach. He did not give the impression of one who wanted to get something off his chest,' said Auguste defensively. 'He said he thought the water would be good for him.'

'Poor devil,' said Rose with feeling. 'He was wrong.'

'So now we must return to our muttons. Hunting Mr Datchery,' said Auguste without enthusiasm.

'If this Datchery is so good at solving mysteries,' said Rose sourly, 'he can come along as soon as he likes.'

Canterbury had been selected for a day visit for the Lionisers on several counts, the chief of which was that it was a pity to miss it, especially since many accompanying male spouses were aware that today was the second day of the cricket match between Kent and the Australians. Plans were made accordingly. The male Lionisers soothed their nagging consciences by reminding themselves that cricket could be classed as a Dickensian occupation in view of the Dingley Dell Cricket Club match against All-Muggleton.

Other parts of Kent, notably Gravesend and Chatham, had more claim to Dickensian associations than did Canterbury, but sufficient of a case could be made to satisfy the more demanding of the Lionisers. In fact the one matter Sir Thomas and Samuel Pipkin did agree about was the

227

importance of cricket, and it was noticeable that a sizeable amount of free time had been built into the programme: 'An afternoon free to wander at will and absorb the delightful atmosphere of Dickens's Canterbury.'

'Perhaps,' breathed Gwendolen, tucking her arm firmly into Angelina's, like the Duchess into Alice's, as she stumbled over the cobbles, 'poor Mr Pegg was Mr Datchery.'

'What makes you say that, Mrs Figgis-Hewett?' asked Oliver sharply.

'Someone was,' she pointed out, 'or darling Thomas would not have claimed to have seen him.'

'Mr Pegg was hardly old enough to play the part. Datchery had a white beard,' said Angelina jokingly.

'My dear,' Gwendolen looked at her pityingly, as one of the cognoscenti to a philistine, 'Mr Datchery was in disguise. Of course,' she breathed, since this failed to have effect, 'perhaps I shall be the next.'

'Whatever do you mean?' asked Angelina, startled.

'If that Mr Pegg was murdered,' she replied shrilly, 'it was for something he knew. He was a witness. Like myself.' She put her finger to her lips. 'My lips are sealed.'

Samuel Pipkin brushed past them quickly with barely an apology.

'To the murder?' asked Oliver slowly. 'Have you told Inspector Rose what you know?'

'Oh, I don't mean I actually *saw* it, Mr Michaels, but he did tell me about Datchery. And that makes me vulnerable.' Her eyes pleaded with him to agree.

Samuel was out of earshot.

In fact he was having a somewhat difficult task as leader of the group. Only *David Copperfield* of Charles Dickens's novels could claim real connections with Canterbury, and as the residences described in it were less than precise, identification had proved difficult. Samuel had the happy thought, however, that the Cathedral at least was unassailable. Some Lionisers, unfortunately for him, hotly disagreed that its place in Dickensian literature merited a visit to it. Protagonists of the visit pointed out that Dickens had personally taken a group of American friends there on a summer's day in June 1869, and moreover David Copperfield dutifully worshipped there. Dissenting voices pointed out that, though this was true, Dickens himself had been greatly disappointed by his visit, considering the standard of the service slipshod. A visit could therefore well be omitted from today's itinerary in favour of all the inns being visited. The Ayes won.

Mr Wickfield's residence and Uriah Heep's dwelling were then sought in vain, though without acrimony, there being no great evidence one way or the other, though there was a body of opinion convinced that Mr Wickfield's residence was to be found in St Dunstan's Street. Fruitlessly they trudged up and down seeking 'a very old house bulging out over the road', and a small detachment of Lionisers rushed into the Diocesan Registry, accusing that office of having harboured the gentleman. When it came to Dr Strong's house, hostilities flared openly. One party was for setting off to Lady Wootton Green, but the opposition, their eyes on luncheon, firmly rejected the idea. Lord Beddington displayed an erudition which astonished even himself, quoting Dickens's manager's story of how Dickens himself had distinctly hedged when asked by his American friends where Dr Strong's house might be. 'It's my belief,' analysed Beddington, with all the weight of the judiciary, 'that the fellow didn't know. He'd made it up.'

A shriek at this heresy from Gwendolen, but the majority of Lionisers decided to abandon the chore and indulge in a visit to the old Sun Inn where Mr Micawber had lodged, and then progress to luncheon at the Royal Fountain Hotel where Mr Dick had slept every other Wednesday, and where the great Mr Dickens himself had laid his head. Honour was thus satisfied, as well as the stomach.

'Personally,' said Samuel Pipkin, ruminating after his third glass of claret punch, 'I think the fellow was drunk.'

'Mr Dickens?' asked a Lioniser, shocked to the core.

'No, no, no,' replied Samuel testily. 'That fellow who was drowned yesterday. He was reeling around. Nearly fell down the steps of the bathing machine. I caught him by the arm just in time. Goodness knows what that Froggie cook puts in his food.' Having delivered this speech, he clearly considered himself absolved from the matter of Mr Pegg's death.

Tactfully Auguste suggested that this afternoon his five remaining pupils should visit Margate. To stay and regard the sands where one of their number had met his end was hardly going to raise their spirits. The bathing attendant indeed seemed to be doing remarkably little business. Perhaps a visit to Margate by train would take their minds off yesterday, and Auguste forced himself to accompany them, feeling he might yet pick up some snippet of information — he hesitated to say clue — to the unhappy events of the last few days.

On the way there the group was quiet. Alfred said not a word and one by one the others too fell silent. Perhaps he had been wrong after all to persuade them to come out. It was only yesterday that James had been one of them, and now he was gone, murdered. How unbelievable it seemed. Surely it would be too big a risk in front of everyone. Perhaps no, however. Did someone pretend to play a joke holding his head under? No, it would have to be someone stronger than he was to hold him down long enough. Someone strong, someone like Heinrich Freimüller. He claimed not to be able to swim though, and assuming that the two crimes were linked, what possible reason would Heinrich have to kill Sir Thomas?

They came out of the railway station and the vista of Margate Bay was before them. As far as the eye could see, there were holidaymakers; it was Broadstairs ten times enlarged. They set off down the slope to the seafront with mixed feelings, and were swallowed up in the crowd. They looked at the remains of the shell grottos on the sands laid by the children over two weeks ago in honour of St James de Compostella, though the reason for the old tradition had been lost in the mists of time. They listened for a few minutes to Uncle Bones and his Minstrels, and some discussion then ensued as to whether Uncle Bones' or Uncle Mack's rendering of 'The Miner's Dream of Home' was superior, but it remained desultory. As a way of both discovering evidence and cheering the spirits of the innocent, the afternoon looked like being a dismal failure. James Pegg may have been a shadowy figure in his life; in his death he dominated.

At three they attended the Variety Show at Lord George Sanger's Grand Hall by the Sea. This was more of a success: Emily liked the performing monkeys, Alfred took to the acrobatic dancers; Alice laughed at the comedy sketches and Algernon pronounced the songs 'capital'. Alice was particularly taken by a duet 'I Love Thee'. Heinrich liked the band. Sid liked the toffee apples. Companionable again, they strolled off in ones and twos to see the menagerie.

'Emily, you are very quiet this afternoon.' Heinrich handed her a 4½d bottle of Eiffel Tower lemonade.

'Am I, Heinrich?' she asked in an artificial voice, paying great attention to her straw. 'I suppose we are all rather subdued. Poor Mr Pegg.'

'But you did not like him, did you, Emily?'

'I don't know why you say that, Heinrich,' she retorted quickly. 'I had little to do with him. Why, I hardly spoke to him after we got down here. But you seemed quite chummy with him. I saw you talking to him only yesterday morning.'

'You are mistaken, Emily,' he said gravely.

They fell uneasily silent and walked slightly further apart as they passed Lord George's big cats. Not for the first time, Heinrich thought that Emily's face was a little feline. His worries grew.

'Alfred, I really am sorry about poor Mr Pegg. He and I didn't always agree, but I know how much you will miss him.'

'Alice,' said Alfred, relieved that at last he could talk. Life stretched bleakly ahead, without relief. He and James were going to do such jolly things. They were going to open a restaurant together; with his name and James's cooking — my word, it would have been a jolly place. A club for those who liked good food. And now he was left alone again. First Beatrice had gone, though he was coming to think that that might be no bad thing, and now suddenly James was gone. What was he going to do? He needed someone, or he was liable to do the most stupid things. He looked at Alice feeding the monkeys. 'I suppose,' he went on awkwardly, 'you wouldn't feel like being my partner, would you?'

'Oh, Alfred, yes of course I would.' Alice threw herself into his arms. 'I'd been hoping you'd ask me.'

He blinked. He hadn't had a lot of time since yesterday. 'It won't be easy,' he told her. 'You don't have James's hand with meat, and although your fish cookery is better, I can do the—'

'Alfred,' she said in alarm, 'what are you talking about?'

He looked at her in surprise. 'The restaurant, of course. The one James and I were going to run.'

'Oh,' she said, deflated. 'I thought you wanted to marry me.'

Alfred stared. He had a one-track mind. Why not settle both things at the same time, after all? 'Of course,' he said speedily. 'I thought you knew that. But we'd better get the restaurant settled too.'

Alice kissed him gravely. 'Yes, Alfred, of course I will.'

Alfred kissed her with mounting enthusiasm, dismissing from his mind altogether the thought of what poor James's reaction would have been.

Sid was having an animated, less romantic, chat with Algernon. 'What were you on about with Pegg that morning?'

'The weather,' said Algernon, leering.

'Come orf it. Bloke's done in—'

'What do you mean done in? It was an accident,' said Algernon in alarm.

'Nah,' said Sid with scorn. 'Leastways, funny sort of accident.'

'Nothing to do with me, anyway.'

'You can swim,' Sid pointed out. 'Whatever yer say, I saw yer out there.' Belatedly he realised it was hardly in his own best interests to reveal his knowledge. If Peckham had removed first Sir Thomas from the scene and then James Pegg, he wouldn't have any qualms about removing Sid. Sid began to inch away, shortly vanishing round the back of the monkey cages. Auguste's company suddenly seemed very desirable.

'I'll tell Inspector Rose what you say, Sid,' Auguste offered. 'You are sure it was he? He claims not to swim well.'

'It was 'im orl right,' said Sid. 'Know 'im anywhere, even in that green striped bathing costume.' Auguste grinned. 'Not that you *know* 'im, if you knows what I mean. I mean, you see 'im cook one of them sauces, see 'im bake a pie. But you don't *know* 'im. Not like what

233

you'd invite 'im to your granny's house and get the silver teapot out.'

Auguste smiled. 'There you are right, Sid.'

On their return to Broadstairs, Auguste walked alone to the Imperial, not sure whether it was Rose or Araminta he hoped to see. He toyed with the idea that he didn't really *know* Araminta either, that possibly she had killed Pegg somehow in a *crime passionnel*. He sighed. His brain was getting dull. What a ridiculous notion that was.

He waited some minutes in the foyer, but neither Araminta nor Rose appeared. Sitting down, he closed his eyes, and as he did so a glimmer of an idea flickered for a moment and faded. He grasped after it without panic. He knew it would flicker again into life, if it had merit. Oil must be added drop by drop as in mayonnaise. Force it and the whole sauce would curdle and be ruined. Slowly, slowly. When he opened his eyes, the idea had not returned, but Rose was in front of him.

'I've news for you, Auguste. This was either murder or the weirdest suicide I've ever come across. I've had the PM and the preliminary comments from the analyst.'

'Analyst?' he echoed with foreboding.

'James Pegg was stuffed full of opium.'

Chapter Eleven

Opium. Auguste tossed and turned in the throes of a waking nightmare. He had gone to bed inescapably aware that he was sharing a house with a murderer, a fact pointed out to him by Rose before they parted last night. Not that he needed reminders.

'It has to be someone from Blue Horizons.' Including you, Naseby would have added. 'No one in their senses is going to fill themselves full of opium and jump into the sea surrounded by other people if he seriously intends to commit suicide. It's hardly possible that any of the Lionisers could have dosed him with opium either. No strangers wandering round your kitchen at Blue Horizons on Thursday, were there?'

'No − yes. Mrs Langham and Mr Michaels came in late in the morning,' Auguste remembered.

'Did they now? And why was that?'

'They wished to help collect evidence and came to report to me.' Put into words it sounded very odd to him now.

Rose regarded him sceptically. 'Very civic-minded of them, I'm sure. Did they come back with any?'

'Yes,' said Auguste defiantly. 'As I told you yesterday, Mr Pipkin had more reason to dislike Sir Thomas than we thought. It is not merely a matter of Shakespeare.'

'Did they have an opportunity to poison Mr Pegg's food while imparting this information?' Rose asked somewhat drily.

Auguste shook his head. 'I cannot see how. It is true they passed through the kitchens, but how would they know which was to be James's food? We did not know ourselves.'

'Blowed if I know then.' Rose sighed heavily. 'It feels as if we're still wandering round that maze in circles, getting nowhither; and yet in a funny kind of way I think we're circling nearer the centre.' He meant this reassuringly. But for Auguste it was yet another reminder that someone he had been close to for the last few months was a murderer.

The maze ran through his dreams as he came up against dead ends, ever circling. At the centre, he could see from on high like an all-seeing god, was a *St Pierre au gratin*, out of which a fresh live John Dory rose displaying its thumb-print of St Peter. Then the Dory turned into Araminta, in the centre of the maze, unattainable, tantalising – smiling.

With a start he awoke, shivering, glad that the night was over. Reason returned, but the dream left its residue of foreboding. Rose, too, had troubled dreams. He also was reaching after something in vain, but the object of his endeavours was intangible. Something done that should not have been done, or something undone that should have been done. Something remained half-finished, but the more he sought to finish it, the more indefinable it became.

'What are you doing, Egbert?' came Edith's sleepy indignant voice. 'That's my night bonnet you're pulling – and my hair.'

He mumbled some apology, but Edith, deducing that something was awry, forced herself to sit up.

'Are you all right, Egbert? I said that Cumberland sauce was too rich for you.'

'It wasn't the food; it was the coffee,' he said, his mind still on Pegg.

'There now, you weren't so foolish as to drink—'

'The case,' he explained.

'Oh, the case,' she said. This explained and excused all. She went back to sleep, saying comfortingly à la Mr Micawber, 'Something will turn up.'

'Something will turn up.' Why could he not rid his mind of the conviction that something already had. Something as slippery as wet fish. Something – yes, something to do with France. Cannes? Iron Mask? The Grand Duke? Rose turned over and went to sleep again, this time peacefully.

Auguste walked six times round the bandstand, watched carefully by a Broadstairs policeman convinced he had a latter-day Fenian bomber before him. Auguste, however, was merely summoning up courage to face the day.

Having done so, he took a deep breath and walked firmly into the Imperial Hotel past the three newspaper men whose pride in their achievements had increased tenfold with their status of having 'known about it' all along. He found his friend taking breakfast early. Rose, determined to remain isolated as far as was possible from the assistance of Inspector Naseby, was still operating from the Imperial, to Mr Multhrop's almost palpable distress. Multhrop was counting the hours to the moment when the Lionisers would depart from his beloved hotel, in the happy hope that all this murder business would then depart with them. The news that not only Rose but five Lionisers were staying on till the crime was solved was far from welcome. Multhrop seemed to blame Auguste for the entire business. He greeted him with a strangled yelp, as though murder incarnate had walked through his doors, and despatched him as speedily as possible to the breakfast room. Rose was alone, Edith not yet having made her appearance.

'The kippers are fresh,' was his greeting.

'Thank you, I am not hungry. Some coffee and – ' he'd almost been going to say a brioche – 'some toast would be delightful.'

Rose, having been informed by Edith that he had to fortify himself, was battling with kidneys and scrambled eggs, though with little enthusiasm. Auguste looked at the congealing eggs and brown shrivelled kidneys, and shuddered. Personally he had no desire ever to see kidneys again. 'I'm going to London for the day,' Rose announced, waving his fork complete with kidney towards Auguste.

'Why?' enquired Auguste, taken aback.

'For a holiday,' answered Rose sourly. 'Naseby arrived, did he?'

'Yes,' Auguste answered briefly. He had no wish to relive the gloating satisfaction with which Inspector Naseby and his platoon had arrived, sealed off the kitchens and banished the group to the upstairs rooms.

'I want to see that kitchen before Naseby takes it into his head to storm it alone. And I want to see your six friends before I go to London.' He ate the kidney, then looked as though he wished he hadn't. 'You've cancelled plans to return to London today?'

'Yes,' said Auguste bleakly. The owner of Blue Horizons had not been amused to hear that the police were barring entrance to his house, and tried to console himself that the value would go up.

'Our friend certainly knows his poisons,' remarked Rose, wondering why Multhrop had a picture of three very dead deer on his breakfast-room wall. 'It wasn't a fatal dose — not meant to be, I imagine. It was intended to make him drowsy so he wouldn't be able to swim. And if that didn't work by itself, then it would be a comparatively simple matter to hold him under. I think it was laudanum — easy enough to get. Wouldn't take full effect for about an hour, and I suppose our friend thought it would be viewed as an accident while bathing. Now this bathing idea — was it planned early?'

'I don't know,' said Auguste, surprised. 'They told me at luncheon, but they had decided before.'

'I wonder whose idea it was. Mind you, that wouldn't be conclusive. Even if it was you, say, Auguste, it doesn't mean necessarily that you're the murderer. The murderer could simply have taken advantage of it.'

'Either way, it does not suggest a long-thought-out plan, but something that was necessitated by something that had recently happened. And it could not,' Auguste added thankfully, 'be that the murderer heard James ask to see me after bathing.'

'No. Tell me again exactly what you ate.'

'A *salade niçoise*.'

'Ah yes, I remember those.' Rose smiled. 'Difficult to add opium to. Then you had the St Pierre thing.'

'A *St Pierre au gratin*. Or if people preferred, a fish mayonnaise.'

'Which did Pegg eat?'

'The St Pierre. We all did, I believe. But it made no difference, since we all ate from the same dish,' Auguste said in despair.

'The same story, eh? Just as in Sir Thomas's case. And this time we've nothing to analyse.'

'I gave the fish mayonnaise to the cat next door,' said Auguste hopefully. 'He still survives.'

'Let's assume it's the drink then. What did Pegg have?'

'I think all save myself and Lord Wittisham drank beer,' said Auguste disdainfully. Holidays were all very well, but that did not mean one threw one's palate wide open to insensitive treatment.

'Tea and coffee afterwards?'

'Coffee.'

'Who served it?'

Auguste thought back. 'We were in a hurry. Everyone wished to go bathing. The two girls, who were serving that

239

day, left the coffee to settle on the table by the window. We all got up to clear the table and get our own coffee. Anyone could have poisoned anyone's cup.'

'And been sure the right person got it?' asked Rose sharply.

'If someone else had been the intended victim, there would surely quickly have been another attempt, or the victim himself would have taken fright. No, I think the murderer succeeded in his aim. Like Mr Punch, he gets his victim every time.'

'You been watching Punch and Judy, Auguste? I wouldn't have thought that up your street at all.'

'I was not impressed by the violence,' replied Auguste simply. 'Especially as there were young children present. "That's the way to do it," this monster claims and bangs people over the head with a stick. First the baby, then his wife, then a crocodile, and various other persons. He sticks to his well-tried method. Our murderer kills by poison. Then there is another death. Again poison is part of the plan. Murder can become a habit, do you not agree? The murderers fall in love with their own cleverness at performing a successful murder. Look at Mary Ann Cotton, look at Dr Cream, and others too. I believe there is a pattern to these murders. First one, then another—'

'That reminds me of my dream,' interrupted Rose suddenly, 'but I can't think how. Two murders don't make a pattern.'

'But with another it may,' said Auguste soberly.

'You think there'll be a third? Then the sooner we get to Blue Horizons the better.'

Naseby was of the same opinion, eager to tour the kitchens and track down incriminating evidence. 'Not that there'll be anything there now,' he announced, marching in ahead of Rose. '*He* had all day yesterday to remove the vital evidence.'

240

'Nothing in the rest of the house?' asked Rose, not bothering to enquire who *he* might be.

'No,' Naseby said.

In agony, Auguste watched as they toured the kitchens, picking up his precious knives, sniffing bottles and demanding to know their contents, sifting through herbs and spices, turning over vegetables.

'We'll have to take all these,' announced Naseby, gathering up armfuls gleefully.

'But they are food preparations,' said Auguste, aghast. 'They are clearly marked Isinglassine, Liebig's Extract of Beef, and Patt—'

'So they *say*. Suppose—' Naseby's eye was caught. 'What's in this cupboard here?'

'This is my own cupboard, with my personal utensils, flavourings, rose-water . . .' He frowned. 'Those I do not recognise,' he said, puzzled, looking at a small group.

'Don't you indeed, Mr Auguste Didier? Well, I do,' announced Naseby, snatching one. 'That's laudanum, that is,' he said triumphantly. 'And that bottle by its side – I think we'll have that analysed. Wouldn't it be a coincidence if it were atropine?'

'But that is my cupboard,' said Auguste, outraged. 'No one would dare open that.'

'Wouldn't they indeed?' Naseby was smug.

'Do you keep it locked, Auguste?' asked Rose, intervening quietly.

'No, but it is my—' He stopped. How foolish he was being. It was a murderer they were dealing with.

'You're partial, Rose. Didier's clearly—' Naseby glared.

'Produce me hard evidence, Naseby,' cut in Rose wearily, 'then I'll consider arresting Mr Didier.'

Rose seemed almost visibly more remote, thought Auguste, sitting uneasily upstairs in the small parlour as they ran through yet again the events of the Thursday luncheon. Naseby had departed with his trophy, leaving one constable on guard outside the kitchen door.

'You ladies served the meal?' Rose addressed Alice and Emily.

'Yes, but we put it on the table in front of everybody and they helped themselves,' pointed out Emily anxiously.

'What did people drink at the table?'

'Everyone helped themselves to what they wanted,' said Alice.

'So it looks like the coffee. Where was Mr Pegg when he got himself some coffee? Anyone remember?'

A silence, and no one looked up.

'Come on now,' said Rose impatiently, 'someone must recollect seeing him pour out coffee.'

'I did,' said Heinrich suddenly. 'Emily and I were at the table when he was getting his coffee, and we got up after—'

'Emily was serving with me,' said Alice indignantly. 'She wasn't sitting down; she was clearing.'

'I was at the table anyway,' said Emily quickly.

'I got my coffee first,' said Algernon, musing.

'Nah, you didn't,' Sid came back at him. 'I did. I remember because it got grounds in it, and I 'ad to wait. Mr Pegg was behind me, waiting for his, and you was behind 'im.'

'That's not right,' said Algernon vehemently. 'Not that it makes any difference,' he said lightly. 'I couldn't have poisoned his cup because when he was walking back to the table with his, I was still pouring mine out.'

'I say, you know,' Alfred frowned nervously. 'I think I was behind Pegg, not you, Peckham. When he turned round, he bumped into me and spilled a bit of his coffee.'

'That wasn't Thursday, Alfred,' said Alice instantly, 'that was the day before. I remember it happening because I was beside you.'

242

Auguste was trying to remember where he had been. He couldn't. It was only two days ago, but getting coffee was an everyday occurrence; the memory of one day was overprinted by the next. Strange that his pupils should remember so clearly.

'There seems to have been a fair old crowd round him one way and another,' observed Rose. 'Whose idea was it to go bathing?' he suddenly shot at them.

They looked at each other, blankly.

'It was — yes, it was Mr Pegg himself,' said Emily suddenly. 'At breakfast time. He said he wanted to go swimming; he'd won a prize at it.'

There was much discussion, but this was finally agreed to be more or less accurate.

Algernon's mind was still on poison. 'I don't see why this coffee is so important. Why couldn't the poison be added at table?' he asked aggressively. 'His attention had only to be distracted by Sid, if he was first back with his coffee, and—'

' 'Ere. Watch it, me old mate,' said Sid threateningly.

'Why should I watch it?' demanded Algernon. 'You had as much chance as the rest of us to poison Pegg's food — *and* Throgmorton's come to that. You were sitting next to poor old Pegg; you could have added something to his salad to look like dressing perhaps.'

'You seem to know a lot about what Mr Pegg ate,' observed Emily tartly.

'I was opposite him,' pointed out Algernon quickly.

Interesting, thought Rose; almost as if they'd forgotten he was there. Like a pack of rats scrabbling for the gang plank. 'Did any of you know Mr Pegg before he joined the school?' Heads were shaken.

'And you knew him best, Lord Wittisham?'

'He was my friend,' stated Alfred once more. 'We were going into partnership. Why should I kill him?'

243

'There seems, unless anyone knows to the contrary, only one reason that anyone would want to kill James Pegg, who seems to have been an honest sort of chap from what Mr Didier tells me. And that's because he knew something incriminating about the murder of Sir Thomas Throgmorton. I'm afraid it's been my experience that friend or not, that doesn't stand in the way when the murderer's own safety is at stake.'

'James Pegg was very quiet at luncheon, Inspector,' Alice informed him, 'so it could have been so.'

'It wasn't me,' bleated Alfred pathetically, looking to Alice for support.

'You wanted to marry Throgmorton's daughter,' pointed out Rose. 'And threatened him, according to Miss Throgmorton herself.'

'Did I?' His face went blank. 'I don't now, though,' he explained. 'I've decided to marry Alice.'

There was a buzz of polite congratulations, though the general consensus was that this was an announcement that could have been made at a more opportune time. Alice's face flushed with happiness.

'My granny allus says,' observed Sid, 'that marriage is like pushing veg through a tammy cloth; if you lets up for a second, you gets a faceful of mush.'

'My granny told *me*,' Emily chipped in, 'that she had a remedy for love-sickness and—'

'And *I'm* telling you,' said Rose mildly, 'that it's ninety per cent sure that one of you is a murderer. You're all, no doubt for good reasons, trying to ignore the fact, but just remember, there's been two murders already. And I have to know which of you it is before you all go down like six – seven,' looking at Auguste, 'green bottles. Some of you know a lot more than you seem to want to tell me. I suggest you do some hard thinking, or I'll arrest the lot of you as accessories.'

There was silence as Rose walked out. Slowly six pairs of eyes turned accusingly to Auguste. He must be, as the maître, responsible. He must solve it.

This afternoon Auguste did not desire even Araminta's company. He required solitude, and distance from the Imperial, from Blue Horizon and its inmates, from Naseby – from everything save his own thoughts.

Broadstairs was crowded with afternoon promenaders, parasols sprouting like bright toadstools. Auguste walked briskly up past Bleak House, mentally congratulating Mr Dickens again for his dramatic choice of holiday residence, and along the cliff path towards the lighthouse and Kingsgate. Some Gothic follies built by Lord Holland were to be found there, so he had heard; follies seemed to suit his mood at the moment.

It was not long before he left all but the most intrepid of travellers behind him and he was almost alone on the cliffs, a blaze of pink and mauve with campions, mallow and snapdragons. He breathed in the sea air deeply. This smell was indeed superb. The sea did not smell like this at Cannes. There the blue Mediterranean wooed one softly into its embrace; here there was danger, excitement, it was bracing; all the difference between gentle herbs and heady spices. Here one knew that the tales they told of smugglers were true; men gathered seaweed by day, and by night came the smugglers. Men like Joss Snelling. They came to cliffs already cut away by seaweed hunters and now pinholed with underground passages, tunnelling into them insidiously – like the case he was now engaged upon. Where and how would danger strike next?

A Fish Fortnight: how had he been foolish enough to imagine this holiday would be a pleasure? How could the school ever return to learning about crabs and crayfish and cod? What would happen to his future after two murders

245

connected with his school? Perhaps he should return to France, admit defeat to working in England. Yet in France too lay an impassable road. Paris could not be for him, not while Tatiana lived there. He could go perhaps to Bordeaux to start a small restaurant. He viewed the prospect without enthusiasm. He could, he supposed, create a simple menu, suitable for those who loved the sea, with all the splendid seafood of the Atlantic coast. Just one or two dishes per course; perhaps he could set a new fashion in sauces, less heavy, less rich. Allow the true flavour of the fish to emerge, as in England. Sauces – his mind returned against his will to his champagne-sauce entrée. His dish of kidneys *poisoned*. How could it have been – and, moreover, *why* should it be? He still felt that if only these questions could be answered, all would be clear. The reason why must surely be that it pointed away from the entrée to another course. Or, he thought suddenly, concealed the fact that it really *had* been in the entrée. He frowned. Surely this was nonsense. Yet the thought persisted and hummed round his brain as the bees in the clover on this lonely clifftop.

He flung himself on the grass and closed his eyes. Ghosts crept through his daydreams, ghosts of old loves, stealing in and out of his heart, ghosts of happy days, ghosts of sad songs, ghosts of the man in the iron mask – he flinched – and now ghosts of Dickens! In the sunshine of the day it was easy to laugh at the ghost of Mr Dickens sitting placidly in the ladies' retiring room at the Albion. He closed his eyes. Shadows of light danced before them, forming themselves into Mr Dickens – who rose to his feet to greet Little Nell. A line from *The Old Curiosity Shop*, which still lay unfinished by his bedside came into his head: 'Always suspect everybody.' So let Mr Dickens show the way. Auguste let his mind play and it revolved with such fantastic ideas, such strange notions, that it was idle to pursue them. They must be nonsense. He did not dismiss them, however.

Like English meat, like English cheese, he left them to mature in his mind. Just in case.

'We were there of course,' Oliver tentatively pointed out to Angelina as he escorted her on a walk over the sands to the Dumpton Gapway.

'Where, Oliver?' Angelina had her mind on the beauty of the day, the sharp fresh smells of the sea, and on Oliver himself. Not on murder.

'In the house where that poor fellow was drugged.'

'So we were,' she replied. 'I did not realise it was the same day. And so I suppose we're suspects, but what reason would any of us have to kill that cook?'

'Why on earth should any of those cooks want to kill Sir Thomas?' countered Oliver reasonably. 'It's almost as if there were two murders, two murderers.'

'Do you think that's possible?'

'Of course. Someone could have taken advantage of the first murder to make the police believe the two were linked.'

'So that's why the Inspector doesn't want us to leave. We – I mean those of us on the committee – could have murdered Sir Thomas.'

'Yes. Only you make it sound rather like a joint committee decision.'

'No. It points to me.' Angelina shivered. 'I don't think I care for being a suspect. But it's more likely that one of those people at Blue Horizons committed both crimes, isn't it?' she asked anxiously.

'We both know, and I'm sure the Inspector does too, that you didn't kill him,' Oliver stated firmly.

'Sir Thomas's murder was planned. It must have been. Could you see Mr Pipkin or Mrs Figgis-Hewett carefully plotting such a crime? She might do something on the spur of the moment like appearing in that wedding dress as Miss Havisham.' Angelina smiled despite herself. 'Looking back,

247

it was rather funny, wasn't it? I felt sorry for the poor Prince. But it's sad too. You won't do that to me, will you?'

'What?'

'Leave me at the church.'

Oliver stopped still, took both her hands and regarded her sternly. 'You're rather forward, my dearest. You haven't yet allowed me to fall on one knee to present you with my heart.'

'You may do so now,' she informed him graciously. To the great interest of one old beach scavenger and three small boys, and to the detriment of his white flannels, he did so. Her acceptance was immediate and enthusiastic, and the ensuing embrace took so long that even the scavenger lost interest.

'Angelina,' remarked Oliver some time later, 'has it occurred to you to wonder just how Gwendolen happened to have the wedding dress with her, if the idea was as immediate as you suggest?'

She stared at him. 'No,' she said, 'it hadn't occurred to me – and I don't know the answer.'

'You didn't like him, Alice, did you?' stated Alfred, point-blank, as they sat in the Victoria Gardens.

'That's no reason to go and murder someone,' she pointed out reasonably enough. 'Oh, Alfred, you are foolish. Why on earth should I wish to kill James?' Alice was offended by his implied accusation. Then she began to worry. It had to be one of them at Blue Horizons. Alfred had swum out after James. Alfred had wanted to marry Sir Thomas's daughter; had threatened Sir Thomas's life. Who more likely for the Inspector to pick upon than Alfred? Alice clung to his arm. I won't let them take you, she vowed to herself. I won't.

'Who do you think did it, Heinrich?' Emily whispered in

248

a small voice as they waited for Uncle Mack to begin. 'It must have been one of us.'

'I do not know,' he replied steadily, keeping his eyes glued to the stage. 'Accident perhaps.' But his voice had no conviction in it. 'Emily,' he turned to her, but could not continue. Should he go to Rose or not?

'I think,' said Emily carefully, 'whoever did this thing is indeed a very wicked person.'

'Yes,' he answered in a strangled voice as Uncle Mack struck up with 'Oh Susannah, don't you cry for me'.

Algernon Peckham was wandering about on the pier on his own. Where should he go from here? He was quite confident that no charge could be laid at his door; he had a high opinion of his own capabilities as a criminal. But he was also growing increasingly interested in his abilities as a cook, which had greatly surprised him. The original reason that he had taken up cookery was receding rapidly in its attraction. If only the police weren't hovering quite so near. If only he were free to choose.

Sid also left Blue Horizons alone that afternoon, but he was not wandering aimlessly. Far from it. Sid had an appointment with a lady.

Edith Rose was growing weary of promenading Broadstairs on her own and had been beginning to think longingly of Highbury. But this evening was offering a brighter prospect than usual. With Egbert absent, Auguste had offered to escort her to dinner in the Imperial's dining room and to the hotel concert afterwards. Mr Multhrop was less delighted at the prospect, clearly thinking that Auguste would arrive secreting a bottle of atropine in his pocket.

Edith carefully rearranged the fichu in her best lace evening blouse for the umpteenth time and sallied forth to meet a formally tail-coated Auguste.

'Is this rich?' she asked Auguste doubtfully, gazing nonplussed at the menu some half an hour later.

Auguste followed her eye and gently removed the menu from her hands. 'If you will permit me to choose, *chère* Edith, I will order for you.'

She yielded her independence gratefully, with mingled fear and pleasant expectation. It wasn't that she didn't trust Auguste, but he didn't know her stomach the way she did and she had to bear in mind that he was French. French stomachs, she was convinced, were built on an entirely different pattern to plain English ones. True, Egbert had somewhat surprisingly survived his visit to France, but this she regarded as an act of mercy on his Creator's part and not a tribute to French cooking.

'What is it?' she enquired, looking with doubt at the *filets de sole Provençale* put before her.

'Taste, dear Edith.'

She obeyed and tasted, then tasted again. 'Is it French?' she enquired. 'I do like it.'

'English,' said Auguste firmly. 'An old English recipe.' The waiter, who disdainfully overheard this remark, began to instruct Auguste on cuisine, an initiative speedily put an end to by Auguste.

Several courses later, Edith set down spoon and fork with a sigh. 'That really was very nice,' she proclaimed in high praise. 'Mind you, I do think the china helps a lot. It tastes better somehow off pretty china. You never get a nice cup of tea except out of a piece of bone.'

'A piece of bone, Edith?' said Auguste, at a loss.

'Bone china, I should have said.' She giggled. 'It must be this nice lemonade you've given me.'

Auguste smiled. These English and their china. But he was glad she liked the dessert wine. He had worried it might be a little strong.

'And now, dear Edith, let us sample the entertainment

250

Mr Multhrop has in store for us.' He took Edith's hand and kissed it.

'Really, Auguste,' she said, pink with pleasure, 'what will people think?'

By the time Egbert Rose returned late on Saturday night, Edith had retired and Auguste was waiting sleepily in the smoking room with a sulky Sergeant Stitch. Stitch had not dined at the Imperial but on inferior fish and chips. He was regretting it. Rose's gaze, as he entered, fell on Stitch. He beckoned, an evil look in his eye. 'I've a lesson for you, Stitch,' he said agreeably. 'Next time, tell me exactly what was said. The full story with no deductions on the part of Sergeant Stitch. Clear about that? Quite clear?'

'No, sir. Yes, sir,' mumbled Stitch, a question mark rearing itself out of the blue over that promotion. 'What did I do, sir?'

'You told me, Stitch, that the groom who stole those bonds was dead.'

'That's right, sir.'

'What you did not tell me, Twitch,' Rose didn't correct his error, 'was that the groom was not just dead, but murdered.'

'Yes, but that was in France, sir,' Twitch pointed out, aggrieved, as though that far-off place should not affect his career. 'And it was years ago. Does it make any difference?'

'Oh, it makes a difference all right. Get the files out in the office, Stitch. We won't be retiring yet awhile. I'll be along in five minutes.'

Stitch, crestfallen, departed, and Rose sank down in a chair. 'After a stiff whisky and soda,' he added to Auguste, summoning the waiter.

'You get used to seeing things around,' he explained. 'My fault entirely. I've seen that French report on unsolved crimes come through so many times, I know it backwards – and forgot all about it. I remembered the story of the

251

necklace because that was a new addition to the list. Forgot the others because they'd been around so long. Groom murdered by wife thought to be English. Poison suspected. Atropine.'

Auguste was no longer sleepy.

'Was there mention of a wife in Sir Thomas's report of the theft? Did Sir Thomas—?'

Rose held his hand up. 'Wait a minute. It's been a long day.' The whisky and soda arrived and Rose took a deep drink. He put the glass down half empty. 'The wife's name was Elizabeth, twenty-six years old at the time. Maiden name on the marriage certificate was Creasy. Married in ninety in France. Probably met her out there. It would be all too neat if she was in Sir Thomas's household too, but I've spoken to Miss Throgmorton who doesn't remember anyone else being involved, and Sir Thomas didn't report an accomplice either—'

'Can I speak to you, sir?' A nervously correct Stitch was drawn up to attention by the side of the whisky and soda.

Rose looked up resignedly. 'What is it Stitch?'

It's Inspector Naseby, sir, he's just telephoned. Those bottles in the cupboard he took. One was laudanum right enough; the other had solution of atropine in it. He wants you to arrest Mr Didier.' So abject was Stitch that even this good news did not enliven his miserable face.

'The trouble with Naseby is,' Rose said viciously, 'that he don't know proof from prog.'

Auguste stiffened, more at Rose's use of such a derogatory word for cuisine than for fear of arrest.

'I'd like to see him stand up at the Old Bailey with a case dependent on two bottles in an unlocked cupboard in a kitchen open to all and sundry,' Rose continued.

Auguste did not share his wish. He could all too clearly see Naseby closing in like an avenging nemesis.

'And sir — ' bleated Stitch, shifting from foot to foot.

'There's someone to talk to you and Mr Didier.'

'It can wait till I've finished this drink,' said Rose firmly.

'I don't think so, sir,' said Stitch humbly. Not quite as humble as Uriah Heep, but still a sight worth seeing.

As they entered the office, a familiar figure turned towards them.

It was Heinrich Freimüller.

'I vish,' he said heavily, 'to confess to the murder of Sir Thomas Throgmorton and Mr James Pegg.'

Chapter Twelve

Sergeant Stitch advanced purposefully towards Heinrich, but Rose motioned him to stop. 'Sit down,' he told Heinrich curtly. 'I want to know why. I want to know how.'

Heinrich sat stiffly on his chair; he cleared his throat and embarked stolidly on his story: 'I put the poison in the soup, as I serve it to Sir Thomas. This is simple. Mr Pegg, I think, does not see me, because I am very careful. Afterwards when the dishes come back to the kitchen, I put some poison in the entrée dish — so that no one suspects the soup,' he explained carefully. 'But later I find I have to kill Mr Pegg, for he did observe me. I think I will not use atropine; if it worked immediately I would be suspect. I have some laudanum, however, for medicine, which contains opium. This will make sure that Mr Pegg will be drowsy when he enters the water and will drown when he swims further out. If he does not drown, I will try again. I put the laudanum in his coffee. This too is easy — I pick the cup up and hand it to him. No one remarks on it. Why should they? Later, I put the bottles in Herr Didier's cupboard. For this I apologise.' He bowed stiffly in Auguste's direction. 'I did not think anyone would suspect Herr Didier.' Auguste looked slightly mollified.

'I'd like to know—' Rose began, but Heinrich was in full flow and continued in the same unemotional voice: 'Mr Pegg swam out, and he was drowned. I stood in the less deep water and watched him. I obtain the atropine from the Embassy stables,' he added.

'Tell me again. Slowly,' said Rose firmly.

'Vy?' demanded Heinrich, puzzled. 'I tell you that I have killed Mr Pegg and Sir Thomas.'

'Just how did you manage to get this atropine from the stables? Not usual for a cook to wander round the stables, is it?' Rose remembered Stockbery Towers and its rigid hierarchies of outdoor and indoor staff.

'I take them out food for a picnic. I find the atropine there, unregarded in a corner. It is an old bottle. I remember it and it gives me the idea.'

'Convenient,' remarked Rose. 'So you put it in the soup and then you handed the plate to Sir Thomas.' He thought for a moment. 'Mr Didier, ask Mr Multhrop for a few of his plates, would you?'

Mr Multhrop viewed the prospect of his plates disappearing into his lost office with great suspicion. 'You won't do anything to them, will you?' he enquired anxiously.

Resisting the temptation to inform Multhrop that he would smear them with atropine and slide them back into the kitchens unobserved, Auguste gravely assured him that they would be completely safe under police control.

'Now, Stitch,' said Rose, 'you be Pegg. Herr Freimüller, show us how you managed it.'

Heinrich awkwardly and self-consciously held the soup bowl in his left hand while Stitch distastefully poured imaginary soup into it. If this was reconstruction of the crime, he was not impressed. Heinrich extracted an imaginary lump of poison from a pocket and secreted it in his large hand, dropping it into the bowl while Stitch, by a great feat of inventiveness, was wheeling the imaginary trolley onwards.

It was at this moment that the crime became vividly real for Auguste, revolted that his soup — albeit only Dickens's mutton broth — was being used for this terrible purpose. Could any of his pupils so have abused their calling? he asked himself. He could not bring himself to believe it.

'What would you have done if Sir Thomas had refused the soup and you were forced to pass the plate to someone else?'

Heinrich hesitated. 'I had asked him,' he said simply after a moment.

'Any particular reason you decided to murder Sir Thomas?' Rose asked ironically.

'Oh yes,' Heinrich said more confidently. '*Herr Inspektor*, I kill him because of an old quarrel. I am not a clever man, and I like cooking. My family do not approve, for they think I should be ambassador, not work in his kitchens.' He smiled ruefully. 'I was a student many year ago at the University of Heidelberg. I met there Sir Thomas; he was just Thomas Throgmorton then. I did not like him. We quarrelled over an affair of honour and fought a duel. It is the custom, you know, in Germany to obtain scars in such honourable contests. This was not that kind of duel. We were fighting in earnest. Sir Thomas won, just; I was wounded, almost killed. I am a clumsy man – ' he glanced at his broad fingers – 'I am not good at fighting with swords. He took the lady, but he did not marry her. I discover years later that he abandoned her and broke her heart. She had killed herself and I vowed that Sir Thomas Throgmorton would pay. I have never married. I come to England and I work at the Embassy. I have almost forgotten about Throgmorton, for time passes and though old wounds may not heal, they close over. Then, suddenly, I hear the name of Sir Thomas Throgmorton. It must be the same man. We are to cook a banquet at Broadstairs for him. This is my opportunity to avenge my Greta. But how? I cannot fight a duel now, then I think of poison, and of the atropine in the stables. I bring it with me just in case. But I will give my enemy a chance.'

'Here comes Mr Datchery,' murmured Rose.

257

Heinrich looked puzzled. '*Nein*, only the two of us were present. I see Sir Thomas before dinner on the Saturday evening. I remind him who I am. We quarrel again. He insults me and I know I have to kill him. Just as the duel used to be our customary method for such disputes, so now I will use the tools of my trade. I will use the food he eats to kill him.'

Auguste shuddered at this heresy. He could not believe it.

Rose regarded Heinrich noncommittally for a few moments. 'Why did you decide to confess?' he shot at him.

Heinrich blinked, taken aback. 'Because,' his eyes flickered to Auguste who was staring at him in suppressed rage at what he saw as personal betrayal, 'I wished to spare further embarrassment to my colleagues. And to Mr Didier.' Auguste did not look grateful for this consideration.

'What do you think, Auguste?' Rose asked wearily as Sergeant Stitch disappeared with Heinrich to Broadstairs police station, the clock chiming midnight.

'What do I think?' exploded Auguste. 'I think he did not do it. Poison food? *Never.*'

'My doubts are somewhat different,' Rose said drily. 'In my experience murderers who confess are longing to tell you why they did it. Eager to justify themselves, so they tell you that first. They don't go into a long litany explaining exactly how they did it, or not till later anyway. But someone who was confessing to a murder he hadn't committed might feel he had to explain the mechanics first.'

Auguste was still fuming, however, on the matter of adulterated soup. 'My friend Freimüller is a chef, and he loves his art. I do not think it possible he would ruin food with poison. Can you imagine Mr Dickens using pages of his manuscript to start a fire? Can you imagine Michelangelo pushing over "La Pieta" to crush a foe? Or Mr Steinway using piano wire to strangle an enemy? The artist does not use his own work for evil purposes.'

'He says he did it, he had reason to do it and that sounded genuine enough. Real emotion there. And he could have done it. That will be enough for the Yard.' Rose looked at Auguste squarely: 'I don't have any choice other than to charge him. So if we're right, we haven't much time to lose.'

'At least we know who Mrs Figgis-Hewett's Datchery was. Remember she said Sir Thomas had told her Datchery had returned?'

'Now he's our Datchery as well. The joker in the pack. I suppose,' Rose added hopefully, 'this Mr Datchery didn't murder Edwin Drood himself, did he?'

'No,' said Auguste sadly. 'Most people do not believe so. He is a device to help solve the murder.'

'Let's hope it works for us too,' said Rose grimly.

Auguste walked back to Blue Horizons, tired, his mind in turmoil. Everything fitted; the case should be over, yet like a soufflé that failed to rise, this dénouement was soggy, unsatisfying.

Sid opened the door into the house, which seemed bleak and unwelcoming as Auguste walked in, no delicious scents emanating from the kitchens. No one had the heart for cooking that evening. No one else was around; they were either in bed or still out. Sid whistled when he saw Auguste's face.

'You look like the broken-hearted milkman, me old china. Wot's Polly Perkins been doin' to you?'

'Alas, it is not Polly Perkins, Sid, whoever that lady might be. I only wish it were an affair of the heart. This is a night made for lovers, not for murder.'

Sid's face was suddenly serious. 'There's not many of us, Mr Didier. It'll be cleared soon.'

'Herr Freimüller has confessed to the murders,' Auguste told him slowly.

''Im? Blimey!' Sid stared. 'Now you does surprise me.

Still, he wouldn't've confessed if he 'adn't dunnit, would he? No one would, stands to reason.'

'And he had good reason to kill Sir Thomas,' Auguste said absently, his tired brain trying to grapple with an elusive thought that strayed through his mind, something to do with Edith, or with Mr Multhrop. Or was it something Sid had just said?

'Tell me again what you said as I came in, Sid,' he said eagerly.

'The ol' broken-hearted milkman?'

'No, you added something.'

'Polly Perkins?' offered Sid. 'Nothing else, me old china.'

'*China*. That's it.'

'China plate − me old mate. Rhyming slang.'

But Auguste was no longer listening. The poison that killed Sir Thomas was not in any of the food. It was on the china. It was as simple as that. To Sid's indignation, Auguste hugged him in true French fashion.

'Sid, you are indeed my old mate,' he assured him gratefully. 'In fact, on this occasion, you are everybody's old mate.'

The simplicity of the evening, however, had vanished by morning. What had seemed straightforward was now revealed as complex, as Auguste mulled it over. The atropine was in crystal form. True, the crystals were colourless, but they were large, not small. How had they not been seen? He himself had inspected the china and table before the dinner commenced. If the crystals were already in bowls or on the plates before the food was added, they would have been obvious, if not to him then certainly to the eater. True, the soup − or indeed the entrée − would have melted the crystals, but they would have been seen before that. And did he not remember that the analyst, according to Egbert, had remarked that atropine required quite a lot of hot water

260

to dissolve it? Would the sauce in the entrée have been sufficient? Or even the soup, come to that. The crystals dissolved in alcohol much more easily, but surely any liquid placed in a glass dish beforehand would have been obvious? Yet it still might prove the answer. His thoughts came back to one person. If only he could see just how, and why, it had been done.

One by one his pupils descended to breakfast. Alfred was first to remark on the absentee. 'Where's old Heinrich?' he enquired. 'Not up yet?'

'I am afraid he will not be taking breakfast with us today,' said Auguste.

'He hasn't been murdered, has he?' asked Algernon, alarmed.

Emily dropped her egg spoon and screamed.

'No,' said Auguste hastily, one eye on Emily, 'but he has confessed to the murders.'

Emily's scream subsided into a low moan. Alice rushed to her, herself pale with shock. 'Have you some smelling salts, Mr Didier?' she cried indignantly. 'The poor girl has had a terrible blow. You know how friendly she is with Mr Freimüller.'

'Some camomile tea,' suggested Auguste weakly, for once at a loss.

'Stronger,' said Alice scathingly, fixing him with a steely eye of English determination. Brandy and smelling salts appeared from different directions.

'Old Heinrich murdered Sir Thomas?' repeated Alfred, bewildered, realisation coming late. 'Why?'

'Revenge for an old quarrel years ago over a woman.'

Emily broke into loud gasping sobs.

'I think I'd better take her upstairs,' said Alice firmly.

Auguste felt ostracised by the indignant glares that were directed at him, as though by breaking the news he shared responsibility.

'We're down to four,' observed Algernon brightly, now reduced to all-male company.

Alfred looked at him disdainfully. 'I don't think that's the right way to look at it, Peckham.'

'What is the right way, when one of your number ensures one of the others kicks the bucket?'

This question baffled Alfred.

'Nah,' said Sid, suddenly intervening. 'I don't see old Heinrich as a poisoner. A German spy, yes, and Pegg his English agent. Yes.' He'd been reading the works of William Le Queux. 'Poison? Nah.'

'Why should he lie about it?' enquired Algernon.

'Perhaps he's one of those eccentrics,' offered Alfred, 'who confess to crimes because they were there at the time.'

'Perhaps,' said Auguste.

'Can we all go home tomorrow?' Alfred continued hopefully. 'Now that it's over?'

'I do not believe so,' replied Auguste. 'I think it may be by no means all over.'

By the time Auguste arrived at the Imperial, Rose had already been in action for several hours. Twitch had been despatched to London to visit the German Embassy and its stables. Naseby had been given charge of a subdued Heinrich.

'You'll be leaving today,' said Naseby, trying to keep a query out of his voice. 'Now that we've got the murderer − or so you say,' he added bitterly, still resenting the loss of Didier in his cells.

'No,' replied Rose simply. 'Soon but not yet.' Naseby's face fell. 'Too many loose ends,' explained Rose kindly.

As far as Naseby was concerned all the loose ends had been tied into the neat little granny knots he always relied on, and for the life of him he couldn't see what Rose considered loose. But he wasn't going to ask him.

'You'll be going then, Inspector Rose,' asked Mr Multhrop happily, 'now you have the murderer in custody?'

'Not yet,' Rose informed him drily. 'One or two details to sort out.'

Mr Multhrop subsided. He should have known he couldn't be so lucky.

'You still hold Freimüller?' asked Auguste as he arrived at the Imperial and joined Egbert.

He nodded. 'He's still talking about duels and laudanum in the coffee. Maintaining he went into a blind rage at the sound of Throgmorton's name and resolved to get his own back in his own kind of duel.'

'An uneven one,' observed Auguste. 'That is what is strange. Have you told Miss Throgmorton yet?'

'She's going into the Factory tomorrow morning to see Twitch. Not that I can see she can help us more than she has. She wasn't born when the Freimüller affair took place − if it did of course, we've still to check it − and she was a child when the groom went off with the bonds. If that's still relevant. His widow must be a rich woman now,' he added absently.

'It depends on what happened out there. Did she murder her husband for money or for some other reason?'

Rose stared thoughtfully at Auguste. 'That's a point. I'll get on to Inspector Chesnais myself.' He eyed Mr Multhrop's telephone with trepidation. The thought of shouting all the way to Paris was daunting. 'She'd be about twenty-eight or -nine now, this Elizabeth Stebbins.'

'We have two − no, three young ladies of that age,' observed Auguste.

Rose nodded. 'Including Mrs Langham, yes, but I don't see our elegant Mrs Langham as the former wife of a groom, do you, for all she knows France and French?'

'No,' said Auguste. 'I agree.'

'That leaves Miss Fenwick and Miss Dawson.'

'There is a fondness between Mr Freimüller and Miss Dawson that I have noticed since our arrival here.'

'It would have to be a very great fondness to put a rope round his own neck,' observed Rose ironically. 'A governess and an army officer's daughter,' he said, looking at his notes. 'Check out their backgrounds, did you, when you took them on?'

'*Mon ami*, you have no idea of business,' said Auguste indignantly. 'I run a school. They are paying pupils. I do not employ them. They do not need references.'

Rose laughed. 'You just need to know whether they can make a *coq au vin*, eh?'

Auguste inclined his head. 'That is not such a bad requisite for a school of cooks.'

Beatrice Throgmorton stalked into Scotland Yard on the Monday morning and was duly escorted to an office where sat Sergeant Stitch, flushed with importance, trying Rose's chair for size. Next year all this would be his, or he was a Dutchman. He rose to his feet and bowed Miss Throgmorton into the visitor's chair with excessive politeness.

'What is all this about, Sergeant?' She had his rank duly noted.

'I am instructed to tell you, Miss Throgmorton, that we have your father's murderer under lock and key. You can sleep easy at nights now.'

It had not occurred to Beatrice to do anything else.

'Who was it?' she enquired bluntly.

'Herr Heinrich Freimüller,' said Stitch impressively. 'One of the cooks.'

'What reason would a cook have to kill my father?' she asked, amazed.

'It appears, so he says, miss, that he fought a duel with your father in Germany many years ago and vowed his revenge,' breathed Stitch, almost betraying emotion. This was very like *The Prisoner of Zenda*. He hoped the lady would not faint at hearing of these dark doings.

She did not. 'Do you mean that man my father told me of – he turned up in *Broadstairs*?'

Even Stitch had to confess it sounded remarkable. 'Yes,' he said firmly. 'Did you recognise him?'

'How on earth could I do that?' asked Miss Throgmorton impatiently. 'I wasn't born thirty years ago.'

'Inspector Rose said,' Stitch hastily moved the blame, 'he had the impression you might have recognised somebody from the past that evening in the Albion Hotel, besides the gardener from the château. Was it Mr Pegg?'

'No,' said Beatrice. 'It was a woman.'

'A woman,' breathed Stitch. This was true detection. Promotion advanced towards him. Feverishly he scrabbled for his notes and read out a list: 'Mrs Langham, Miss Fenwick, Miss Dawson. Any of those names familiar?'

'Mrs Langham I've met of course. The other two mean nothing, though I think we had a cook called Dawson once.'

'A man or a woman?'

'A woman. Years ago. Even if you had not already caught your murderer, Sergeant Stitch, old Mrs Dawson would hardly be of use to you.'

'Old?'

'She was about sixty when she left. I don't remember what exactly, but I believe she left under some cloud.'

'I don't think,' said Rose grumpily, 'I'll ever feel the same about the seaside.'

Edith, visiting the shops for the umpteenth time, was inclined to agree with him. She did not even have Mrs Figgis-Hewett's company since she had informed Edith with a flush of excitement on her cheeks that she was to accompany Lord Beddington to luncheon in Ramsgate. He had invited her, she emphasised, and wasn't that nice? To take her mind off dear Thomas, she added hastily, in case there should be any doubt as to the reasons for her acceptance. Edith had agreed that it was indeed for the best; she spoke truthfully, considering that another gentleman friend might be the best tonic for Gwendolen. And from what she had seen of Lord Beddington, a union with one who could sleep peacefully throughout the eruption of Vesuvius might be most suitable to withstand the onslaught of Gwendolen's voice.

Fortunately, as Edith trailed into Bobby's in Margate for the sixth time, she had a feeling she would not be here much longer. Firstly, someone had confessed to the murder. True, Egbert still seemed to be investigating the case, but she had known Egbert for a long time: whenever a case was nearing its finale there was an inner excitement about it like a coiled spring. And that excitement had been there since yesterday.

'I've just had Twitch shouting down the telephone at me. Nothing of interest about Freimüller yet.' Rose related the conversation to Auguste, commenting gloomily, 'Twitch is getting too lively by half. I'll have to get him his promotion in self-defence. Only thing puts me off is that I'll most likely be put up to Chief Inspector. I'd still have him round my neck.'

'Why should Freimüller confess?' asked Auguste. 'Do you think he could really be the murderer and hopes to make us think that someone else did it?'

Rose was doubtful. 'He'd have to be very confident. Suppose it was a Naseby case. He'd be only too happy to press ahead. He wouldn't want to go upsetting any apple carts. No, I think the pot is boiling — it remains to see what the stew is like.'

'My friend, if you must use cooking metaphors,' said Auguste severely, 'please use them properly. The pot is smiling, not boiling, and as to apple carts, these are not easy to—' He broke off.

266

'What's the matter? Don't you like stale sandwiches?' Rose eyed Mr Multhrop's offering, brought into the office for them both, without enthusiasm.

'No, it is an idea, just an idea . . .' Auguste thought all round it, turned it upside down to examine it, tested each ingredient. Rose waited patiently. This had happened before and he'd learned to value the process, however maddening it was at the time.

'I do not see quite how or why,' said Auguste, at last and unhappily. 'It makes no sense, but nevertheless I shall visit the library.' He told Rose what was in his mind.

Rose's face was alert. 'I wonder. I just wonder.'

'My friend,' Auguste told him, 'it could fit as tight as a Toulouse sausage skin.'

The Prince of Wales was at luncheon at Sandringham. For once it did not disturb him in the least that Alexandra was late. He was a happy man; he was a man about to leave for Marienbad in three days' time, where all the cares of this dull world where Kaisers won British yacht races would be forgotten. He would forsake dull court circles. At least in Marienbad, society was diluted with a few more colourful characters. Even if it was all family, there were Montenegrans, Hapsburgs, Romanovs − he wondered if Tatiana Maniovska would be there this year. With the death of the Czarevitch, the Romanovs would be in mourning. Still, Tatiana lived in Paris, not Russia, so she might be there. He hoped so. He was fond of Tatiana and he hadn't seen her since Cannes last year. He frowned. That brought back a few unwelcome memories. Wasn't that where that cook fellow claimed to have met him? Come to think of it, he owed the cook fellow something for smuggling him out of the hotel last week. Deuced awkward from all points of view if he'd still been there when police and newsmen and so on came along. He'd actually been sitting next to

Throgmorton, after all. Goodness knows what Mama would have said. Having to take luncheon with her again the next day at Osborne House seemed a small penance to pay compared with having to listen to her strictures on the frequency with which he got involved in scandals of the seamier kind. And it was never his fault, that was what aggrieved him so much. He did his best to keep out of trouble, but it seemed inexorably to follow him.

He must do something about a present for that chef one day.

Apart from the fact that both were in formal attire, there was nothing to distinguish Rose and Auguste from hundreds of other late promenaders on the seafront. They were on their way to Blue Horizons after a busy afternoon on both sides, Rose with Naseby and on the telephone.

'The widow was left without much money. She didn't murder for money, so Chesnais says,' Rose reported.

Auguste had had a rewarding afternoon at the library. Now there was little doubt in their minds. Only proof was lacking.

'If it fails,' said Rose as they reached Blue Horizons, 'we'll have to play a waiting game. But if we succeed we'll at least know where we are with Freimüller.'

Sid, who seemed to have appointed himself sheepdog for such occasions, was sitting, arms akimbo, astride a chair in the parlour doorway. His four sheep were waiting inside. Alice's arm was round Emily on the sofa; and Alfred sat bolt upright on a balloon-back chair, and Algernon lounged in an armchair with a nonchalance he did not feel — if his fingers twisting nervously on the arm were anything to judge by.

'As you know,' Rose began, 'Herr Freimüller has been arrested for the murders of Sir Thomas Throgmorton and James Pegg. He has told us how he did it, and given an explanation of why.'

A moan from Emily.

'But we have to check his story, so our investigations are continuing.' Rose looked round the blank faces listening to him. 'He tells us that he served the poison in the soup. He held the plate while Pegg put the soup in, and he then added the poison. James Pegg saw him and threatened to give him away, so he put opium in his coffee and watched him drown. Anyone any comments?'

There was an appalled silence.

'I don't think James would blackmail anyone,' said Alfred, unusually forcefully. 'He would come to tell you.'

'Where did he keep the poison?' asked Emily suddenly.

'In his pocket.'

'Then there'd be traces of it in the pocket,' said this latter-day Lady Molly. 'I know Heinrich is innocent. Have you checked the pockets?'

'The laboratory has done so, Miss Dawson. There is no trace of poison.'

'Then he's innocent!' shouted Emily. 'You must free him.'

'Not yet. He still holds to his story, but the new evidence gives credence to our view that he may be protecting someone. It would have to be someone he's very fond of. Someone like you, Miss Dawson,' Rose observed quietly.

Emily stared at him as all eyes turned to her.

'No!' cried Alice, outraged.

Emily said nothing.

'Cor,' said Sid, expelling a long breath.

'It wasn't me,' Emily said flatly. 'It wasn't, it wasn't, it *wasn't*,' shriller and shriller.

Rose ignored her. 'We learned a day or two ago of a young lady called Elizabeth Stebbins, though I doubt if that's her real name; she murdered her English husband in France. He had been Sir Thomas's groom and stolen a great deal of money in bonds which were never recovered. We wondered whether perhaps, just perhaps, this young

269

murderess – who used atropine – had also been in Sir Thomas's household. She'd be about your age, Miss Dawson. And Miss Throgmorton told us she remembers an old cook by the name of Mrs Dawson.'

'Grandmama,' moaned Emily. 'Oh no. She has nothing to do with it.'

"Hasn't she, Miss Dawson? Didn't you visit her at Throgmorton Park? Didn't you get to know the staff there? Meet a young groom?'

'No!' bawled Emily, as Alice withdrew her arm, moving slightly away from her.

'Then why did your grandmama leave under a cloud?'

'It's nothing to do with her. *Nothing*. I'll tell you, and then you'll be sorry. Her eyes weren't good enough any longer. She was confusing plants, and she put some wrong berries in the blackcurrant jam and one or two people – ' her voice faltered – 'were taken ill.'

'What plant, Miss Dawson?'

'Deadly nightshade,' she whispered.

'The atropine plant,' said Rose with satisfaction. 'I thought you were anxious about something. Why didn't you tell us?'

'You would have thought it was me,' cried Emily. 'As you do now,' she wailed.

'So I would, if it hadn't been for Mr Didier, and something he saw on the day Sir Thomas was killed. He saw a donkey cart pass Sir Thomas with Miss Fenwick and Lord Wittisham in it, and Sir Thomas noticing it and shouting something.'

'He asked what I was doing here,' said Alfred forlornly. 'But I've told you that.'

'Yes,' said Auguste. 'He wanted to know what you were doing here. You had omitted to mention you'd be in Broadstairs, you had threatened to kill him. He saw you later that day and you reiterated your threat and then carried

270

it out by poison in his brandy. You have served in India. You know all about atropine. You put poison in the entrée dish to make us think it was the food and not the drink to blame.'

'No!' He was on his feet glaring, a ferret at bay.

'Then you were forced to kill your friend James Pegg because he'd heard you quarrelling with Sir Thomas. Whom else would he protect? He was an honest man. He'd have come straight to me or the Inspector about anyone else.'

'No!' Alfred yelled.

'You swam out after James Pegg,' said Rose inexorably, 'and held his head down knowing he wouldn't struggle because you'd put laudanum in his coffee.'

Alfred looked wildly round for James Pegg to come to his aid in his hour of need, but he wasn't there. He looked desperately to his other protector. She did not fail him.

'I think it is me you want, Inspector, do you not?' Alice Fenwick, her face as composed as ever, stood up and walked to where Sergeant Stitch awaited her. As she reached the doorway, she turned.

'I would have made you a wonderful wife,' she said anxiously to Alfred. 'I really would.'

Everyone seemed to be gathered at the Albion Hotel that Monday evening, though Gwendolen Figgis-Hewett kept well away from the ladies' retiring room, in case Mr Dickens, too, was interested to hear about how the murders were solved. Mr Multhrop, who when news of the arrest reached him realised that his ordeal was all but over, was somewhat concerned that this evening cooks were to mingle with Lionisers, but was relieved to discover that in their evening clothes cooks looked not much different from real human beings. Araminta was sitting demurely by his side, a vision in rose pink chiffon and about as practical.

Algernon Peckham wore a haunted look, as if now that

271

the murders had been solved, Scotland Yard's attention might well be turned to a small matter of a necklace. Heinrich Freimüller sat dazed next to Emily who still sniffled a little through shock. Auguste had apologised very nicely and said it had been necessary in order to free Heinrich, but she did so hate Grandmama's little secret being general knowledge. She didn't want the story to follow her wherever she went in her new career. Career? Suddenly that seemed rather a dismal word. Alfred, looking even more dazed, sat next to Sid whom he seemed to have appointed as his temporary keeper.

Gwendolen sat next to Lord Beddington, her arm firmly through his, Angelina with Oliver and Samuel Pipkin next to Edith Rose. They seemed to have struck up an animated conversation about *The Pickwick Papers*.

The landlord eyed the bottle of hollands wistfully, but was mindful of the fact that Scotland Yard had forbidden it to be served at least until after dinner.

'Alice Fenwick,' began Rose, 'though I doubt if that will turn out to be her real name, was a housemaid in Sir Thomas's establishment ten years ago. She was, and has remained, ambitious and determined. She furthered these ambitions by whatever means she could; she found out about the bonds, stole them, and persuaded the groom, who was in love with her, to take them to France. Any suspicions Sir Thomas might have had were countered by the fact that she was – um – having an intimate relationship with him. She blackmailed him by threatening to tell his sick wife of their relationship, and he consequently did not report her in connection with the theft. She duly left his employ some months later, travelled to France and once there married the groom. They changed their names and disappeared. Unfortunately, the money being in his name, he had spent a large part of it, and she decided at last she would gain her freedom and preserve what money was left. She poisoned him and removed herself to England as an independent, young, unmarried woman, ready to – um – move up classes, so to speak.'

'You mean she was Throgmorton's *mistress*?' asked Alfred, stunned. A murder he could understand, but this was a new, and terrible, concept. 'But, dash it, she was an officer's daughter.'

'No, a sergeant's daughter. He was a sergeant in the Indian frontier wars, killed in eighty-seven. She was born out there, came to England after his death and went into service. But it was in India she learned of the powers of their datura plant, which is as common to them as deadly nightshade is to us,' Emily gripped Heinrich's hand, 'and the ease and frequency with which it was there employed. In France she discovered it was the same poison as used by grooms to treat horses – if not in the same form.'

'Why did she do it?' asked Alfred plaintively.

'Quite simple, Lord Wittisham. She was determined to marry you, and if Sir Thomas saw her before the event, there could be no chance of that. But once married to you, it would never occur to him, even if they met, that it could be the same woman. The nobility never marry housemaids, or so would be his reasoning.'

'But couldn't she just have avoided him?'

'No doubt she hoped to do so, but she could not be sure. And in the end of course he did recognise her and sealed his fate. Mr Didier put me on to that. He saw you in the donkey cart, Lord Wittisham. He also saw *her*. You thought, and Auguste thought, that he was speaking to you, for *you* answered. It was natural enough. But he wasn't. He was speaking to Alice Fenwick – not that he knew her by that name.' Rose looked at his rapt audience. 'I should have realised because when he next saw Lord Wittisham late that afternoon he asked him what he was doing down here – his attention had been elsewhere when Lord Wittisham answered that same question from the donkey cart. Once he'd seen her, he was determined to see justice done, his wife being dead, and accused her when he saw her in the hotel before dinner.

'Unfortunately for her, James Pegg overheard at least part of the conversation. He probably did not realise the significance of what he'd heard, but it was enough to perplex him. Then you, Lord Wittisham, announced you were going to marry Beatrice Throgmorton. Alice was horrified but Pegg, of course, was delighted. You were safe. He only wanted to protect you, Lord Wittisham. When Miss Throgmorton decided not to marry you, you turned back to Miss Fenwick, and Pegg was put in a dilemma. He decided to tell us all about it, and foolishly told her so on the Wednesday evening. He was drowned before he could do so.'

'I was not alone in the morning and so he was going to tell me,' said Auguste bitterly, 'after we had bathed.' He glanced at his demure-looking Delilah in pink chiffon. 'Alice drugged and drowned him,' he went on. 'When Mrs Figgis-Hewett was screaming for help in the water, Alice bobbed up *behind* her, which showed she had no fear of water, could swim, and indeed was probably on her way back from drowning James Pegg.'

'But how did she poison Sir Thomas?' asked Algernon, partly out of genuine interest and partly to keep the Yard's attention firmly on murder.

Auguste looked modest as he produced his *coup de théâtre*.

'Alice was a very determined young woman, but not one of many original ideas. This poisoning required great planning ability. I recalled how much store she set on Mr Harmsworth's excellent magazine for information. She had a great interest in murder, and in the graphic stories and pictures that adorn the magazine's pages. It had already occurred to me that the poison might be safer employed if it were on the china plate, and not in the food itself. And how better, as Alice herself had laid out the dishes, as she confidently informed us. Yet I could not see how the poison would remain undetected.

'So I paid a visit to the library and looked through the past issues of the *Harmsworth Magazine*. There I found a most interesting article on poison devices; it told me of poisoned gloves, of poisoned boots, of poisoned shirts, even of a poisoned hockey stick. But what interested me most was a Chinese device. The Chinese had a most interesting way of disposing of their victims to avoid the problem of food tasters. The poison was put not in the food itself, but in the cup or bowl. The bowl was heavily coated with a colourless soluble poison which dissolved when hot tea was poured in. Alice did not wish to use a poison that would be certain to act immediately and draw attention to the dish straightaway, before the dirty dishes could be washed, and gambled that atropine usually takes a little time to work. She was used to the poison, having poisoned her husband. It was colourless and soluble. She coated the bowl with atropine, dissolved in alcohol and set into a colourless jelly which adhered to the sides and bottom of the bowl and would not be noticed because it was both firm and thin. She then poisoned the left-over kidneys to divert attention *not* to the later courses, but away from any suspicion that it was the bowl that had been poisoned.

'Did I not say,' Auguste concluded rather complacently, 'that no pupil of mine could poison food of our creation? Particularly a dish of mine,' he added.

'That reminds me, Auguste,' said Rose offhandedly. 'Miss Fenwick has a message for you. She said to tell Mr Didier I'm sorry I used commercial jelly.'

'But why did you do it, Heinrich?' asked Emily, walking in the conservatory shortly afterwards amid the potted

275

palms, in a state of mingled relief and romantic joy. 'You didn't really think I'd done a murder, did you?'

'I did not know. I was afraid,' said Heinrich simply. 'You knew much about poisons. You did not like Sir Thomas, and you let it slip that you knew him before we came here. You said he had a weak stomach, but no one had told us that.'

'But murder!' said Emily, still rather shocked. Then she reflected. 'You did this for *me*, Heinrich?'

'Yes,' he said heavily. 'I lost my Greta to Sir Thomas. I let her go, and she killed herself. I would not allow another woman to be lost to Sir Thomas also. And certainly not a woman that I—' He hesitated.

'Yes, Heinrich?' Her grip tightened.

'That I lof,' he finished. 'But I am so much older—'

'Oh Heinrich.' She hardly dared breathe.

'But if you would become Frau Freimüller, we will cook great banquets together. You with your patisserie and me with my meat pies. You like?'

'Oh yes, I like *very* much.'

'What should I do, Sid?' asked Alfred Wittisham plaintively, over a third glass of hollands.

Sid considered. 'I reckon there's a fortune to be made down at the docks for someone who can cook decent grub.'

Alfred brightened. 'Do you think I could do it?'

'They'll think you're the cat's whiskers down there, mate,' Sid assured him, correctly.

Alfred beamed. 'Will you help me?' he asked confidently.

'Well, my dear,' said Gwendolen Figgis-Hewett, unable to take offence at anything today, 'I brought the wedding dress just in case, you know. You see,' she hesitated, with a sidelong look, 'dear to me though Thomas was, it is true he had rather a sharp tongue. I was just a little upset that

276

he asked me to portray Mrs Leo Hunter from *The Pickwick Papers* reading the Ode to an Expiring Frog. Can you imagine anything more unsuitable?'

Angelina, who had escorted her to the ladies' retiring room, just in case Mr Dickens should be lurking, gravely assured her she could not.

'And I was so cross I thought it would serve him right,' Gwendolen went on vehemently. 'Then I thought, well, Agnes was much more suitable for someone my age, but in the event, he was so *unpleasant* – you do understand, don't you?'

'I do,' said Angelina gravely, and kissed her.

'Oh, my dear,' said Gwendolen, pleased. 'I wonder if – perhaps you might – just a quiet ceremony. But if you would be my bridesmaid . . .'

'A word with you, Mr Peckham,' said Rose, tapping him on the shoulder. 'About that necklace.'

Algernon started like a rabbit faced with a piecrust.

'Mr Didier tells me you've the making of a brilliant cook,' Rose continued unexpectedly.

Algernon nodded helplessly.

'I dare say you had it in mind to tour the great kitchens of Europe in order to nip up a few drainpipes. That right?'

A nod of the head, swiftly followed by several shakes.

'I've persuaded Higgins to part with the necklace, Peckham. My advice is stick to the cooking. Or we'll be waiting right at the end of that drainpipe, with the Comtesse de la Ferté's necklace to drop over your head. Understand?'

Algernon Peckham did. A vision of a small restaurant in Wiltshire with brilliant dishes with a touch of France about them floated before his mind. Even meat dishes . . .

'This Alice doesn't sound a very nice person, Egbert,' Edith pronounced her severest sentence.

'She had a lovely face, Edith,' Auguste said wistfully.

'Now that isn't everything, Auguste,' said Edith gently. 'As you well know. So had Lucrezia Borgia, no doubt. And Adelaide Bartlett. And Florence Maybrick. Even Maria Manning—'

'You seem to know a lot about husband-murderers, my dear,' observed her husband drily.

'Oh, Egbert.'

'Would she have murdered Wittisham had they married, do you suppose?' said Rose.

Auguste considered. 'I doubt it. She might well, as she claims, have made a wonderful wife. And to think I nearly—' He bit back his words, remembering Edith's presence. But memory of the night that he had nearly held a murderess in his arms was vivid. And he too had considered her as a wife.

'What will you do now, Auguste? Continue with the school?' asked Rose.

'I shall return. My pupils wish to finish the course. We shall not give up. And when it is over I shall take a holiday. *Not* at the seaside,' Auguste added, almost able to smile at himself. 'There are too many lovely temptations. The sun distorts one's usual judgement.' It might have been an excuse.

'Why did you first suspect Alice Fenwick, Auguste?' asked Edith.

'It was something your Mr Dickens said. "Always suspect everybody." But I realised there were two people I had never suspected. Perhaps it was Emily? Perhaps we should suspect the least likely person to have committed murder. And so she was, so timid, so shy. But then suddenly I thought, no, not her, but *Alice*. Alice, so calm and comforting, so reliable. She was so reliable, she was always *there*, and somehow above suspicion, for we thought of her as ill-treated by Lord Wittisham, not as a murderess of Sir Thomas. And so . . . ' He could not finish.

'I have to thank you, Auguste, once more,' said Egbert Rose quickly, seeing his distress.

'Thank Mr Dickens,' said Auguste with a smile.

'Araminta,' Auguste asked, seeing her alone, lovely, desirable, by the dance floor, the band playing a gentle melody of love, 'may I have this dance?'

'Oh, Mr Didier.' She was upset to have to refuse. 'I am engaged—'

As she spoke, her partner came to claim her, looking somewhat embarrassed. It was Sid.

'He's more my age,' Araminta explained kindly as she floated away in his arms.

Auguste walked slowly home along the deserted seafront. Everyone it seemed had their partner. All save him. He stood gazing out over the dark ocean, and wondered about himself. What did life hold for him? He had been wrong about Araminta; he had been wrong about Alice. No more should dreams of women fill his thoughts; only perhaps those of the one he could not have. But what instead? What remained for him in life?

He listened to the splashing of the waves on the sands. Out there were all the wondrous fishes of the sea, waiting for the Williams and Josephs of this world. And for the Auguste Didiers. Tomorrow before they departed he would show his pupils how to cook a true *bourride* of Provence. In art there was refuge, there was peace. Not murder.